P.E.P.

SQUAD

E.T. O'HELY

MERCIER PRESS

IRISH PUBLISHER – IRISH STORY

FOR EMMA, CHRIS, BEN
AND ESPECIALLY MATTIE

MERCIER PRESS

Cork

www.mercierpress.ie

© Eileen O'Hely, 2014

ISBN: 978 1 78117 195 0

10 9 8 7 6 5 4 3 2 1

A CIP record for this title is available from the British Library

Printed and bound in the EU

CONTENTS

1	PROPOSAL	5
2	SIMULATION	16
3	ORIENTATION	34
4	APTITUDE	58
5	FITNESS	73
6	DRAMA	86
7	ROACH	95
8	ABSEILING	109
9	ASSAULT	128
10	BREAK-UP	141
11	AUDITION	155
12	HORSEPOWER	170
13	DUNEBOARDING	185
14	MAZE	198
15	MUSICAL	212
16	SKYDIVING	227
17	BRIEFING	249
18	SNOW	266
19	PLAN B	283
20	CAVALRY	300
	EPILOGUE	317

1

PROPOSAL

'Jess! You look fantastic!' said Saoirse as Jess stepped out of the changing room.

Jess looked uncertainly at her reflection in the mirror. Apart from her school uniform, she never wore skirts, and as far as she was concerned the mini skirt Saoirse had talked her into trying on showed way too much leg. Not that Jess had bad legs. As a runner and gymnast her legs were perfectly toned, and as she was half Egyptian her skin had a year-round tan. The simple fact was that, although Jess had great legs, she just felt more comfortable with a pair of tracksuit trousers covering them.

Saoirse stood behind Jess and gathered her dark hair into a ponytail. 'Even better,' she said. 'You really should dress like this, you know – it suits you.'

Jess's fringe fell below her eyebrows. If it wasn't so late in the term, the school would be sending a note home to her parents advising them to get it cut.

Saoirse's eyes dropped to her wrist. She gasped and let go of Jess's hair.

'What's wrong?' asked Jess, turning to her friend.

'The CSPE exam starts in fifteen minutes!'

'What?' exclaimed Jess, grabbing her friend's wrist and looking at the watch herself.

'I don't have a spare helmet, but I can give you a ride,' offered Saoirse.

'I've got a better idea,' said Jess, 'race you!'

Two minutes later, Jess was back in her school uniform, sprinting towards the front exit of the shopping centre while Saoirse headed for the car park.

As a gaggle of pensioners with walking frames emerged from a café, Jess swerved to avoid them, tweed skirts billowing in her wake. Dead ahead a toddler was crouched in the middle of the concourse, struggling to open a red plastic packet. When Jess was three feet away the bag exploded, little brown spheres scattering in all directions.

'*Maltesers!*' gasped Jess as her foot landed on a clump of them and skidded out from underneath her. Jess threw her weight forward and managed to regain her balance, surfing one-legged on the Maltesers rolling beneath her school shoe until they crumbled away to a malty, choco-latey mess.

She sprinted down the ramp to the exit, her feet taking on a mind of their own, pumping one in front of the other at a pace that was almost out of control. When she was only metres from the exit, a shop boy lost control of a train of trolleys and got them jammed in the doorway.

Jess was running too fast to stop and the trolleys were completely blocking the exit. She had no choice but to jump, doing a perfect swan dive across the trolleys and landing in a forward roll on the pavement outside.

Not even pausing for breath, she darted along the footpath, dodging prams and little old ladies' shopping carts (what was it with old women and kids today?) and leapfrogging over postboxes and rubbish bins.

Her biggest hurdle came when she got to the bus stop. The footpath was packed with people looking at their watches and stamping their feet. A bus hadn't come for some time and they were clearly annoyed about it. Pushing through them would be impossible.

Jess considered detouring around the bus stop on the road side, but there was too much traffic to make that an option. The only way left was to go over it.

She leapt on top of the rubbish bin next to the bus shelter and grasped the edge of the toughened glass. Hoisting herself up onto the roof, she ran across the top of the shelter, acutely aware that the people below could see right up her skirt. When she got to the other side she jumped, somersaulting over the heads of the remaining people and landing four feet away. As she hit the ground, Jess heard a familiar whine and glanced over her shoulder.

Saoirse's baby-blue Vespa was heading towards her, weaving in and out of the traffic. Jess put on a fresh burst of speed.

As she ran hard to keep ahead of the Vespa, her heart was pounding and her muscles complaining about being jolted into action without a proper warm-up. But she had one advantage. While the Vespa had to stick to the roads, Jess could go cross country.

Coming up on the left was a children's playground. Jess hurdled the boundary fence with ease, scaled the ladder of the slippery dip, then surfed down the slide on her heels. She leapt directly from the slide to the see-saw, running up the slope and keeping her balance easily as she got to the centre and her weight made it flip in the other direction. She slid down the other side and bounced on the very end of the see-saw. The rebound gave her the extra spring she needed to clear the fence on the opposite side of the playground.

Only one more road to cross and she'd be there.

The lights were red and the carriageway was clear, but cars were parked bumper to bumper along the verge. Jess did a sideways roll across the bonnet of an Aston Martin and ran through the gates of Kilmaire College just as the blue Vespa caught up with her.

Jess smoothed down her skirt and straightened her tie while Saoirse parked the Vespa and took off her helmet.

'Plenty of time,' said Saoirse, shaking out her hair.

'Wanna bet?' said Jess, heading at a run towards the hall, where a man with a crew-cut was pulling the doors closed.

'Wait!' yelled Jess as she and Saoirse ran across the schoolyard.

The man's steely blue eyes bored into them.

'Miss Leclair and Miss Ahearn, presumably,' he said flatly.

'Are we too late?' panted Jess.

'Almost,' continued the man, whose haircut and physique suggested he belonged in the army rather than supervising Junior Certificate exams at a private girls' school. Jess had tried to blot out the sound of his heels clicking up and down between the rows of desks all week as she sat papers in English, Irish and Mathematics, and, to tell the truth, she found him a little scary. 'Let's get a move on.'

Jess took a few minutes to settle into her Civic, Social and Political Education exam, but she got so involved in writing her essay in the final section that she didn't realise the rest of the class had left early.

'Time's up, Miss Leclair,' said the exam supervisor, standing directly in front of her desk.

'Oh, sorry, Mr … um …' began Jess.

'Parry,' said the supervisor, adding Jess's exam paper to

the pile he was holding. 'I was wondering if I could have a word?'

'I guess,' said Jess, leaning back in her chair and folding her arms.

'How do you like school?' asked Mr Parry.

Jess was expecting to be grilled about her late arrival, so the question surprised her and she wondered where this was going. 'It's not my favourite place to be, but it's OK,' she admitted.

'You're doing very well academically. Straight As for everything, champion for your age group in gymnastics and cross-country – you're even top of your class at the community Arabic school you attend on Saturday mornings. And glancing over your Junior Cert papers, I've yet to see a wrong answer.'

'Hang on – how on earth do you know all that?' asked Jess, wondering whether exam supervisors were really permitted to look over Junior Cert exam papers – let alone determine whether the answers were correct – and, even if they were, how he could know all that other stuff about her.

Rather than answering her, Mr Parry pulled a brochure out of his suit pocket and handed it to Jess.

'What's this?' asked Jess, glancing at the flyer for what looked like a posh high school called Theruse Abbey. It was filled with pictures of smiling teenagers in immaculate school uniforms looking studious in class, playing instruments and doing various sporting activities in equally immaculate sports gear.

'False advertising,' said Mr Parry.

'What? You mean the students at this school don't actually smile the whole time?' replied Jess, flicking through the brochure.

'No, what I mean is that the school is a cover.'

'A cover for what?' asked Jess.

'A training academy for secret agents.'

Jess looked up at Mr Parry. 'Funny. Seriously, why are you showing me this?' She set the brochure on the table in front of her.

'I am serious,' said Mr Parry. 'That's the brochure we give to parents of prospective students. *This* is the brochure we give to the students,' he continued, handing a sceptical Jess a second brochure.

The photos were of the same teenagers, but this time they were dressed in camouflage gear of different colours. As well as sitting in classrooms and science labs, they were abseiling down cliffs, practising martial arts and doing target practice with what looked like real guns.

'OK,' said Jess slowly. 'What has this got to do with me?'

'Let me start from the beginning,' said Mr Parry, pulling the chair out from under the desk in front of Jess and sitting down. 'Theruse Abbey is a training academy for exceptional students like yourself who go on to work for P.E.P. Squad after graduation.'

'P.E.P. Squad?'

'Planet Earth Protection Squad. The most secret spy network in the world,' explained Mr Parry.

'You're kidding me. The most secret spy network in the world couldn't come up with a better name than P.E.P. Squad?'

'Admittedly the founder is a rather … unique individual,' said Mr Parry.

'And how come I've never heard of it?' asked Jess.

Mr Parry laughed.

'It's only the amateur government-run spy agencies like MI6 and the CIA that the public hears about. We're a *secret* organisation. We're the best in the world because we recruit the best and we recruit them young. This may surprise you, but the teenage mind is ideally suited to acquiring secret-agent skills. The brain is still developing and is far more adaptable to learning than an adult brain. The nucleus accumbens, the pleasure centre of the brain, develops quite early, while the prefrontal cortex – which, among other things, curbs dangerous behaviour – develops late, so teenagers are keen to indulge in thrill-seeking activities that many adults think are too risky. This makes you guys far easier to train in basic field-agent skills such as base jumping and high-octane sports – or even your free running,' said Mr Parry, looking at Jess pointedly.

'How did you–' began Jess.

'You came to our attention some months ago. As well as Junior Cert results, we monitor the results of national academic competitions, like mathematics competitions and the Young Scientist of the Year competition, and we look at the results from interschool athletic meets. When we find individuals like yourself who excel in that type of thing, we dig a little deeper.'

'You mean you've been spying on *me*?' asked Jess.

Mr Parry spread his hands almost apologetically.

'It's what we do best.'

Jess frowned, wondering exactly how much the man sitting opposite her knew about her. 'And you're telling me I should consider going to this secret-agent school?'

'I know a good candidate when I see one,' said Mr Parry, lacing his fingers behind his head and leaning back in his chair. 'You have all the attributes we look for. Are you interested?'

Ignoring his question, Jess peered around the room suspiciously.

'What are you doing?' asked Mr Parry.

'Looking for hidden cameras. This can't be real,' said Jess.

'I can assure you it is,' replied Mr Parry. 'Don't tell me you're not interested.'

'Oh, if it's real then I'm interested,' said Jess. 'It sounds cool. But even if I believed you, my parents would never go for it.'

'What if I told you they already have?' said Mr Parry.

'What?' exclaimed Jess. 'You're telling me that my ridiculously overprotective parents want to send me to a school for spies? No way. I'm going to be stuck at this place for the next three years. My dad's on the school board.'

'Actually, your parents were surprisingly easy to persuade. After all, they think you're going there,' said Mr Parry, gesturing to the first brochure. 'We arranged to interview them a while ago – letting them think they came to us, of course.'

'How, exactly?' asked Jess.

'We have very skilled recruiters. In your parents' case it was easy. Your father's a dentist, so we arranged to have a new client discuss the school with him.'

'And he fell for that?'

'It piqued his interest enough for him to google the school and talk to your mother about it. They were quite impressed with the tour.'

'They've been to the school?' said Jess with surprise. 'What did they say about the shooting range?'

'It's a simple matter to disguise the shooting range and other speciality training equipment on parent tour days,' said Mr Parry. 'As to what your parents thought, they were sufficiently impressed to submit the application forms for you.'

'Without telling me?' said Jess sceptically.

'They wouldn't be the first parents in the world to arrange a school transfer without telling their child about it until after the fact.'

Jess said nothing. The thought that her parents would do something like this behind her back had taken her totally by surprise.

'Now I know this is a lot to take in,' said Mr Parry, standing up. 'One of the problems we have in recruiting students of your calibre is convincing them that something seemingly so outlandish really exists. So I want you to go home, have a think about it and we'll discuss it again tomorrow. Any questions?'

Jess shook her head and started towards the door of the exam room, deep in thought.

'Good,' said Mr Parry. 'Oh, and Jess.' She turned back. 'Try to be on time for your exam tomorrow.'

2

SIMULATION

As soon as Jess got home she googled Theruse Abbey. The top hit was the school's official website, which looked a lot like the first brochure Mr Parry had shown her. There were also Wikipedia entries for the abbey itself and the school. She scrolled down the list further and found entries in the *Golden Pages* and even an entry for Theruse in the government listing of secondary schools. But there was nothing out of the ordinary.

Jess decided to try a different tack. She typed the address on the back of the brochure into Google Maps, which brought up an image of a headland on the south-west coast of Ireland. There was quite a narrow land bridge out to a cape which spread out to form a roughly triangular shape. Jess switched her view to satellite and zoomed in. There was a grouping of buildings and playing fields that could have belonged to a school at the mouth of the cape. Of course there was. Her parents had been there and seen it. The rest of the area was a mix of trees and open grassy areas, with what appeared to be rocky cliffs stretching down to the sea. She clicked on *Get Directions* and typed in her home address. The school was over four hours' drive from where she lived. Definitely too far for trips back and forth from Dublin every weekend, which was probably why Mr Parry was doing his recruiting in Dublin.

Next she logged on to Facebook and tried to set her secondary school to Theruse Abbey. Facebook came back with 'No information has been provided … yet' and prompted her to *Create a Page*. She logged out.

She then typed P.E.P. Squad into the search engine. She got over three million hits but they were all related to American cheerleading, various bands or some low-rating horror movie from the nineties. No mention of a spy organisation.

Having run out of ideas for any other research, Jess decided to start studying for her History exam the next day. She opened her textbook and flipped to the chapter on the Easter Rising, but she couldn't concentrate and had a second look at the prospective students' brochure. Although almost any school would be better than Kilmaire, Jess was starting to get really excited about the idea of Theruse Abbey and a career as a secret agent.

The next morning, Jess left early for school. When she got to the end of her street a man stepped out in front of her.

'Good morning, Jess,' said Mr Parry.

'Oh, hello,' said Jess, a little surprised.

'How did the research go?'

'What research?' asked Jess.

Mr Parry gave her a look.

'You hacked my computer?'

Mr Parry smiled.

'If you didn't go home and immediately try to find out all you could about Theruse Abbey and P.E.P. Squad, then you wouldn't be P.E.P. Squad material.'

'Oh,' said Jess.

'So, have you made up your mind?' asked Mr Parry.

'Yeah. I'd like to give it a go.'

'Excellent,' said Mr Parry, walking to the driver's side of a car parked on the side of the road. 'Hop in.'

Jess hesitated. Mr Parry was effectively a stranger – a taller, stronger stranger – and she wasn't sure hopping into a car with him was the best idea. Noticing her reluctance, he smiled.

'Caution is a good trait to have in our line of business. Got a mobile phone?'

Jess nodded.

'Know how to use the GPS?' he asked, reaching into the car and passing Jess a GPS unit. 'Now, you can watch where we're going, and the police are just a phone call away. You can even sit in the back seat if you like.'

Jess opened the back door and checked to make sure the child safety lock wasn't engaged before hopping in and fastening her seat belt. Mr Parry started the engine and pulled out into the rush-hour traffic, not going noticeably faster than Jess could have walked. However, when they got to the turn off for Kilmaire College, Mr Parry drove straight ahead.

'Uh, weren't we supposed to turn …?' began Jess, her thumb poised to dial 999. Then she noticed the smile on Mr Parry's face and relaxed. 'You're not taking me to school, are you?' she said.

Mr Parry shook his head.

'What about my History exam?' asked Jess.

'You got 96 out of 100. Apparently your knowledge of Neolithic peoples leaves a bit to be desired,' said Mr Parry. 'We've got a different type of test planned.'

Jess turned to look out the window and smiled. They were heading towards the city and traffic was becoming heavier. As they neared the centre, Mr Parry turned a corner into a narrow laneway. It was a dead end, with graffiti spray painted over the brick walls and nothing but an industrial bin and a steel door with no handle.

'This is us,' said Mr Parry, stopping the engine and getting out.

Jess followed as he walked up to the door. He looked around to make sure no one was watching and then placed all four fingertips of his right hand on the rightmost brick above the door. There was a click and the door swung outwards.

Mr Parry ushered Jess inside.

They were in a small, windowless booth, with an LED screen mounted high on the wall in front of them.

'Agent Parry and prospective student Jessica Leclair,' announced Mr Parry.

A laser beam shot out from the wall in front of them, scanning their bodies down and up.

'*Identity confirmed*,' sounded a metallic voice.

The wall in front of them slid open to reveal a grey, dimly lit foyer, empty apart from an attractive woman with dark hair swept back into a ponytail.

'Hello, Marianna,' said Mr Parry.

'Nice to see you, Wayne,' said the woman, clasping his hand in both of hers before turning her attention to Jess. 'You must be Jessica. I'm Marianna Enigmistica,' she continued, rolling the r in her name the way Italians do.

'But all the students call her Signora Enigmistica,' prompted Mr Parry.

'Nice to meet you, Signora Enigmistica,' said Jess.

'Welcome to P.E.P. Squad's Dublin branch office,' said Signora Enigmistica. 'As well as our regular duties and research and development, we also do the final testing phase of enrolment here.'

'Testing phase?' said Jess.

'Well, we need to see if you really have what it takes. Lieutenant Parry's been known to get it wrong occasionally. Think of this as a practical exam for a language. Only this practical will be somewhat more energetic,' said Signora Enigmistica, winking at Lieutenant Parry.

'Lieutenant?' said Jess.

'I spent a little time in military intelligence,' said Lieutenant Parry vaguely.

'And if he's wrong about me?' asked Jess, turning back to Signora Enigmistica.

'Then we give you a glass of Memory Wipe, tell your parents that you have not been accepted for admission and all of this goes away.'

'What's Memory Wipe?'

'A special cocktail that erases a select portion of memory, depending on the concentration,' said Signora Enigmistica, matter-of-factly.

'Don't worry, I hear it tastes quite fruity,' said Lieutenant Parry, noticing the look of alarm on Jess's face. 'Besides, I know a good candidate when I see one.'

Jess didn't like the idea of ingesting a drink that could mess with her brain, especially in the middle of exams. She hoped she wouldn't need it.

'Come with me now, Jess. You'll see Lieutenant Parry again after the test.' Signora Enigmistica strode through a doorway that had magically appeared in the foyer, and along a corridor. Jess hurried after her. They ended up in a room with a black cylindrical booth in the centre. The cylinder was about three metres high and four metres in diameter. To the side of the room was a single desk with a computer console and a Chinese room divider.

'Take everything off – and by everything I also mean underwear – and put this on,' said Signora Enigmistica, pointing Jess in the direction of the room divider and passing her a black body suit, complete with gloves and little booties to cover her feet. It was made of an extremely lightweight fabric Jess had never come across before, which somehow seemed to feel both hot and cold at the same time.

First looking around for hidden cameras or secret doors that might slide open, Jess slid her shoes and socks and knickers off and pulled the bottom half of the jumpsuit up under her school uniform. She slid the bodice up under her dress so that it covered her chest, before pulling off her uniform. Then it was a simple matter of undoing her bra and slipping her arms into the sleeves of the suit. There was also a hood, which she pulled over her head, leaving the skin on her face the only part of her body that was exposed. The suit was very, very tight.

'Um, excuse me,' said Jess, poking her head around the Chinese screen. 'I think I might need the next size up.'

Signora Enigmistica walked over and gave Jess a once-over, saying, 'Looks like it fits perfectly. Put these on.'

She tossed Jess a pair of trainers. The second the laces were tied, the teacher said, 'Ready?'

Jess followed her towards the booth.

'This is state of the art in virtual reality. No need for clumsy helmets and handsets,' said Signora Enigmistica, pressing a button on the outside of the booth to make a previously invisible door slide open.

'How does it work?' asked Jess, stepping inside. Tiny green pinpoints of light appeared all over her jumpsuit.

'The floor, walls and ceiling have special sensors. When you start to move, the software calculates where you should be in the programme matrix and moves the cell surfaces to compensate,' explained Signora Enigmistica. 'Walk to the left.'

Jess walked to the left and the floor moved to keep her in the centre of the booth.

'Faster,' said Signora Enigmistica.

Jess broke into a jog and the floor kept up with her.

'What happens when I want to stop?' asked Jess.

'Just slow down. The floor will follow,' said Signora Enigmistica.

Jess slowed down gently and still stayed in the centre of the booth. She stopped abruptly and the floor stopped with her.

'This is cool,' she said.

'Yes,' said Signora Enigmistica, with the slightly amused air of someone who has seen far more amazing things in her life. 'The cell can simulate gradients and the suit itself can simulate obstacles, so if you're running straight towards something then you'll feel the impact when you crash into it.'

'Good to know,' said Jess.

'Now, we are going to run a simulation to test your physical and mental agility while under immense pressure. Try to complete the test in the shortest time possible. Ready?'

Jess nodded.

Signora Enigmistica closed the door.

It was pitch black in the booth. No light snaked in from the edges of the door. It was also soundproof. Jess was starting to feel decidedly uncomfortable when the wall in front of her brightened as though someone was turning up a dimmer switch. It was an image of Signora Enigmistica, so lifelike that for a second Jess thought the teacher had re-entered the booth.

'How are you feeling, Jess?' Signora Enigmistica's voice echoed around the booth.

'A little nervous but OK.'

'Touch the inside of your left wrist with your right forefinger,' Signora Enigmistica instructed.

Jess did so and felt a small, hard lump.

'That's a microdot that we've had sewn into the suit. Your mission is to deliver that microdot to this man,' said Signora Enigmistica, holding up a photo of Lieutenant Parry, 'on the third floor of this building,' she continued, flashing a photo of the Dublin GPO. 'Since you'd be sitting your Junior Certificate in History if you weren't here right now, I don't need to tell you the name of the building. Good luck.'

The image of Signora Enigmistica faded and was gradually replaced by a noisy cityscape.

Jess found herself next to an air-conditioning vent on top of a tall building on the southern bank of the Liffey. She guessed it was O'Connell Bridge House, as she could see O'Connell Bridge and Street stretching out in front of her with the GPO less than halfway up the street. Once she got to street level, it'd be only a five-minute walk. The task seemed straightforward. Too straightforward.

She headed for the only access point she could see, a door in the middle of the roof. Suddenly it opened. A man in a suit and tie stepped out onto the roof. He looked like an ordinary businessman, apart from the gun he was pointing at her.

The instant before the man opened fire, Jess rolled for cover behind the air-conditioning vent. A volley of bullets clattered against it. The gunfire ceased momentarily and she heard two sets of footsteps running towards her. That meant there were two gun-brandishing businessmen and they could split up and approach her from either side of the vent. She had to move, fast.

Jess scrambled towards the edge of the roof nearest her and stopped short. She was at the far edge of the building from O'Connell Bridge. Below her was a drop of at least seven storeys to the lower, adjoining part of the building she was on. Even with all her free-running training, there was no way she'd survive the jump. However, to the right she could see that the top few storeys of the main building narrowed in like steps. She could possibly jump down one tier at a time, if she could make it to the edge. But that would mean exposing herself to fire.

A sequence from one of her dad's favourite old-school martial-arts movies entered her head. Those guys never ran in a straight line – they always cartwheeled and flipped so as not to provide an easy target. Although Jess had only come second in the floor routine at the interschool gymnastics championships, she hoped her final tumbling run would be a winner today. She took the longest run up she dared. The instant she saw a gun-wielding arm in her peripheral vision, she launched into a series of back flips towards the edge of the building. Both men fired at her. Although their bullets missed, they flicked up chips of concrete into her legs and arms. And they *hurt*.

Talk about feeling the impact, Jess thought bitterly to herself as she landed her final flip about a foot from the edge of the building and dived off the top, turning a single somersault in the air and landing on her feet in a low squat. It was a long drop and her ankles rammed painfully into the ground, but she ignored the pain and repeated her somersault over the edge, landing equally painfully on the next floor down.

She pressed herself up against the wall and looked through a window. More gun-brandishing businessmen were inside the building and running towards her. She had to move. She peered over the edge of the building. There was a window-cleaning platform another floor down with a canvas tarpaulin stretched across the bottom of it. Having already proven to herself that she could land safely, although painfully, over such a vertical distance, Jess decided to take the plunge. Being so small, the platform didn't offer her much room for error or rolling space to break her fall, but it was either that or crash out of the test.

She took a deep breath and dived off the side of the building – but she didn't calculate the spin correctly and landed heavily on her back on the platform.

Again, the pain was very real, but she had no time to recover from it. Her pursuers had come to the edge of the roof and were firing down at her. She rolled as close to the building as she could for protection, her ears ringing from the impact of bullets on metal.

Surprisingly the men didn't seem to be aiming for her. Jess wasn't sure what they were doing until one of the bullets made a different sort of twang as it hit the cable from which the platform was suspended.

She watched in horror as the bullets severed the wire strand by strand. She looked around desperately and noticed the control box on the opposite side of the platform. If she could just reach the Down button. Jess stretched out her arm, but the gunmen were quicker and blew the control box apart.

The platform started to tilt and she knew it wouldn't be long before the cable broke completely, sending her plunging to the street below. She was still well over thirty metres high. There was no way she could survive the fall.

As the platform tilted, a loose corner of the tarpaulin billowed in the breeze. Jess reached down and touched it. It certainly felt real enough through the glove. She closed her fingers around it and yanked. To her surprise and relief, the tarp came away from the platform floor. Working quickly, the tilt of the platform growing ever steeper as bullet after bullet severed more strands of cable, Jess undid her trainers and tied a corner of the tarp around each foot. She stuffed her feet in their tarp socks back inside her trainers and retied the laces quickly. Then she grabbed the other two corners of the tarp in each hand and jumped.

Base jumping was something that had always appealed to Jess, but she'd never expected to be trying it for the first time with a home-made parachute. Spreadeagled, Jess felt a jerk as the updraft caught in the tarp, yanking her upwards. She felt the corners of the tarp start to slip out of her shoes and looked at how far she had to go. Nine storeys, eight, seven ... Jess looked from the building to the ground below. The breeze from the river was pushing her towards a street lamp.

Five storeys, four ... Jess tried to steer the makeshift parachute away from the lamp but the right edge caught on it. The sudden stop yanked the tarp out of her hands and pulled her trainers off. She crashed barefoot onto a coffee cart below.

As she picked herself up she heard the audible pedestrian-crossing signal and dashed across Burgh Quay, nearly getting mowed down by a lorry that ran the red light. A big crowd was gathered on O'Connell Bridge, watching a street performer who was asking for a volunteer from the audience to assist with a magic trick. As Jess tried to push her way through the crowd, the magician grabbed her and manhandled her into his supposedly magic box.

Jess quickly felt around the inside of the box but

couldn't find any lever or fake wall that would free her. Luckily the box was made of a lightweight material and reasonably roomy. Determined not to waste any more time, she raised her leg and kicked as hard as she could against the front of the box. The wood cracked. One more kick and she was free.

Jess shot out of the box and raced north across the bridge and up O'Connell Street. The lights at Eden Quay were red, and O'Connell Street was blocked by traffic. Jess wove in between the unmoving traffic, trying to cross the road diagonally, and almost got taken out by a bicycle courier. She ran up the west side of O'Connell Street, having to dodge the usual Dublin bustle. The pedestrian lights changed to orange and Jess put on an extra burst of speed to try to make it across Abbey Street, but she was fractionally too late and a left-turning white van screeched around the corner in front of her. Jess pulled up just in time, feeling the breeze from the van's passing against her face.

As she waited for the lights to change, she heard footsteps pounding on the pavement. At least six suited gunmen were running towards her down O'Connell Street from the direction of the GPO, blocking her access to the front of the building. Thinking quickly, Jess ran around the corner after the van, picking her time to weave through the moving traffic as she crossed Abbey

Street. She could hear the gunmen behind her, but she had a good lead on them. She ducked into William's Lane when suddenly a motorcyclist turned in behind her, gunning his engine and chasing her along the footpath. Jess made a beeline for a large rubbish bin, leapfrogging it at the last second. The motorcyclist ploughed straight into it and was launched through the air, landing spreadeagled and clearly stunned only millimetres from Jess.

She put on a fresh burst of speed, turning up Prince's Street and entering the GPO through the side entrance. She was searching desperately for a way up to the third floor when red lettering appeared in front of her, hovering in mid-air. *Time Remaining: 10 …*

What the hell? thought Jess.

9 …

Time remaining is in seconds?

8 …

Signora Enigmistica definitely didn't mention a time limit.

7 …

Jess saw a stairwell on the opposite side of the main hall and ran for it.

6 …

When she was halfway across the hall, three gun-brandishing businessmen came in the front door. They took aim, but Jess dived onto the highly polished floor and slid the rest of the way to the stairs on her belly as gunfire raked the floor behind her.

5 …

Jess slammed into the riser of the bottom stair and half crawled, half ran up the stairs.

4 …

One more level to go.

3 …

Footsteps clattered up the stairs behind her.

2 …

Jess ripped the microdot out of her sleeve.

1 …

Jess reached the top of the stairs, where Lieutenant Parry was waiting with his arm outstretched. Jess held the microdot out towards him. At the same moment she felt the muzzle of a gun between her shoulder blades. Then everything went black.

The door of the booth opened and Signora Enigmistica appeared with a glass of green liquid. Jess took a few seconds to adjust to the new reality.

'Did I pass?' panted Jess.

'Looked to me as though you were about to get shot. It's lucky you ran out of time when you did: it would not have felt pleasant,' answered Signora Enigmistica, the look on her face indecipherable.

'You didn't say anything about a countdown,' said Jess,

finally noticing the glass in Signora Enigmistica's hand. 'Is that Memory Wipe?'

'Drink it and see,' said Signora Enigmistica, holding the glass out to her.

Jess took one last look around her and drank.

3

ORIENTATION

Jess woke up feeling not particularly well rested but very excited. Signora Enigmistica and her simulation booth felt like a hazy dream. But that was all months ago, before the summer holidays. Now it was the first day of autumn term. Jess dressed in her Theruse Abbey formal uniform and smiled at her reflection in the mirror.

The same day that she'd passed the simulation test, an envelope addressed to her parents had arrived with the Theruse Abbey emblem on it. Jess had found the lengths to which her parents went to prepare her for the 'news' quite amusing. They cooked her favourite dinner – complete with self-saucing chocolate pudding for dessert – and waited until Jess couldn't eat another bite before bringing up the subject.

Jess had tried not to smile as her parents looked at each other, both hoping the other would speak first. Finally, she couldn't stand it any longer.

'What's up?' she demanded.

Her parents looked at her like naughty children caught in the act.

'You've been acting weird all evening. Does one of you have cancer or something?'

'No, no, nothing like that,' exclaimed Mrs Leclair.

'Then what's with the burritos and the chocolate pudding? It's not my birthday, so that can only mean bad news.'

'It's not bad news,' said Dr Leclair.

'In fact it's good news,' said Mrs Leclair smiling sadly.

'Then why are you pulling that face?' Jess asked her mother.

'Well,' said Dr Leclair, 'you know how you're always complaining about how much you don't like Kilmaire College?'

'Yes,' said Jess cautiously.

'We kind of went behind your back a little and enrolled you in a different school,' said Mrs Leclair.

'Not Loreto—' began Jess.

'No, it's not a girls' school. It's a school you probably haven't heard of before,' said Dr Leclair, passing Jess the parents' version of the Theruse Abbey brochure.

'What's Theruse Abbey?' asked Jess, skimming through the pages as if it was the first time she had seen it.

'It comes highly recommended and it's mixed,' said Dr Leclair.

'Yeah, I can see that,' said Jess. 'Where is it?'

'That's the thing,' said Mrs Leclair. 'It's out west.'

'What? Blanchardstown?'

'No. Really west. Near Dingle,' said Dr Leclair.

'Dingle! But that's—'

'Four hours away. You'd have to board,' said Dr Leclair.

'Jess? How do you feel about that?' asked Mrs Leclair, laying a gentle hand on her daughter's forearm.

'Um, it's a bit of a shock,' said Jess. 'How did you even hear about this place?'

'A walk-in client who needed some emergency work done. He saw your picture, asked your age and told me all about the school. He even had a brochure with him,' said Dr Leclair.

I'll bet he did, thought Jess. Instead she said, 'You've enrolled me there already?'

'We could tell you're not happy at Kilmaire,' began Mrs Leclair.

'And this new school seems to cater well to students with your temperament. The teachers are enthusiastic, and the students seem happy and challenged,' continued Dr Leclair.

'The only thing is that it is so far away,' said Mrs Leclair. 'But looking at all the possible options, this one seems to be the best.'

'So what do you think?' asked Dr Leclair.

'It's a lot to take in,' Jess replied, which was quite honest. A mere thirty hours before she had been totally unaware of Theruse Abbey or P.E.P. Squad and thought she was doomed to spend the next three years at her current school. Now she had a life of thrills and espionage to look forward to.

'We really do think it's for the best,' said Mrs Leclair.

'Look,' said Dr Leclair. 'You don't have to decide now. This is only an offer of enrolment – you don't have to accept it. And it's not too late to apply to other schools.'

'I'll think about it,' said Jess, sliding out from her seat at the table, taking the brochure with her. She barely managed to run upstairs and close her door before bursting into fits of laughter.

As she zipped up her suitcase and looked around her room for the last time, she felt incredibly nervous.

'Jess! Are you ready?' Mrs Leclair called from downstairs.

'Coming,' said Jess.

She dragged the suitcase downstairs, glad that her textbooks and most of her uniform would be waiting for her at school. It just wouldn't do to have copies of books with names like (she was guessing) *How to Disarm and Disable Enemy Agents* lying around, and her parents might have become suspicious if they'd had to launder combat fatigues.

The four-hour drive to Theruse Abbey seemed to last four weeks. It wasn't just that Jess was excited about her new school and anxious to get there, but her mother droned on and on about how far away she'd be, and how much she'd miss her, and how they could come and collect her at any time if she was feeling homesick.

'Now, they say that it's easier for the students to adjust to boarding school if we limit phone contact to once a week,' said Mrs Leclair for the eighth time.

'You told me that already,' said Jess wearily, catching her father's eye in the rear-view mirror as he shook his head.

'But that doesn't mean I won't be thinking about you every single minute …'

'Aiysha, relax,' said Dr Leclair.

'But she's our baby,' said Mrs Leclair, wiping her eyes. 'I just didn't expect it to be this hard.'

'You'll be fine, Mum,' said Jess, while thinking, *If only you knew.*

They finally made it to the school and joined a short line of cars waiting to turn into the gates. A teacher was standing at the gate with a clipboard.

'Who do we have here?' asked the teacher.

'Jessica Leclair,' said Mrs Leclair.

'Leclair … Jessica … here you are. Transition year. Welcome to Theruse,' said the teacher. 'The car park's down the driveway and on the left. The welcome assembly starts at 2 p.m. sharp in the auditorium, just inside the main entrance of the abbey. Students only, I'm afraid, Dr and Mrs Leclair. It makes the separation, especially for first-timers, easier. Have you labelled your suitcase, Jessica?'

Jess nodded.

'Just leave it in the foyer before assembly. You can say your goodbyes there,' said the teacher, waving them through.

They drove up the gravel drive between freshly manicured lawns. The school building was a beautifully restored abbey, with various towers jutting over a high stone wall. They drove through an archway in the wall, following the red-and-white painted sign to the car park.

'Well, here we are,' said Dr Leclair as he pulled into a parking space. 'Looks like most of the parents are saying their farewells here. Do you want me to carry your suitcase for you?'

Jess scanned the car park quickly. It was fairly empty. The few kids who were there were waving goodbye to their parents and walking over to the abbey alone.

'No. I'll be fine,' said Jess, hopping out to grab her suitcase from the boot.

Both her parents got out of the car.

'I know it's school policy for you to stay here over midterm,' began her mother, 'but if you're really missing us–'

'I'll be OK, Mum. Honestly,' said Jess, as a couple of boys, so alike they had to be brothers, walked past.

'I'll miss you so much,' wailed Mrs Leclair, flinging her arms around her daughter.

The boys looked over at Jess and grinned.

'Mum,' hissed Jess, 'you're embarrassing me!'

'Sorry,' said Mrs Leclair, taking a step back and sniffing. 'Now I know they said once a week, but you know you can call us any time if you need to.'

'Yes, Mum,' said Jess. 'Are you sure *you'll* be OK?'

Mrs Leclair nodded as she wiped another tear away.

'Mum. It's only boarding school. It's not like I'm joining the army or anything,' said Jess, wondering whether the army would be less gruelling than what awaited her in agent training. 'I'll be back at the end of term for sure.'

'I know,' said Mrs Leclair. 'But you're my baby …'

'Mum!' groaned Jess, worried that her mother would make a scene.

'Alright. I'm all right,' said Mrs Leclair, dabbing at her nose with a tissue. 'Take care, darling.'

'I will, Mum,' said Jess.

'Work hard, *ma petite*, and enjoy yourself,' said Dr Leclair, kissing Jess on the cheek.

'I will, Dad.'

She pulled up the retractable handle of her suitcase

and dragged it through the car park, following the tiny trickle of students making their way towards the building. As she reached the door, she turned and waved at her parents, who were still standing by the boot of the car. Then, with a growing sense of anticipation, she stepped through the front door, dumped her bag with the others in the foyer and walked into the auditorium.

The stage was semi-circular and three sections of seats descended towards it. Jess did a quick calculation and worked out there was seating for at least two hundred people, although less than fifty of the seats were taken and all of the students were seated in the first few rows. Jess chose to sit in the fourth row. As she walked towards the centre, she immediately regretted her decision, as the boys she'd seen in the car park were sitting in the middle of the row. Her first urge was to sit down immediately and pretend she hadn't seen them, but then she thought that wasn't the sort of thing a gutsy secret agent would do and decided to sit right next to them.

'Hi,' she said. 'I'm Jess.'

'I'm Ben,' said the boy seated beside her, offering his hand.

'And I'm Matt,' said the boy next to him, reaching across his brother to shake hands with Jess.

Now that she was up close to them, she was sure they were twins. Both were blond-haired and quite tanned, with broad Australian accents. The only distinguishing factor between them was muscle mass, with Matt looking like Ben on steroids.

'Before you ask,' said Ben, 'yes, we're identical twins and, yes, we're from Australia.'

'Before you ask, yes, that was my mum and, yes, she's always like that,' replied Jess.

'Nice to know she cares,' said Matt.

'That's one way of looking at it,' said Jess, feeling her cheeks burn just at the thought of her mum's display in the car park. 'How did you Aussie guys end up at a school in Ireland?'

'Both our parents work in the oil industry. We've been in Kuwait for the last three years. Rather than sending us to what they consider to be one of the exclusive international schools in Kuwait—'

'Oh, the irony,' interrupted Matt, smiling broadly.

'—our parents wanted us to be educated at a normal school in an English-speaking country. Ireland's only seven hours away by air, which is half the distance to Australia, so it was the obvious choice,' finished Ben.

'Yeah, we'll get to go back and thaw out in the holidays. Seriously, do you ever get summer in this country?' asked Matt.

'We had two sunny days in a row last week in Dublin!' said Jess defensively.

'Not a good idea to offend the natives,' Ben muttered.

'So how did you hear about this place?' asked Jess.

'This seemingly random chick approached us at GameCon to see if we'd design a game for this new VR cell her company makes.'

Jess had no idea what they were talking about. 'What's GameCon? And what's a VR cell?'

'GameCon's a convention for computer-game industry professionals,' explained Matt. 'And VR stands for Virtual Reality.'

'What were you guys doing at a convention for computer-game industry professionals?' asked Jess.

'We, uh, own a gaming company,' said Ben.

'Oh,' said Jess. 'How old are you?'

'Fifteen,' said Ben.

'I'm four minutes older,' volunteered Matt.

'Hang on,' said Jess, remembering the simulation in the final testing phase of her recruitment. '*You* guys wrote that game with the gunmen on the roof of O'Connell Bridge House?'

'No, we didn't write that one, but we did get to play it,' said Ben. 'Pretty annoying, really. It's amazing technology and I had all these great ideas for how we could develop it further but, as you know, it was just the last step in recruitment and no one seemed all that interested in my suggestions.'

While Jess and the boys had been chatting, more students had arrived. However, the auditorium was less than half full when the back doors closed and a hush fell around the hall.

Down on the stage a group of adults filed in and sat on a row of chairs that spanned its width. They were men and women of all different nationalities, but the one thing they had in common was that they all looked very, very fit. Jess recognised Lieutenant Parry and Signora Enigmistica. They were sitting either side of a young woman with beautiful, long, shiny hair, who kept glancing apprehensively at the students.

Jess wondered why the chair in the very centre was empty until a tall man dressed in a torn tuxedo with an open bow tie hanging around his neck jogged in from the left wing. One side of his face was grazed, and there was an open cut above his eye. The majority of students in the audience chuckled as he made his entrance, but Jess saw Lieutenant Parry's smile tighten as the man passed him on his way to the microphone centre stage.

'Good afternoon, cadets and staff. For those of you who don't know me, I'm Vladimir Metsen, founder of P.E.P. Squad and Principal of Theruse Abbey. Welcome to a new academic year, and an especially warm welcome to those joining us for the first time. In three years, or rather two years and ten months' time, you too will have the opportunity to ruin expensive designer suits like this on covert missions.'

Jess and the twins found themselves giggling along with the other students.

'Only two months ago we said goodbye to our very first graduate class, and they have already demonstrated their expertise in worldwide operations. Some of their missions included preventing a plane hijacking, stopping a jailbreak in Iran and quelling an insurgency in the Balkans. However, alongside these successes, I regret to inform you that one of our operatives, Aoife Maguire, was killed on a mission in Morocco.'

Several horrified gasps echoed around the auditorium.

'Most of you will remember Aoife for her sense of humour, her, shall we say, *unconventional* outlook on life and, perhaps less fondly, for her amazing roundhouse kick in tae kwon do.'

'I've got a pin in this arm from sparring with Aoife,' the boy sitting in front of Jess whispered to the girl next to him.

Jess shuddered.

Metsen's face took on a serious mien.

'Let me remind you that what we do here at the abbey and after graduation is very real and very serious. Unfortunately sometimes even brilliant operatives like Aoife die in the field. If any of you are having doubts, as always you are free to leave at any time, as long as you grab a glass of Memory Wipe on the way out.'

A murmur rippled through the audience, but nobody moved from their seat. Jess couldn't help thinking that Metsen was treating the girl's death somewhat casually, if not coldly.

'This year, in addition to our Irish cadets, we welcome new cadets from Russia, the Ukraine, South Africa and Australia to our family. Even though the calibre of Irish recruits is just as high as usual, we couldn't pass up the opportunity of inviting these exceptional individuals to join our special community. I trust that our broader student base will provide an enriching learning experience for all.

'Now for some school notices,' continued Principal Metsen. 'Due to Ms Maguire's death, we have revised the syllabus. Our language programme will now include more language labs specialising in regional dialects and colloquial language. We are also introducing a new sub-ject called "Advanced Counter-Surveillance", which will be compulsory for sophister-year students.'

There was a loud groan to the left.

The principal snapped his head around.

'Mr Foley. Unless you want to end up dead as a P.E.P. Squad operative or knock back a glass of Memory Wipe, I suggest you revise your attitude.'

After a few moments glaring at the unfortunate boy, Principal Metsen smiled broadly again.

'Now to more pleasant news. It is my absolute pleasure to welcome Miss Ball to the teaching staff.'

The woman sitting between Signora Enigmistica and Lieutenant Parry stood up and made a small curtsey.

'Miss Ball is our new Head of Arts and will be directing this year's school musical: *The Wizard of Oz*. There will be a sign-up sheet outside Miss Ball's office and auditions will be held later in the term,' continued Principal Metsen.

'School musical!' chuckled Matt.

'Now I'll ask our transition-year cadets to stay seated. Freshman- and sophister-year cadets, please collect your bags and go to your dormitories to change into your regular uniforms. I'll leave the rest of you in the capable hands of our transition-year coordinator, Lieutenant Parry, while I slip into something less shabby.'

The principal virtually had to shout the last few words as two-thirds of the cadets left the auditorium with much chattering and laughter. Most of the teachers stood up and left too. Once the doors had banged shut the room was deathly quiet. Only twenty-four students were left.

Lieutenant Parry walked to the front of the stage and sat down, dangling his legs over the orchestra pit.

'Firstly I'd like to offer you all a warm welcome

and congratulations on being accepted into the P.E.P. training programme. I know a good group of candidates when I see one, and I can tell you're all going to thrive in this environment,' he said with a broad smile. Then the smile disappeared. 'I'm not going to lie to you. The next three years are going to be tough. You need to acquire a truckload of skills before we can, with any conscience, send you into the field as P.E.P. Squad operatives. You heard yourselves just now that one of last year's graduates didn't even make it through the summer before being killed on a mission. And Aoife was a brilliant, *brilliant* student. I recruited her myself,' said Lieutenant Parry, pausing for a moment as he collected himself. He seemed genuinely upset by Aoife's death – unlike Metsen, who had ploughed on through his welcome speech without blinking. 'No matter what we throw at you here, it can't always match what's waiting for you out there. The training course is tough because it has to be. In the real world of espionage there are no second chances.

'So exactly what is it we're going to teach you, I hear you ask,' continued the lieutenant, looking around. 'Think about the skills that a spy needs to have: fluency in multiple languages, a geekish understanding of the latest technology, the fitness of an Olympic athlete, the list goes on. But on top of that, your parents think you're attending an ordinary Irish school. They will expect to see evidence of your passing exams in all the normal subjects, as well as your participation in our Arts programme and other extra-curricular activities. The course load at Theruse Abbey is heavier than in any other educational institution in the world, and the physical education component is more gruelling than SAS training.'

'Bring it on,' said Matt, cracking his knuckles, while Ben made an audible gulping sound.

'Any takers for Memory Wipe at this stage?' asked Lieutenant Parry, looking at the group of cadets.

Nobody moved.

'Good,' said Lieutenant Parry. 'Now let me introduce you to our Head of Sciences: Herr Klug.'

A tall man wearing rimless glasses stood up.

'Science and mathematics are subjects on which we place great emphasis here at Theruse Abbey,' he began in a flawless English accent, to Jess's surprise. 'Everything from administering advanced first aid to hacking into security systems to defusing bombs relies on a thorough understanding of all facets of these fields. You can choose to sit the Leaving Certificate exams for any mathematics or science subject in your sophister year, though by the end of *this* year your knowledge in everything from biology to chemistry to technology will far exceed what is required for passing the higher-level Leaving Certificate.'

'That sounds like two years of Science squished into one year. I'm screwed,' muttered Matt.

'More like a *double load* of two years of Science in one year,' corrected Ben. 'You're doubly screwed.'

'In your freshman and sophister years, should you so desire, you can take an undergraduate course in Science to earn a BA degree. The degree will be awarded by Trinity College, although all subjects will be taught here at Theruse Abbey.

'Only a small percentage of espionage is based in the field. An equally rewarding career as a P.E.P. Lab scientist is also on offer to our graduates,' continued Herr Klug. 'Developing gadgets, accessing and analysing intelligence, making advances in bioengineering – it all happens at P.E.P. Labs. Just something to keep in mind. I look forward to seeing you in class.'

Herr Klug nodded to the students and sat back down in his chair.

'Thanks, Herr Klug,' said Lieutenant Parry. 'In addition to Science and Mathematics, you'll also see Herr Klug in Fieldwork Fundamentals, and if anyone opts to learn the tuba or the euphonium, he will be your instrument teacher. Also, let me warn you right now, he is a tough and unforgiving driving instructor. Now I'd like to introduce Master Qing, the Head of Socioeconomics.'

A short man wearing a traditional Chinese tunic

padded silently across the stage in matching slippers.

'Welcome, cadets, to Theruse Abbey,' he said without a trace of an Oriental accent. 'As you have already seen, a lot is expected of you. The Socioeconomics Faculty encompasses History, Geography, Economics and Politics. It is the interaction of these disciplines that shapes society. Similarly to the Science Faculty, on completion of your transition year you will have been taught enough to pass the higher-level Leaving Certificate exams in Economics, History and Geography. In freshman and sophister years we hold weekly seminars to keep students up to date with world events, including those not reported in the media.'

Master Qing nodded to the class and returned to his seat.

'All that on top of a double load of Science,' Ben whispered to Jess.

'And I don't think he's the last one to speak either,' said Jess.

'Crap,' said Matt.

'Thanks, Master Qing,' said Lieutenant Parry. 'You will also see Master Qing in your daily Fitness Training and if ever a language teacher is called out on assignment, Master Qing will fill in for them. Now I'd like to introduce you to Ms Pimsleur, Head of Languages.'

A petite woman of indeterminate ethnic origin stood up.

'I'd like to take this opportunity to congratulate you on your commencement here at Theruse Abbey,' she began. 'Some of you are looking a little overwhelmed, so I'll be brief. The list of languages on offer is quite extensive. At a minimum we expect you to attain an ordinary-level Leaving Certificate standard in all six of the official languages of the United Nations. Although some of you may be in more advanced classes, the teachers for transition year are: Mr Hamid for Arabic, Miss Kwan for Chinese, Mr James for English, myself for French, Señor Carreras for Spanish and Ms Dvoynev for Russian.' Each teacher nodded as Ms Pimsleur introduced them. 'Native speakers of those languages must sit the higher-level exams. Everyone must pass the higher-level exam for Irish.'

'*What?*' exclaimed Matt, loudly enough for everyone in the auditorium to hear.

'Did you have something to say, Mr …?' began Ms Pimsleur, looking directly at Matt.

'Sykes,' said Matt. 'Matt Sykes.'

'Very James Bond,' chuckled Lieutenant Parry.

'Did you have something to say, Mr Sykes?' continued Ms Pimsleur.

'Why do we have to study Irish?' asked Matt.

'You're one of our international students, I take it?'

Matt nodded.

'First and foremost,' explained Ms Pimsleur, 'Irish is the only compulsory subject in the Irish school system at Leaving Certificate level. Second, it gives us a great advantage as secret agents. There are less than one hundred thousand native speakers, and there are less than two million people worldwide who speak any Irish at all. This makes the ability to communicate in Irish one of our greatest assets – kind of a code without a code, if you see what I mean.'

Matt nodded, but the look on his face spoke volumes.

Ms Pimsleur turned her attention back to the rest of the students.

'Unlike Science and Socioeconomics, the language programme is continuous over the full three years at Theruse Abbey. And as Principal Metsen already pointed out, we have also made some revisions to the programme, running more language labs in local dialects. Field agents will have to pass additional tests before being admitted to a region, even after graduation. Any further questions?'

The class remained silent.

'I'll see you all in French class. Enjoy your time here.'

'Just quietly, if I were you I'd hope you never see her in combat training. Ms Pimsleur is a black belt in five separate martial arts disciplines,' said Lieutenant Parry. He made a show of shielding his eyes and squinting out into the audience. 'Are you all still awake out there?'

A ripple of assent ran through the teenagers.

'In which case, I'll reintroduce you to Miss Ball, Head of Arts.'

Miss Ball sat down on the front of the stage next to Lieutenant Parry.

'I don't know about you, but my head is spinning with the amount you have to learn in just three years. Luckily we have a wonderful Arts programme so you can relax and indulge your artistic side. Like languages, Arts classes are held throughout your entire time at Theruse Abbey, so you can really build on your skills. Our courses are divided into Visual Arts, Music, Drama and Dance, which we combine to showcase your talents in the school musical, held at the end of the spring term. Regarding the musical, transition-year students start off-stage, being responsible for costumes, make-up and props; freshman-year students play in the orchestra; and on-stage roles are generally reserved for our sophister-year students. Auditions are open to all, of course, and I'd welcome any of you who want to try out.

'We also encourage our students to master at least one musical instrument. You never know when playing in a string quartet could be a useful cover. In any case, it's a good string to have to your bow, so to speak,' said Miss Ball, blushing at her accidental joke.

'Visual Arts includes a lot of theory, which is essential

knowledge for spies, as artwork fetches millions on the black market. Practical skills are also useful, for example if you need to make a quick disguise or forgery. Dance is excellent for balance and general fitness, and Drama will give you skills to master going undercover. But aside from enhancing your spy skills, most importantly the Arts will allow you to relax and develop to your full potential.' Miss Ball dropped her voice, but the acoustics in the hall brought her words to the ears of the assembled cadets. 'Was I allowed to say that?'

'Yes,' chuckled Lieutenant Parry. He turned to the seated teachers. 'Thank you for your time this morning.' The teachers stood up and filed offstage, leaving only Parry and the transition-year students in the hall.

'Now,' said Lieutenant Parry, 'before I ask for a show of hands for Memory Wipe after that information overload, let me tell you about what I consider to be the most important subjects here at Theruse Abbey. We start each morning with a Physical Education programme. In addition to cardio fitness, muscle training and endurance, we also teach you self-defence and combat techniques from a range of martial arts and military disciplines. Saturdays are devoted to my personal favourite, Fieldwork Fundamentals, where you learn to master all sorts of extreme sports such as rock climbing, abseiling, skiing, scuba diving, white-water rafting – you name it, you'll learn it.'

The mood in the auditorium lifted.

'Almost without exception, every transition-year cadet's favourite subject is Espionage 101. In Espionage you will develop your spy toolkit. You will learn about gadgets and gizmos with Herr Klug, advanced martial arts with Master Qing, code making and code breaking with Signora Enigmistica … It's a really fun subject. And lastly, the most important part of transition year, as at every other school in Ireland, is work experience.'

An excited whisper buzzed around the auditorium.

'Before you get too excited, it won't be quite as glamorous as Tom Cruise in *Mission Impossible*, but we will send you on a real mission, although not one that is truly dangerous, and you will be involved in the planning, gadget briefing, execution and debriefing phases.'

'You mean we have to kill someone?' asked a slim blonde-haired girl with a thick Russian accent.

'What? No,' said Lieutenant Parry. 'By *execution* I mean proceeding with the operation.'

Jess heard a grunt from a few rows behind her. She turned to see a moody-looking boy with unruly dark hair. He had even broader shoulders than Matt, and his face had the same ultra-fit look as the teachers'.

'Your week-long work-experience operations will be staggered throughout summer term, depending on the skills and fitness levels required. These are compulsory and you must pass to continue here at Theruse,' continued Lieutenant Parry. 'Are there any questions?'

'What do we do on Sundays?' asked a freckle-faced girl with brown curly hair and a South African accent.

'I don't want to bring the mood down,' said Lieutenant Parry, 'but most cadets at Theruse spend Sundays catching up on homework or doing instrument practice. Anything else? No takers for Memory Wipe?'

The cadets looked around but all remained quiet.

'Right then. Make your way to the west wing, where you'll find your dorms. Rooms are twin share and your name will be on the door. Your uniforms are in your rooms. Get changed and quickly familiarise yourself with the floor plan on the back of your dorm doors. Master Qing expects you in the transition-year homeroom for your aptitude test in half an hour.'

4

APTITUDE

Jess, Matt and Ben joined the flow of transition-year students towards the west wing. The cadets' names were written on the dormitory doors. Jess's was on the very first door at the top of the stairs, along with the name Emily Harris.

'This is me,' she said to the boys. 'I guess I'll see you at the aptitude test.'

'Unless we decide to swallow some Memory Wipe first,' said Ben gloomily.

'Come on, man. You'll have a college degree by the time you graduate high school,' rallied Matt. 'Plus I need your help with all the study and I really want to stay – the girls here are totally hot. Present company excluded,' he added, winking at Jess.

Jess narrowed her eyes, but Ben leant over and whispered, 'He thinks he's giving you a compliment,' steering Matt away before he could say anything else stupid.

Jess opened the door and checked out her dorm. There were two beds against adjacent walls, two cupboards with inbuilt drawers, two bookshelves, two desks and an en suite bathroom. Her suitcase had been placed on the end of the bed near the window. She was just undoing the zip when the door burst open. The freckle-faced South African girl who'd asked about what to do on Sundays stood in the doorway.

'Hi. I'm Emily, and you must be,' she said, glancing at the door, 'Jessica.'

'I prefer Jess.'

'Jess it is then,' said Emily, flopping down on the other bed. 'Can you believe all that?'

'I'm in shock,' said Jess.

'I don't care what anyone says, I'm trying out for Dorothy.'

'Excuse me?'

'The lead part in the musical. They should give the role to the most talented person, regardless of what year they're in,' said Emily, deadpan.

Jess just stared at her.

'I'm *joking*,' laughed Emily, rolling onto her side. 'I can't even sing! The look on your face! Can you believe the amount of stuff we have to learn?'

'It's a bit more than I thought I was signing up for,' admitted Jess.

'It wouldn't be too bad apart from the languages. Five – no, six – foreign languages in three years, including

Irish. My old school taught Afrikaans and German. Fat lot of good that does me. How about you?'

'We learnt Japanese,' said Jess. 'But my mum's Egyptian and my dad's French, so I've got a head start on French and Arabic at least.'

'Chinese and Russian should be a piece of cake for you then,' said Emily, sitting up. 'Right, what do our real uniforms look like?'

Jess and Emily yanked open a cupboard door each.

'Oh, no.'

'You're kidding me.'

'Yellow *so* isn't my colour.'

'Do you think this means we're in Gryffindor?' giggled Emily as the girls put on their yellow combat fatigues.

'I think Gryffindor's more of a goldy colour with red. Hufflepuff's yellow,' said Jess.

'Hufflepuff it is then,' said Emily.

'These boots feel weird,' said Jess, pulling on a pair of chunky boots that were surprisingly light.

'They're made of a lightweight nanofibre spun from the web of the Amazonian Bokyich spider and are impervious to water, bullets and mosquito stings,' said Emily.

'Really?' said Jess. 'How do you know that?'

'I'm making it up,' laughed Emily, pulling her boots on. 'Did you know they've taken gullible out of the dictionary?'

'Why?' asked Jess. Emily raised her eyebrows as Jess continued, 'What word do they use for gullible now?'

'I think they've just stuck a photo of you in there,' said Emily, giving Jess a pitying look.

Jess thought for a moment and realised two things: one, that her roommate had just made a joke at her expense and, two, that she didn't really like her new roommate.

There was a knock at the door.

'You ready?' Emily asked.

Jess nodded as she tied her laces.

'Yes?' said Emily, opening the door only halfway.

'Hi, I'm Matt,' said Matt, extending his hand to Emily, who looked at it like it was covered in Bokyich spiders. 'I was looking for Jess.'

'Hey there,' said Jess, hurrying to the door before Emily offended one of her new friends. 'Time to go?'

'Aptitude test starts in five,' said Ben, poking his head around the door. 'I'm Ben, by the way,' he said, raising a hand towards Emily before Matt shot him a warning look and he lowered it again.

'OK, Ben-by-the-way. Lead the way,' said Emily.

Jess glanced at the floor plan on the back of the door as she exited her dorm. Instead of turning left to take the most direct way to the transition-year homeroom, Ben turned right and led them a roundabout way through a series of corridors and stairwells.

'Are you sure you're going the right way?' asked Matt.

'If you'd even bothered to look at the map you might be qualified to criticise,' snapped Ben as they passed a staircase.

'Down here,' said Jess, noticing a group of yellow-clad cadets waiting outside a door at the bottom of the stairs. Just as they joined the back of the group the classroom door opened. Master Qing stood in the doorway.

'Come in and choose a seat. Any seat will do.'

Jess was disappointed to see that the room was like most of the classrooms at her old school. She'd been expecting all sorts of unconventional gadgets, but there was nothing other than a whiteboard at the front, a teacher's table and rows of student desks.

Master Qing stood at the front, idly folding origami throwing stars while the cadets filed in and took their seats.

'As you know, you have been offered a place at Theruse Abbey because you are all outstanding,' said Master Qing once they were settled. 'This afternoon's test is to measure exactly how outstanding. The test is designed for you not to finish. Also there are heavy penalties for answering questions incorrectly, so do not guess and do not rush.

'The test will measure your level of knowledge in Arabic, Chinese, English, French, Irish, Russian and Spanish, as well as your numerical and verbal ability.

62

The answers are multiple choice. Are there any questions before you begin?'

Nobody made a sound.

'Then good luck.'

Master Qing tapped the top of his desk, and twenty-four screens slid up out of the cadets' desks while touch keyboards materialised on the desktops.

Excited murmurs went around the classroom, apart from the moody-looking boy from assembly who, Jess noticed, looked distinctly unimpressed.

On the computer's prompting, Jess typed in her name.

Instantly a garbled collection of characters, some of which resembled Greek characters she'd learnt in maths classes at school, appeared on the screen. She put up her hand.

Before she'd even fully stretched her arm up, Master Qing had appeared silently beside her.

'Yes, Ms Leclair?' he said, making Jess jump slightly.

'I think there's something wrong with my computer. The display's all garbled.'

Master Qing looked at her screen. 'That is only garbled if you don't know how to read Russian,' he said. 'It is obvious you do not, so move to the next question.'

With her cheeks burning, Jess pressed 'Enter' and the next question appeared on her screen. Thankfully this one was in English.

Sharon has a brother. Last year she was four times as old as her brother. Next year she'll be twice as old as him. How old are Sharon and her brother now?

Easy, thought Jess, typing 5 and 2.

The next question was a picture of a left-facing dog made up of matches. The instructions were in Spanish, but Jess could guess from her knowledge of French that the task was to make the dog face the other direction by moving only two matches. She completed the task easily and moved onto the next question, which was on Arabic grammar.

Jess continued making her way through the aptitude test methodically, leaving out only the occasional question in Spanish and all of the ones in Russian and Chinese. Then her computer froze.

'Machine is frozen,' complained the blonde-haired Russian girl who'd been confused about Lieutenant Parry's use of the word *execution* in the auditorium.

'That is because the two hours are up,' said Master Qing.

'Two hours?' exclaimed Ben.

'It goes quickly, doesn't it?' said Master Qing. 'We will compile the test results and you will be issued with your individual timetables during dinner, which will be served in the refectory in fifteen minutes. I presume you remember the way from memorising the maps in your dorms.'

'Fantastic. I'm starving,' said Emily as her stomach made a growling sound. 'Let's go.'

'I'll catch up with you,' said Matt.

'You're not hungry?' asked Jess.

'He's got an appetite for something else,' said Ben, nodding towards the Russian girl.

Emily smiled. 'Good luck, *bru*,' she said, before turning to Ben and Jess. 'Now, which way is dinner?'

'This way,' said Ben. 'The refectory's on the ground floor.'

The closer they got to the refectory, the more cadets they saw in red and green fatigues and the more intimidated Jess felt. There was a certain worldliness about the more experienced cadets, and Jess felt even more nervous than she had during the teachers' introductions at the welcome assembly.

The refectory was a long, high-ceilinged room. The teachers' table sat beneath a large stained-glass window with the Theruse Abbey crest. There was a servery along one side of the room and the rest of the space was filled with tables and chairs.

Some cadets were already eating. Others were pushing trays along the serving bench, choosing dishes from the bains-marie.

'Wow! Pizza!' said Ben, reaching for the plate with the biggest slice and putting that on his tray.

'What's so exciting about pizza?' asked Emily, taking a bowl of minestrone.

'I thought they'd have us on some special diet, like green vegetables drizzled with fish oil.'

'Sounds tasty,' said Jess, taking a portion of lasagne and a bowl of green salad.

A tray slammed down on the bench beside her. It was Matt and he was alone.

'What's wrong, bro?' asked Ben, struggling to keep a straight face as he grabbed a slab of tiramisu from the dessert chiller. 'You didn't strike out, did you?'

'It's early days,' sighed Matt. 'I would have been in with a chance if this other dude hadn't been chatting her up in Russian. She'll come round,' he said hopefully, taking a bowl of ice-cream.

'Sure she will. Just like that girl at the ice-cream parlour,' laughed Ben, pointing at Matt's dessert choice.

Jess nearly dropped her tray on the way to their table as Ben told her and Emily about some of Matt's failed conquests.

'And there was this one girl,' Ben said, shaking so hard with laughter as he was sitting down that his bread roll and cutlery threatened to fall off his tray, 'waiting at a deserted taxi rank, late at night, in the rain. Matt didn't even get through his opening line before she pulled out the pepper spray–'

'Sounds like you boys have a few things to learn about cultivating potential assets,' said a deep voice behind them.

The cadets looked up to see Lieutenant Parry thumbing through some papers with an amused expression on his face.

'Well, at least I try,' muttered Matt, shooting Ben a filthy look.

Lieutenant Parry handed the papers out to the cadets.

'These are your timetables. There are no electives for first years, so the only variation is in your language-class assignment.' He turned to go, then spun back around and said in a loud whisper, 'And Jess, just so you know, you topped the aptitude test. Told you I know a good candidate when I see one.'

Jess blushed and pretended to study her timetable avidly as the others looked at her.

She also felt she was being watched from another direction. She glanced up and saw Principal Metsen and Señor Carreras at the teachers' table. Although not looking at her, the principal was facing her direction and she got a decidedly creepy feeling from him.

'I bags you as my study buddy,' said Emily, elbowing Jess.

Jess made a mental note to check for bruising later.

'Cool! We start off with Espionage 101 tomorrow,'

said Matt. 'I can't wait.'

'Espionage isn't first thing tomorrow,' corrected Lieutenant Parry.

'Yes it is, at nine o'clock,' said Matt, pointing to his timetable.

Lieutenant Parry tapped the top of Matt's timetable. 'Fitness Training is first thing in the morning, before classes start. And in case you were wondering, it's not optional.'

'Six-thirty start,' whistled Matt.

'Is that a problem?' asked Lieutenant Parry.

'No. I'm up for it,' mumbled Matt.

'Good to hear it,' said Lieutenant Parry. 'The rest of you?'

'Bring it on,' said Emily.

As Lieutenant Parry went off to distribute more timetables, Jess, Emily and the twins examined their own.

'This course load looks pretty heavy,' said Matt.

'Look at it this way,' said Emily. 'More class time with your Russian soon-to-be girlfriend.'

'Hmph,' said Matt, shoving a forkful of spaghetti into his mouth and slurping up the dangling noodles.

'Yeah, that's the way to win her over,' said Emily, winking at Jess. 'Anyway,' she continued, 'how did you guys find out about Theruse Abbey?'

'GameCon,' said Matt.

'Although the initial screening was through Facebook,' added Ben.

'You didn't tell me that bit,' said Jess.

'A guy friended me and set me a hacking challenge,' said Ben.

'So someone unknown to you sends you a hacking challenge via social media, and you just do it, no questions asked?' said Emily.

'Isn't hacking illegal?' asked Jess.

'Only if you get caught. And I've never been caught,' said Ben, smiling deviously.

'What are you, some kind of überhacker?' Emily asked.

'He's a genius,' said Matt. 'He can break into anything.'

'*Almost* anything,' said Ben somewhat sheepishly. 'Couldn't find any trace of P.E.P. Squad online. Even trying to do a reverse trace through Facebook got me nowhere.'

'And the hacking challenge …?' prompted Jess.

'Oh, right. It was tough, but I managed to break into this supposed supercomputer, and all I could find on it were details about me and Matt.'

'What sort of stuff?' asked Emily.

'Academic records, our business …'

'You've got your own business?'

'Ever heard of BMgaming?' asked Matt.

'*Racing Demons* – of course! You're not … Wow!'

'What's *Racing Demons*?' asked Jess.

'Come on! You must have heard of it. It's my favourite game of all time,' said Emily.

The three of them looked at Jess, forks poised in front of their mouths.

'What can I say? I'm not a gamer,' said Jess. 'What's so special about it?'

'It's the highest-selling product our company makes,' said Matt.

'It's the highest-selling product *any* gaming company makes,' said Emily. 'Did you guys write it?'

'We both worked on the storyline, Matt did the graphics and I did the *real* programming,' said Ben.

'Sounds like you're the brains of the outfit,' said Emily. 'Is he here as some sort of pet?'

'That's a bit harsh!' said Matt.

Jess fought back a smile. Emily's sense of humour was quite funny when she wasn't on the receiving end of it.

'I think he's the one who got me in, actually,' said Ben. 'Matt's held the title of Kuwaiti under-eighteen wrestling champion continuously since he was twelve. He's a machine in the ring.'

'I'll bet he is,' said Emily. 'But back to your hacking the supercomputer …'

'Oh, right. Well, I must have passed the first round because Ms Pimsleur came up to us at GameCon and got us to play that game–'

'What game?' asked Emily.

'The one in the VR cell with the gunmen on the roof,' said Ben.

'Didn't you play it?' asked Jess.

'I didn't play any game. I was offered a scholarship here after I won the South African Go-Karting Con-structathon for the second year running. I guess dodging bullets is the same as dodging other racers in home-made go-karts.' Emily shrugged, then flashed a grin. 'Plus, I'm really smart. But my therapist says I need to work on my interpersonal skills.'

'You have a therapist?' said Matt.

'If you were the only girl in a family of six older brothers, you'd need a therapist too,' said Emily, matter-of-factly.

'What about you, Jess?' asked Ben.

'Gosh, I'm nothing like you guys,' said Jess awkwardly. 'I don't own a company or win national championships or anything. Lieutenant Parry just came to my school posing as an exam supervisor.'

'But why did he choose you? What's your special skill?' asked Emily.

'I don't know. I do OK at interschool sports, and I get top marks all the time.'

'Yeah, we heard. In fact, I think the whole canteen heard,' said Matt.

'Refectory,' corrected Ben.

'Whatever.'

'Well, I'm glad you're here,' said Emily.

Jess was so stunned that Emily had paid her a compliment that her mouthful of lasagne tumbled back out onto her plate.

'Although maybe one of those Swiss finishing schools could also have been a good choice,' laughed Emily.

Jess looked across at Emily and saw a smile playing around her roommate's lips. She'd topped the aptitude test, made some friends and her roommate was turning out to be not completely bad after all. As far as first days go, this had been a good one.

5

FITNESS

An ear-piercing bleeping woke Jess at 6:15 the following morning.

'Morning,' she yawned at Emily as she struggled into her yellow fatigues. When there was no response she continued, 'Did you sleep all right?'

'I don't do chit-chat this early in the morning,' said Emily in a monotone from underneath her duvet. 'Don't take it personally.' She groaned and then struggled out of bed, grumpily shrugging on her clothes.

The girls laced their boots and joined the stream of cadets heading from the dormitories to the gym. The green- and red-clad cadets all seemed quite revved up.

'How can anybody be cheerful at this hour?' grumbled Emily.

'Does that count as chit-chat?' teased Jess.

'Don't push it, Leclair,' said Emily in a less-than-friendly tone.

Jess fought back a chuckle. Turning Emily's medicine back on her was kind of fun.

The door to the gym was open and it was quickly filling up with cadets. All the walls were mirrored. Half the floor was covered in padded gymnastic mats and the other half was bare floorboards, which were slightly springy. The rear of the gym was full of weight machines and cardio equipment. There was a large, empty area on the right-hand side with a raised podium at one end. Punching bags lined the other side of the gym, along with ropes and rope netting that stretched all the way to the ceiling.

Signora Enigmistica stood in the middle of the padded floor, dressed in a tracksuit with a whistle around her neck.

'Grab a bike, a walker or a treadmill or jog around the room half-pace for ten minutes, then we'll start aerobics,' she shouted.

Jess chose a treadmill and was pleased when Ben hopped on the one next to her.

'What does she mean half-pace?' panted Ben, his legs moving wildly to keep up with the conveyor belt. 'I've got this on its lowest setting, and it's faster than I've ever run in my life!'

'Then how do you stay so skinny?' asked Jess, jogging lazily with her treadmill set eight levels higher than Ben's. 'If last night's anything to go on, your diet's terrible.'

'I don't get to eat like that all the time,' puffed Ben, sweating. 'Plus thinking burns up a lot of energy.'

They spent the rest of the run in silence as Ben hadn't the breath to spare for talking.

'Ten minutes is up!' called Signora Enigmistica. 'Time for aerobics. Everybody grab a step.'

Jess and Ben joined the group of cadets gathering plastic platforms and bases.

'If it's your first time, don't bother with the base,' a girl in red told them.

Jess and Ben dropped the bases back and set their platforms next to Matt and Emily at the very back of the room.

'Hi, Emily,' said Ben.

'Don't bother,' warned Jess, but it was too late to stop Emily snarling at him.

'What did I do?' Ben asked Jess.

'Apparently she doesn't do mornings,' explained Jess.

Signora Enigmistica turned on a ridiculously bouncy Europop track at full volume. 'We'll start off easy with some side steps … one … two … Now grapevine left …' she said, crossing her right leg behind the other before stepping the left leg out wide, 'and right!'

Jess, Emily and the boys narrowly avoided crashing into each other as they tried to copy Signora Enigmistica. The colourful sea of cadets in front of them moved as one, apart from the odd yellow-uniformed cadet banging into the person next to them.

'Step basic!' called Signora Enigmistica.

After a few beats, everyone in the room was marching up on the step and back down again in time.

'Watch the change. Grapevine left … right … step basic … grapevine right … left … step basic!'

'I think I'm getting the hang of this,' said Matt, his feet tapping in time with Signora Enigmistica.

'Yay for you,' said Emily sarcastically, as she kept getting the direction of her grapevines confused.

'Knee repeater … straddle … over-the-top … indecision!' called Signora Enigmistica as she danced her way effortlessly over and around the step.

The red- and green-uniformed cadets continued along in perfect time, while the yellows, in particular Emily and Ben, did their best not to fall off the step and break their ankles.

'At least no one can see us back here,' puffed Ben.

'And around the step. Now turn to the back!' said Signora Enigmistica.

The whole class rotated clockwise, apart from Emily who spun anti-clockwise and crashed into Ben.

'You two, middle back!' yelled Signora Enigmistica. 'Back here for an aerobics tutorial after sprint training!'

'Sprint training?' gasped Ben.

'I blame you for this,' grumbled Emily.

'What?' squeaked Ben, struggling to keep up with the routine.

Fifteen sweaty minutes later Signora Enigmistica turned the music off.

'I'll hand you over to Lieutenant Parry now. You two,' she said, eyeballing Ben and Emily, 'don't forget to come see me after sprint training.'

'Reds, rope climbing. Six roofs each – Ms Pimsleur will be checking,' yelled Lieutenant Parry. 'Greens, boxing with Master Qing. Yellows, over here with me for suicide runs.'

'Sounds enticing,' muttered Ben as they walked over to the floorboard area where Lieutenant Parry was standing. Six rows of field markers, spaced evenly apart, stretched from one side of the floorboard area to the other.

'The concept of suicide runs is very simple,' explained Lieutenant Parry, demonstrating. 'You run along to the first marker, touch the ground, then run back to the start and touch the ground again. Then run along to the second marker, touch the ground, run back to the start and touch the ground. And so on right up to the sixth marker and back.

'Now everyone get into teams of four and line up behind one of the rows. When you've all completed your runs, sit down. The last team standing will get to see me after class.'

Jess, Emily and the twins lined up together.

'Go,' yelled Lieutenant Parry.

The six front runners took off. Jess was first in her group. She'd done lots of suicide runs in her athletics training and completed the course with ease. Matt was a lot slower. He was fit but bulky and, although Jess had finished first, by the time Matt had finished their team was coming last. Emily brought them back into third, then it was Ben's turn. He started off well, gaining on the second-place team, but by the time he got to the fourth marker he'd developed a stitch. At the end of his turn, he only just managed to beat the moody-looking dark-haired boy over the line.

'You four see me after class,' said Lieutenant Parry to the last-placed team before blowing his whistle and yelling, 'Rotate!'

The groups of cadets moved on to the next station. Ben and Jess paired up for boxing.

'I'm glad I'm not with Emily,' said Ben, throwing such light punches Jess couldn't even feel them through the thick impact pad. In contrast, Emily was pummelling the pad so hard that she had Matt backed right up against the wall.

Jess could hardly feel her arms after the boxing and only made it all the way to the roof twice on her rope climbs. She was completely drenched with sweat by the time they were dismissed to have showers and breakfast.

Jess was dressed and brushing her hair by the time

Emily made it back to the dorm. Jess turned her back as soon as she heard the door handle turn to avoid making eye contact.

Emily was a lot more civil when she came out of the bathroom.

'I reckon I burnt about a thousand calories just then,' said Emily, sounding like her normal self. 'Let's go load it all back on.'

But breakfast was quite a different set-up to the previous evening. Instead of being able to help themselves to whatever they liked, they saw that the servings of food were packaged with the allocated cadet's name on them.

'What's this about?' asked Emily.

A woman placing the freshly cooked meals in their packets smiled at her.

'Optimum-performance portioning. Meal servings are strictly controlled to keep you in peak physical and mental condition. It's always toughest just after the holidays.'

'Ben was right,' said Jess as they walked to their table. 'Fish oil on green veggies.'

'More like the food pyramid in three easy sachets,' said Emily, plonking down her tray and pouring the allocated amount of milk onto her serving of something that vaguely resembled muesli.

'Mind if I join you, ladies?' asked Matt.

'Where's Ben?' said Emily, looking around.

'I think he passed out in the shower,' Matt replied, tucking into his food with relish.

'He'd better get here quick,' said Jess. 'Espionage starts at nine, and I get the feeling they don't take kindly to latecomers.'

'I wouldn't worry about it – he's an eating machine,' said Matt between mouthfuls.

A clattering of cutlery and crockery made them turn around. Ben's breakfast tray was wobbling like crazy.

'Let me take that,' said Jess, helping Ben put the tray down on the table before everything slid off it. Unlike everyone else, whose meals were made up of cereal, toast and fruit, Ben had an extra plate with bacon, eggs and sausage.

'How'd you score all that?' asked Matt, his mouth full of toast.

'They said I need building up,' said Ben, picking up his knife and fork with shaking arms but immediately setting them down again with a groan. 'After all those failed attempts at rope climbing, I don't think I can use my arms.'

'Hurry up and eat that, or I'll eat it for you,' said Matt, spearing a piece of Ben's bacon with his fork.

'I wouldn't if I were you,' warned Jess. 'They've probably got hidden cameras in the cutlery to make sure you only eat what you've been allocated.'

'And I bet they weigh your poo to make sure their calculations are right,' said Emily.

'Emily!' said Jess.

'It'd be quite simple, really. They could put an inbuilt fingerprint scanner in the buttons on the toilets to identify whose waste it is, then channel it to the lab for individual analysis,' continued Emily, as Jess threw her spoon down in disgust. 'It'd be the perfect way to tweak the optimum-performance portions. The food's probably all genetically modified anyway–'

The bell that rang to signal ten minutes until the start of morning classes interrupted her, to everyone's relief.

'Time to go,' said Matt, stealing a sausage from Ben's plate on his way out.

After brushing their teeth, Jess, Emily and the twins joined the growing group of excited yellow-uniformed cadets back in the gym where that morning's Espionage 101 class was going to be held.

'Good morning, cadets,' said Master Qing. 'I trust you all enjoyed Fitness Training this morning? Now it is time for the real work to begin. As you are aware, this subject is called Espionage 101. In this class you will learn many vital skills that you may need to use in the field to complete a mission, save your life or save the life of another. Please assemble yourselves into four rows of six.'

The cadets got into four rows with Jess, Emily, Matt and Ben in their usual spot at the back.

'On Mondays throughout this term,' continued Master Qing, 'I will teach you the martial art Aihi Choo. It is one of eight martial-art disciplines of which I am a Grand Master. Aihi Choo is primarily hand-to-hand combat. The movements are smaller, faster and more powerful than in similar disciplines, therefore more effective against an opponent.

'Before we begin, I have a very simple rule. Here at Theruse Abbey there are many strong personalities. Your course load is heavy. That can lead to some stress. Let me make it perfectly clear that the practice of Aihi Choo is only permitted inside this classroom, under my strict supervision. Is that understood?'

All the cadets nodded.

'Very well,' said Master Qing. 'We will start with the warm-up.'

He pressed his right fist against his open left palm and bowed deeply. The cadets bowed back. Then Master Qing launched into a series of movements, shouting each movement's name as he did so, expecting the class to follow.

By the end of the warm-up Jess's already aching arms had gone completely numb. She was beginning to regret not finishing her breakfast.

'Gather round,' said Master Qing softly when the warm-up was over. 'Today we will practise felling an opponent.'

He beckoned to Jess.

'Have you studied a martial art before, Ms Leclair?' asked Master Qing.

'No,' said Jess.

'Good. Sometimes it is harder to unlearn than to learn from scratch,' said Master Qing. 'Now, the secret to felling an opponent is to get in close and use their weight against them,' he continued, moving quite close to Jess. 'This can be difficult if your opponent is armed, particularly with a short, stabbing weapon. So the secret is to be swift.'

Master Qing took another half step towards Jess and the next thing she knew he'd snaked a foot behind her leg and kicked her feet out from under her. Jess found herself flat on her back staring at the ceiling.

'Notice how I stepped swiftly behind her, without allowing her time to react?' said Master Qing, helping Jess to her feet. Jess looked at the teacher warily. She had been expecting a little more warning and a lot less thump.

'Now, find a partner and practise. Remember, use your opponent's weight against them.'

Jess and Emily paired up. Ben turned to Matt, but he had joined a large group of boys clustering around the blonde-haired Russian girl, whose name was Svetlana.

'I get on my back for no man,' said Svetlana, instead choosing to work with her roommate, Lauren.

During the class Jess found it was a lot easier to fall over when Emily was on the attack than to hook her own leg in behind Emily's knee and try to knock her over. In the course of their little duels, Emily only fell once, and Jess thought that had more to do with Emily sneezing than her own Aihi Choo skill.

With ten minutes to go, Master Qing split the class in two and sent them to opposite sides of the gym.

'Line up along each wall,' said Master Qing. 'Now, the person at the head of each line, come into the centre, bow, then try to fell your opponent.'

The first two sparrers were Svetlana and Matt.

As Matt sauntered towards Svetlana he shook his head, saying, 'I can't fight a girl, sir.'

Svetlana used his temporary distraction to step up to Matt's side and he was soon flat on his back.

'That's right,' she said, smirking. 'You *can't* fight a girl.' She turned to go.

'Stay there,' said Master Qing. 'This is a knockout competition. What is your name?'

'Svetlana Hanikova.'

'And your name?' asked Master Qing, turning to Ben who was next in line.

'Ben Sykes,' Ben gulped.

'Good luck, Ben Sykes,' said Master Qing with a vague smile on his face.

Ben was better prepared than Matt and kept eye contact with Svetlana as he approached her. They started circling each other. As soon as he was close enough Ben seized the opportunity to shoot his leg behind Svetlana's, but she turned quickly and managed to kick his leg out from under him instead, toppling him over.

And so it went. Svetlana exhausted all the cadets on one side of the hall, and then did the same with those originally queued up behind her. Only Emily managed to engage Svetlana in a lock for a few moments, right knees entwined, hopping around the mat like two boxing kangaroos, before she ended up on her back like the rest of the class.

'Wow, Svetlana,' said Emily when the bell went. 'You must be pretty happy.'

'Not really,' said Svetlana, holding up her left hand to show Emily four perfectly manicured fingernails and one with a jagged tear. 'I break nail.'

6

DRAMA

The refectory was a very different place at lunchtime. While it had buzzed all over with excitement and expectation during breakfast, the lunching cadets, particularly those wearing yellow uniforms, were completely subdued.

'I'm surprised Lieutenant Parry wasn't standing at the door with a big jug of Memory Wipe,' said Emily.

'How on earth are we supposed to learn so much stuff in one year? It's not just a double load, it's a triple load of a double load,' said Ben, massaging his temples.

'I don't know about you, but my legs are killing me,' said Jess, feeling her thighs seize up as she bent to sit in her chair. 'I need to stretch, but I don't have the energy.'

'At least this is an improvement on breakfast,' said Matt, shovelling in forkful after forkful of his huge helping of spaghetti marinara. 'I was beginning to think I'd never see decent food again.'

Once the cadets had finished eating, they sat back in their chairs without speaking to each other. They were too exhausted and overwhelmed. The tolling of the bell in the abbey tower marking the start of afternoon classes sounded ominous.

'What have we got?' asked Matt.

Ben looked at his timetable.

'Drama,' he groaned. 'That was always my worst subject.'

'Yeah, the only time you ever got an A minus,' grumbled Matt.

They joined the other transition years waiting in the auditorium, scattered along the first row of seats.

A pair of high heels clicked across the stage.

'What are you doing down there?' chided Signora Enigmistica. 'Drama takes place on the stage, not in the stalls. Come.'

The cadets climbed up on the stage and gathered around Signora Enigmistica.

'Welcome to Drama. As with the majority of subjects at Theruse Abbey, we will be starting off studying material for the Leaving Certificate syllabus for Drama. But by far the most important aspect of the class is to teach you acting skills so that you can blend in flawlessly on any undercover mission anywhere in the world.

'Today we will be starting with one of my favourite Shakespeare plays, *Hamlet*. What I like most about this play is its title. The plot of *Hamlet* is not one of Shakespeare's originals but is based on much older stories from other cultures. In fact, the word Hamlet is a very basic anagram of the name of the Danish Prince Amleth, from Saxo Grammaticus's version of the story.'

There was a snort from among the students. Jess turned to see that it was the moody-looking dark-haired boy. It was the first time she had been close to him. He had a sneer on his face and an attitude to match.

'Do you have something to add, Ivan?' asked Signora Enigmistica.

'I was just thinking that, for someone as revered as Shakespeare, neither the play nor the attempt at disguising the title is particularly creative,' said Ivan.

'Unlike when we use anagrams as codes in the field, Shakespeare probably didn't care if his prince's code name could be easily deciphered. On that note, do you have any suggestions on how to ensure that the anagrams we use can only be deciphered correctly by those we want to, Ivan?' asked Signora Enigmistica.

'Oh, I don't know. Build some sort of texting device that works as an anagram translator with private key encryption?' he suggested.

Signora Enigmistica smiled.

'Very good. That's exactly the type of device we use in the field, although such devices weren't available four hundred and fifty years ago when Shakespeare was alive. Now,' she continued, turning to the rest of the class, 'let's test your knowledge of *Hamlet*. Who can give me a quote? Jess?'

'To be, or not to be,' said Jess.

'Naturally,' said Signora Enigmistica. 'Anything slightly less mainstream?'

'The lady doth protest too much, methinks,' said Ben.

'To sleep, perchance to dream, ay there's the rub,' said Emily, in a perfect mimic of Mel Gibson's voice.

Signora Enigmistica was duly impressed.

'Excellent, Emily. I had to double-check that Mel Gibson wasn't hiding behind you. Can anyone else do that?'

'They may take our lives, but they'll never take our freedom,' said Ivan, sounding exactly like Emily had but with a Scottish accent.

'Very good,' said Signora Enigmistica. 'Can you do a female voice?'

'You're a human being, you live once and life is wonderful, so eat the damn red velvet cupcake,' said Ivan in a husky female voice with an American accent.

Signora Enigmistica looked at him.

'Emma Stone,' said Ivan.

Signora Enigmistica looked around the class as the other transition years nodded their heads.

'Something for me to google later,' she said. 'Right. Back to our Danish prince …'

After classes had finished for the day, Jess and Emily were holed up in their dorm ploughing through homework. As well as having to learn to recite Hamlet's famous soliloquy, they had a worksheet to complete for Chinese, an essay to write for History and a map to draw for Geography.

Jess leant back in her chair and stretched and yawned widely. Then, as her eyes took in the clock, she straightened up quickly.

'Hey, Em, it's half past six. We'll be late for dinner.'

'What's the rush? I'm sure they won't let anyone else touch our green veg and fish oil,' said Emily distractedly.

Jess's stomach let out a loud growl. Both girls giggled.

'OK, OK, I'm coming!' said Emily.

As they got to the refectory, they saw Ben and Matt coming from the direction of the gym. They were both very sweaty.

'What, this morning wasn't enough for you two he-men?' Emily commented.

'I was spotting Arnold Schwarzenegger here in the gym,' said Matt.

'Why?' asked Jess.

'Let's just say that Krivlyakaev guy gave me extra incentive to bulk up,' said Ben.

'Who's Krivlyakaev?' asked Jess.

Matt and Ben looked at each other uneasily.

'Mr Private Key Encryption from Drama,' said Ben

finally. 'Look, I don't want to talk about it. Can we just drop it?' he said, stalking off towards the servery.

'What happened?' Emily asked Matt.

'Krivlyakaev threatened him,' said Matt quietly.

'What?'

'Why?'

'When?' said Emily and Jess together.

'After Drama,' said Matt. 'Ben thought it'd be cool to chat about encryption keys or something. Krivlyakaev pretended to be interested and offered to shake Ben's hand, but instead he bent Ben's arm behind his back and called him a limp cabbage.'

'A limp cabbage?' Emily laughed.

'It must be a huge insult where he comes from. You could tell from his tone,' said Matt.

'Then what happened?' asked Jess.

'Krivlyakaev said something I didn't quite catch – Ben was moaning pretty loudly – but it went along the lines of if Ben didn't stay away from him, next time he'd break his arm. Unsurprisingly, as soon as classes were over Ben said he wanted to hit the gym.'

'Good for him,' Emily declared approvingly.

'I wonder what Krivlyakaev's problem is?' said Jess crossly, furious that the Russian had threatened her new friend for no apparent reason.

Matt shrugged. 'Who knows?'

They got their food allocations and sat down with Ben at what was quickly becoming their regular table. Ben was tucking into a massive plate of roast beef and vegetables, with a double helping of black forest gâteau. The others' meals varied only in size. Matt had a very thin slice of cake, Jess had a regular serving and Emily didn't get any dessert at all.

'Well this is unfair,' she said, looking at the others' desserts enviously.

Jess dug straight into her cake.

'It's really not that good,' she said, licking the cream off her fork. 'It's very chocolatey, and the cream's quite sweet, and the cherries – well, why would you put fruit in a chocolate cake?'

'Let me judge for myself,' said Emily, reaching towards Jess's plate with her fork.

'No,' said Jess, whipping her plate away. 'They're going to analyse my poo later, remember, and if a single chocolate shaving's missing they'll know.'

'Just a bit,' begged Emily.

'No. And it's for your own good,' said Jess, quickly spooning cake into her mouth. 'You're in the military now and you have to learn self-discipline. Not eating cake is good for your moral fibre.'

'Not letting me share some will be extremely bad for your moral fibre,' threatened Emily.

But it was too late. Jess had already finished her slice.

Emily turned her attention to Matt's dessert.

'Not on your life, lady,' said Matt, putting his fork up protectively.

Emily looked over Matt's shoulder and said, 'Who's that guy talking to Svetlana?'

Matt turned around and Emily helped herself to a large chunk of cake.

'Where is she?' said Matt, looking around for Svetlana.

'Jus over dare,' said Emily, her mouth full, while she helped herself to another forkful.

Matt gave up looking and turned around to find his dessert bowl empty, except for a few crumbs.

'Sucker!' said Emily gleefully. 'And I agree with Jess. It wasn't very good.'

Matt glared at Emily for a moment, then turned to Ben. 'Bro,' he wheedled.

'Nuh-uh!' said Ben. 'If this is what I need to help me stand up to creeps like Krivlyakaev, then you couldn't possibly deprive me of it and live with yourself, could you?'

Matt gave up and dropped his fork on his empty plate.

'You're too easily manipulated, Matt,' said Emily. 'You just gave in to emotional blackmail, and you lost out on your rightful piece of cake because of your crush on the Russian ice queen.'

'I'd like to thank you all for teaching me a valuable lesson today,' said Matt, eyeing the others carefully. 'Next time, when we're on real a mission and it's eat cake or save my friends, you know what my decision will be.'

7

ROACH

As the week wore on, the punishing physical activity and heavy subject load began to take their toll on Jess. When the 6:15 wake-up call went off on Friday morning, it was the most unwelcome noise she had ever heard. Her entire body ached and her brain was spinning from all the lessons and homework assignments. As a result she was feeling less than happy.

'Uurgh,' groaned Jess.

'What did I say about chit-chat?' grouched Emily, hurling a pillow at Jess, which smacked her right in the head.

Despite the pain she felt in every muscle, Jess leapt out of bed and ripped Emily's duvet off her.

'Oi! Give that back,' yelled Emily.

'Go get it,' said Jess, throwing the duvet out into the corridor.

Emily stormed through the door and Jess slammed it behind her and locked it.

'Hey,' yelled Emily, rattling the handle. 'Let me back in!'

'Oh, I'm sorry, does that count as *chit-chat*?' said Jess, pulling off her pyjamas and changing into her combat fatigues.

'Jess, you let me in right now or I'll–'

'You'll what? Be late for class? Because I'm not opening this door until you apologise.'

'Apologise? For what?' yelled Emily.

By this time a few bleary-eyed cadets were poking their heads out into the corridor to see what all the noise was about.

'Oh, I don't know,' Jess yelled back, lacing her boots. 'Throwing pillows at me. Not letting me *breathe* too loud in the morning in case it disturbs you. What else would you like me to add to the list?'

'Come on, Jess. People are staring,' pleaded Emily quietly.

'Apology first,' said Jess, tying her hair in a ponytail.

'Fine. I'm sorry,' said Emily. 'Can I come in now?'

'Not until you promise to change your attitude,' said Jess.

'Change my … what are you? My mother?'

'Worse. I'm your roommate. I have to put up with you twenty-four/seven, and if I can't even let out a groan in the morning, then … um … that's your problem and you have to deal with it. Young lady,' Jess added, with a giggle.

Emily sighed. 'OK. I'm sorry. I'll work on my attitude,' she grumbled.

Jess unlocked the door and Emily barged in. 'But only with you,' she hissed. 'If anyone else tries to talk to me in the morning, they're dog meat.'

Not wanting to push her luck, a smug Jess kept quiet on the way to Fitness Training.

'How's it going?' asked Lieutenant Parry, standing at the door of the gym with a welcoming smile for the tired cadets. 'Any takers for Memory Wipe yet?' His expression changed when he saw Jess and Emily arrive. 'I understand there was a bit of a commotion in the dorms this morning. All sorted now?'

'Just peachy,' said Jess, putting her arm around Emily's shoulders and smiling broadly.

'Great,' said Lieutenant Parry.

With tired, overworked muscles, the morning's training session seemed even harder than the previous ones, and no one had any energy left to talk during breakfast. Even Ben was finding it hard to get excited about their next class, a special Espionage 101 lesson in the electronics lab, run by Herr Klug.

Herr Klug, on the other hand, was very excited, bouncing on his toes as he waited for the exhausted cadets to take their seats.

'Good morning, cadets. I have a real treat for you

today,' he said. 'We will be testing a revolutionary new bug from P.E.P. Squad research labs: the ROACH 2000.'

Out of the corner of her eye, Jess saw something scurry across her desk. Ugh! A cockroach. She slammed her electronics textbook down on it and immediately a high-pitched wail erupted from the speakers on Herr Klug's desk.

Herr Klug winced as he muted the volume, then turned to the class and smiled. 'Ah. Miss Leclair. It would seem you have located the missing one.'

Jess looked under her textbook. Instead of the guts of a smeared cockroach, a tiny pile of broken electronic circuitry lay on the desk. She shrugged apologetically and handed the remains to Herr Klug, who looked like a child whose toy had broken on Christmas morning.

'ROACH is short for Remote Optical Audio Channelling. Two thousand is the number of the prototype – this is the two-thousandth version the lab has made. And from the relative ease with which Miss Leclair spotted it and destroyed it, we will have to start work on model 2001,' continued Herr Klug, shaking his head. 'Never mind. This morning we will be testing the ROACHes. They are remote controlled. Please take one ROACH wristband between two.'

Half of the cadets went up to Herr Klug's desk, where he had a box of what looked like watches. Emily brought one back to the desk she was sharing with Jess. It had a digital display and underneath the display was a tiny joystick.

'You can release the ROACHes by flipping open the display,' said Herr Klug, demonstrating. 'Press the joystick in to activate them.'

Emily flipped the display open to reveal the little ROACH inside. She lifted it out and placed it on the desk in front of her. When she pressed the joystick it started twitching. The image of the world as seen by the ROACH popped up on the display.

'Cool!' said Emily.

Jess shuddered. Although she knew the ROACH was just a tiny electrical gadget, the gleam of its wings and the way its antennae twitched made it seem like a real bug.

Emily moved the joystick to the left and the ROACH went left; she moved it to the right and the ROACH scurried back in the other direction. She moved the joystick in circles and the ROACH chased its tail.

'This is neat!' said Emily.

'What happens when it gets to the edge of the desk?' asked Jess, sitting well back from the desk and looking at the ROACH with revulsion.

Emily moved the joystick back to the right, and the ROACH walked right off the edge of the desk before tumbling to the floor. It landed on its back, its six little mechanical legs wiggling helplessly in the air.

'They can walk up and down surfaces up to forty-five degrees, but any steeper and they tend to take a tumble,' laughed Herr Klug.

Telling herself that it was not a real cockroach, Jess picked up the ROACH and set it on its feet. Then it was off again.

'The signal should have a range of several hundred metres, depending on the density and ferromagnetic properties of the surfaces between you and the ROACH,' said Herr Klug. 'The ROACH transmits optical and audio signals back to the wristband. The optical output comes up on the display, and there is a wireless earpiece for the audio.'

'So it's a real bug,' said Svetlana.

'No, it's a robotic listening device with optical capability *disguised* as an insect,' said Herr Klug. 'Your assignment is to test the signal strength of the ROACH, taking note of the distance from you to the ROACH and the type and thickness of material between you and the ROACH.'

'Hey, Jess,' said Emily, 'can you pick ours up again and hold it on the other side of Matt's head?'

Again, Jess fought back her impulse to stamp on it and picked up the ROACH, holding it on the opposite side of Matt's head to where Emily was standing.

'Signal's extremely clear,' said Emily, tapping the earpiece in her own ear. 'It's like there's absolutely nothing between the ROACH and the receiver,' she added cheekily.

'Ha, ha,' said Matt, clearly unimpressed.

Meanwhile Ben was busy building a fort out of textbooks to see how the thick books affected the ROACH's signal.

'Please be as adventurous as possible,' said Herr Klug from the front of the classroom. 'The more research you do, the better your grade, and the more help you'll be giving our research labs.'

When the class was over, Emily picked up the tiny ROACH and popped it back inside the control unit.

'This is a great gizmo. I'm going to test it on Monday morning in English. See if the signal can reach all the way from the classroom to my bed. But for now,' she said, glancing at her timetable, 'it's time to get in touch with our artistic sides.'

Jess was surprised to see that the Art teacher was Miss Kwan, their Chinese teacher.

'I can see by the looks on your faces that you weren't expecting me,' said Miss Kwan. 'But I can assure you that we won't be holding any of the Art classes in Chinese until next term.'

The whole class drew in their breath nervously.

'I'm *joking*,' said Miss Kwan and the cadets all relaxed. 'Instruction in Chinese begins in summer term.'

Ignoring the horrified looks on the cadets' faces she continued. 'This term we will be learning many of the techniques you will need for your contribution to the school musical. Anyone who wasn't too overwhelmed by the course descriptions at assembly will remember that transition-year cadets are responsible for props, costumes and make-up. Our first learning unit is cosmetics.'

All the boys groaned.

'It might interest you to know that the top prosthetic make-up artists in the world are all male,' said Miss Kwan, making the boys sit up with interest. 'Although that isn't a viable career option for any of you, of course, because you're all going to be spies when you graduate.

'Today we'll start with faces. In the field we tend to use prosthetic masks if we want to disguise an operative or, in rarer cases, have the operative impersonate an asset or a target. So most often, the masks will look entirely human. Your task will be to create one of these masks for yourself. But as Art class is a chance for you to indulge your artistic expression, feel free to add some sort of disfigurement to your mask or even make it look like an animal or alien – the only limit to what you can do is your imagination.

'For this exercise you'll be working in pairs. Could the cadets on this side of the room please stand up, take a latex head cap and a jar of Vaseline from the front desk, then introduce yourself to someone on the other side of the room who you haven't worked with before.'

'Wow, having to make new friends,' muttered Emily as their side of the class stood up. Unsurprisingly, Matt paired himself with Svetlana (who looked less than happy about it) while Ben steered well clear of Krivlyakaev, opting for Lauren. Jess introduced herself to a tall boy named Aidan.

'You will, of course, be making each other's masks,' said Miss Kwan once the class had settled. 'For this we use a method called lifecasting. To start with, place the latex cap over your partner's hair and cover any facial hair, including eyebrows, with Vaseline.'

'Do you want to be the moulder or the mouldee?' Aidan asked.

'Mouldee doesn't sound too appealing,' said Jess. 'Not that I think you'd do a bad job,' she added hurriedly. 'It just makes me think of mildew.'

'Right,' said Aidan. 'I guess I'll be the first mouldee then.'

Jess pulled the latex cap over Aidan's hair, making sure it covered the edge of his hairline. Then she carefully coated Aidan's eyebrows and his attempt at sideburns with Vaseline.

'Has everyone finished step one?' asked Miss Kwan, walking around the class handing out strip bandages and bowls of something slimy. 'Now we begin on what is called a hard mother mould. The first step is to cover your partner's face with alginate. When it sets, the alginate will become the base of your mask. Even when set it's very flexible, so we'll build up a hard shell with quick-set bandages. Spread them evenly over your partner's face, working outwards from the nose.'

Jess grabbed a handful of alginate and slapped it on Aidan's face.

'That's freezing,' complained Aidan, trying to shake it off.

'That's not helping,' said Jess, rolling the next goopy handful between her palms to try to warm it up a little.

Once she'd covered Aidan's face with alginate, she smoothed strip after strip of quick-set bandage over it, building it up until it was quite chunky. Pretty soon half the class looked like the invisible man.

'When you've finished, leave the cast on your partner's face for about ten minutes to harden, then you can swap,' said Miss Kwan.

Jess applied the final strip of plaster then went to see how her friends were doing. Ben's plaster mould was so perfectly smooth that it looked like he'd covered Lauren's face in white foundation cream. She couldn't recognise who Emily was working with, but Matt looked like he was in seventh heaven, having Svetlana as a literally captive audience.

'Isaat en inutes et?' came a muffled cry from Jess's desk.

'Oops!' she said. 'Sorry, Aidan, let's see how this worked.'

Jess peeled the mask off Aidan's face.

'That feels better,' he said, rubbing his cheeks. He glanced at the lumpy mask. 'Handsome fellow.'

'It's amazing how that doesn't come across when you're not covered in plaster,' said Jess dryly.

'That's it. Grotesquely disfigured space alien for you!' said Aidan.

'Those of you who have finished can put your moulds on the drying racks by the window, then take a skull cap for your partner,' said Miss Kwan.

Aidan smiled gleefully as he brought back the materials to make Jess's mask. 'Your turn to go mouldy, gross alien girl,' he said.

Aidan had Jess in stitches describing how he was going to decorate the mask, while he spread the bandages over her face. 'Over here I'll do a big collection of boils, where leaking reactor fluid from your spaceship's nuclear engine broiled your skin,' he said as he smoothed the bandages over her cheeks, 'and these will be the bases for the tentacles sprouting out of your forehead here, here and here – stop laughing! You're cracking the alginate – and I'll build the nose up to look like a cross between a manatee and a toucan – hold still. How am I supposed to work with such amateurs? And as for your chin ...'

Jess was a little disappointed when Aidan finally took the mask off and there was nothing but a plain, white plaster face.

'What's wrong?' asked Aidan.

'You'd built it up so much, I was kind of hoping to see all the grotesque alien-girl stuff,' Jess admitted sheepishly.

'That'll be in the real mask. This is just the mould, remember? I've got a whole week to plan exactly how hideous I'm going to make you,' smiled Aidan.

'If your masks are dry, you can fill them with gypsum cement to make the positive mould,' said Miss Kwan. 'You will need to make two positive moulds. Once you've finished, you may go to lunch.'

The mask Jess had made of Aidan's face was dry enough for the cement, but the cast of her own face still had some time to set.

'Go ahead,' said Aidan. 'I'll amuse myself watching the plaster dry.'

Jess was mixing a bowl full of cement when she heard Aidan's voice whisper in her ear, 'How are you enjoying working with the attractive Mr Aidan Lyons?'

Jess spun around, splashing cement all over herself to see Emily grinning at her.

'How do you do that?' asked Jess.

'Mimic people or spot when they've got crushes?' grinned Emily.

'I don't know what you're talking about,' said Jess, feeling her cheeks go red.

'You mean it's escaped your notice that he's the cutest boy in the year?' continued Emily.

'Not so loud,' hissed Jess, looking over at the drying racks where Aidan was prodding the mask to see if it was dry. 'He's good to work with. Doesn't throw too many pillows at me. Who did you end up with?' she asked, trying desperately to change the subject as Aidan picked up his mask and headed towards them.

Emily grinned an evil grin. 'Krivlyakaev.'

'You chose him?'

Emily nodded.

'Why?' asked Jess.

'I thought it would be a good chance to gather some intelligence. See what his problem is. Turns out overinflated ego, god complex and when he feels threatened intellectually he turns to violence,' said Emily.

'He told you all that? What did you do? Dip the bandages in truth serum?'

'Nah,' said Emily. 'My eldest brother's a psychologist. I was reading through one of his textbooks when I was six and found this chapter about how you identify basic personality types.'

'How do you do that?' asked Jess.

'Now that would be telling,' said Emily mysteriously.

'What would be telling?' asked Aidan, setting his mask on the bench and spooning cement into it.

'Aidan, this is Emily, my nerdy roommate who reads psychology textbooks for fun,' said Jess.

'Hey, I like reading ahead. It gives me an edge,' said Emily.

'Emily, this is Aidan, who wants to turn me into some freakishly disfigured space alien,' continued Jess.

'That shouldn't be too much of a challenge, considering she looks like a freakishly disfigured space alien already,' said Emily, winking.

'Your homework,' said Miss Kwan from the front of the room as the bell rang, 'is to draw life-sized sketches of your mask design, face-on and left and right profiles, in full colour. We'll begin clay sculpting next lesson.'

8

ABSEILING

Despite the physical and mental exhaustion, Jess was becoming conditioned to waking early and Saturday was no exception. She opened one eye and looked at the alarm clock on her desk, cursing herself when she saw that it was only 6:14. She pulled the duvet over her head in a desperate effort to get back to sleep.

Then all hell broke loose.

A high-pitched bleeping – much louder than their alarm on previous days – broke out, followed by a howl from Emily's bed on the opposite side of the room.

'Agh! I can't believe we didn't turn the stupid *dinges* off. It's the weekend!' cried Emily, pulling her own duvet over her head.

'*Dinges?*' said Jess as she got out of bed and padded over to the alarm. 'Is that South African for something that dings?' She hit the Snooze button, but the noise continued.

'No, it's a *thing*, you Uitlander.'

'I'm not even going to bother with that one,' muttered

Jess, banging the alarm's Off button repeatedly and finally pulling the cord out of the wall. Only then, as the noise persisted, did she realise that it was not coming from their machine. 'Emily, that's not our alarm.'

'What?' said Emily, poking one eye out from under the covers.

There was a sharp rap at the door.

'Do you think there's a fire?' asked Jess, running to the door.

'There'd better be,' grunted Emily.

Jess opened the door to find Signora Enigmistica standing on the other side, dressed in her tracksuit with a whistle around her neck.

'I thought you girls might try to sleep in this morning. Up you get!' she said, walking into the room and pulling Emily's bedclothes back.

'What are you doing?' cried Emily.

'The same thing we do every morning. Fitness Training!' said Signora Enigmistica. 'Come on. Get dressed!'

'But it's Saturday,' grumbled Emily, reaching for the duvet.

'Oh, Saturday. I forgot,' said Signora Enigmistica, holding it out of Emily's reach. 'Of course we don't exercise on Saturdays. We also don't eat breakfast, lunch or dinner.'

'We get the message,' said Jess. 'Two minutes.'

While Emily and Jess were getting dressed they could hear Signora Enigmistica rapping on all the cadets' doors.

As they left their dorm they bumped into Ben and Matt.

'If Lieutenant Parry had said anything about no sleep-ins on Saturdays I never would have signed up,' said Matt grumpily.

'And if I'd known he was *a true pantyliner*, I would never have signed up either,' laughed Ben, after glancing at a small electronic device.

'You what?' said Emily.

'Gadget boy's latest invention,' said Matt, rolling his eyes. 'An anagram generator.'

'But *a true pantyliner*?' asked Emily.

'Anagram for Lieutenant Parry,' said Ben.

'When did you get time to make that?' asked Jess.

'Lifting weights is so mindless I had to do something to stop my brain from imploding, so I wrote the code in my head,' said Ben.

'Nerd,' said Emily.

'Now there's no need for name calling,' said Ben, typing into the gadget again, '*my Irish earl*.'

'What?' snapped Emily irritably.

'Anagram of Emily Harris,' said Jess when Ben refused to answer.

'By now you should know better than to be *that chic*

111

in the morning,' growled Emily, running ahead with the other cadets, who were starting their workout by doing laps around the gym.

'She's getting a bit friendlier in the mornings now,' observed Ben.

'I'd hardly say so,' said Jess. 'Try typing *that chic* into your gadget.'

'Hitch cat … ah, chit-chat. She still doesn't like it,' said Ben.

'If you two have time for chit-chat,' said Herr Klug as he jogged up behind them, 'then you have time for fifty squat thrusts after your warm-up.'

Ben was about to protest but shut his mouth when Emily ran past him smirking.

Emily was still grinning when they got to breakfast.

'Nothing makes me happier than watching people doing punishment for too much chit-chat in the mornings,' she trilled as she smeared her toast with her allowance of thirteen grams of butter.

'Maybe you could just do some squat thrusts in your room before the alarm goes off and leave me out of it,' Ben grumbled at Jess.

'If you hadn't been playing with that gadget, then this

never would have happened,' Jess grumbled back.

'OK if I chow with you guys?' asked Lieutenant Parry.

'Go ahead,' said Matt through a mouthful of Weetabix.

'How are you all enjoying your first week here?' asked Lieutenant Parry.

'It's pretty tiring,' said Jess, sprinkling her allocated one hundred and six grains of sugar on her porridge.

'These early mornings are a killer,' said Matt.

'You'll get used to it,' said Lieutenant Parry. 'How about the classes?'

'It'd be OK without the languages,' said Emily.

'I still can't get my head around Chinese,' admitted Jess.

'Espionage 101 is good,' said Ben. 'Especially the gadgets lesson.'

'Now why doesn't that surprise me?' said Lieutenant Parry. 'I guess you'll be applying to work in the research labs instead of being a field agent when you graduate?'

'You bet,' said Ben, crunching on his bacon.

'No Memory Wipe needed for this table then?' continued the lieutenant.

'I think someone slips me a gallon of it before every Chinese lesson,' grumbled Jess.

'Well, forget about classes for now,' said Lieutenant Parry. 'Saturdays are all about Fieldwork Fundamentals.'

'Oh, yeah,' said Matt. 'What are we doing today?'

'One of the rules of Fieldwork Fundamentals is for you to be prepared for anything, so it'd be unfair for me to tell you,' said Lieutenant Parry, 'even if you are my mentees.'

'Is that Irish for *boets*?' asked Emily.

'I have no idea what you just said,' said Lieutenant Parry, taking a gulp of coffee, 'but to be clearer, I am your mentor and you are my mentees. If you're having problems with school work, or any problems at all, or want some career advice, I'm here for you.'

Jess felt pleased. She liked Lieutenant Parry the best out of all the teachers she'd so far come across at Theruse Abbey.

'Do you mentor all the first years?' asked Ben.

'Just you guys. We get a handful of you each. I'll actually be your mentor for your whole time here.'

'Could have done worse, I guess,' said Emily, grinning.

'Too right,' said Lieutenant Parry. 'I like to meet up as a group once a week. Group discussion does wonders for boosting morale. You can of course meet me for one-on-one appointments as well. You guys have a think and let me know the time that suits you best.'

He stood up and took a final swig of his coffee. 'But right now I've got the whole lot of you for Fieldwork Fundamentals. We're meeting at the back entrance at nine. Don't be late.'

Jess finished her porridge quickly and went off to

brush her teeth, leaving the others behind. She was still slightly annoyed with Ben and Emily for the squat-thrust incident. Rather than waiting for them, she took the rear stairs down to the back entrance so she wouldn't risk bumping into anyone returning from the refectory.

She had been so busy during the first crazy week that she hadn't spent any time outside in the school grounds. As the week wore on the rain had been torrential. Even the scheduled outdoor classes had been relocated inside.

'There's no point having you all come down with the flu in the first week of term,' Signora Enigmistica had said.

In stark contrast this morning was glorious. As Jess stepped out through the back door the smell of salt air hit her immediately. In the distance she could hear the crash of waves hitting the cliffs that surrounded the abbey grounds. She closed her eyes and felt the sun on her face, letting her body soak up the fresh air for the first time in a week. Standing alone in the sunshine, Jess felt like she'd found her own private Nirvana.

'Hi.'

The voice startled Jess so much she jumped.

'Sorry,' said Aidan. 'I didn't mean to scare you.'

'Oh, no. I was just ... um,' said Jess.

'Hi, Aidan,' said Emily loudly as she walked up to them, then whispered to Jess, 'I was wondering why you were in such a hurry after breakfast.'

Jess shot Emily a furious look, but Aidan's roommate had also arrived and the two of them were chatting so he missed the remark. Gradually the rest of the transition years arrived and finally Lieutenant Parry turned up, carrying three huge canvas rucksacks that he dropped on the ground with a heavy *thunk*. 'Welcome to Fieldwork Fundamentals. Today we'll be—'

'Dropping heavy bags on the ground,' Matt whispered just a little too loudly.

Lieutenant Parry's head snapped around.

'Congratulations, cadet. You've just earned the right to carry one of these,' he said, picking up a rucksack and tossing it at Matt, who stumbled under its weight as he caught it.

Krivlyakaev laughed.

'Another volunteer, fantastic,' said the lieutenant, flinging a second sack at Krivlyakaev.

The pack slammed into Krivlyakaev with a wallop, but he was ready for it and caught it with his feet firmly planted on the ground.

'I just need one more.' Lieutenant Parry looked at the gathered students. 'How about we see if a girl can carry one?'

He tossed the final pack to Emily, who stood her ground and caught it without shifting her feet.

'Well, don't just stand there, get moving,' said Lieutenant Parry, starting off across the lawn and heading into the trees.

'What we doing today?' asked Svetlana, as the group rushed to keep up with him.

'Abseiling and, depending on how much time we have, Australian rappelling. You'd be surprised the number of times it comes in useful to scale a high wall or abseil down the side of a building when you're on a mission,' replied the lieutenant.

The fresh air and the thought of doing an adventure sport put the cadets in high spirits as they hiked through the trees. The sound of the waves grew louder until all of a sudden they reached the edge of a thicket, only metres away from a cliff.

Some metal stakes had been hammered into the ground midway between the thicket and the top of the cliff.

'Here we are,' said Lieutenant Parry. 'Has anyone not been rock climbing or abseiling before?'

Everyone except Krivlyakaev put up their hands.

'Then I'm glad you're here, Ivan,' said Lieutenant Parry. 'You can be my wingman. You can put your bag down now. You too, Matt and Emily.'

Matt, Emily and even Krivlyakaev dropped the sacks with relief.

Lieutenant Parry opened one of the sacks and tipped it

upside-down. A stack of orange helmets and what looked like loops of seat belt straps fell on the ground.

'This is your safety gear,' he continued. 'Standard mission combat gear includes a belt with a retractable wire and grappling hook, but that's for the professionals. While you're learning, we use regular abseiling gear, which includes ropes, harnesses and, of course, helmets. It's old school, but it's safe and ideal for training.

'We'll start with the helmet. Make sure it fits nice and snug.'

Jess put one of the bright orange helmets on her head and pulled the chin strap tight.

'Now this,' said Lieutenant Parry, holding up a D-shaped metal clip a little smaller than the palm of his hand, 'is a carabiner. You open it by unscrewing this,' he continued, demonstrating. 'You can then clip it onto the rope, screw it shut tight again and that'll hold you.

'This,' he said, holding up a contraption that looked like loops of seat belt strung together, 'is your climbing harness. One loop for each leg and the big loop for your waist,' he continued, stepping into the harness. 'The straps on the legs and the waist are adjustable. They should be pulled tight in a way that is firm, yet comfortable.'

Although Lieutenant Parry had made it look easy, when Jess tried to step into her harness she got into all sorts of trouble.

'Having trouble threading all your alien tentacles through the right loops?' teased Aidan. His climbing harness was already done up.

'Yeah. Accessories aren't really my thing,' said Jess, feeling a bit useless.

'I think you've got your left leg through the bit where your waist should go,' said Aidan.

'Ah,' said Jess, sliding the whole harness off to start again.

'Let me,' said Aidan, picking up the harness and untangling it. 'Right leg in here. I said *right* leg.'

'Oh, sorry,' said Jess, putting her left foot down and stepping her right leg through the loop.

'Now your other right leg …'

Jess stepped into the harness and Aidan threaded the waistband around her waist.

'Just as well putting one of these on wasn't on the entrance exam,' joked Aidan.

Jess liked the attention but wished she didn't always come across as such a klutz around Aidan.

'When you tighten the belt, make sure you thread it back through the buckle to make it look like a C for closed,' said Lieutenant Parry.

'If you just thread it through once, the buckle looks like an O. If it's O for open, it can come loose,' said a voice Jess hadn't heard since the welcome assembly. It was

Principal Metsen. 'Good morning, cadets.'

'Good morning, Principal Metsen,' chorused the cadets.

'Continue,' he said, nodding at Lieutenant Parry.

Lieutenant Parry paused for the briefest moment before continuing. Jess got the feeling that Metsen rubbed him up the wrong way.

'There's a carabiner at the front of your harness. Make sure you secure yourself to the rope before attempting any of the exercises today.

'The rope acts as your safety line and also as your brake. To make things simple, we'll all do this the same way, even you left-handers out there. Hold the rope in front of you with your left hand. This will be above you as you go down the rock. The rope behind you acts as your brake. Hold it in your right hand. When you want to stop, pull it hard to the left. OK?'

The cadets nodded.

'Would you prefer top or bottom?' Lieutenant Parry asked Principal Metsen.

'It's your class. I wouldn't want to interfere with the way you run it,' said the principal.

'I'll take the top, then,' said Lieutenant Parry, setting up the ropes while Principal Metsen put on his climbing harness and helmet. He clipped his carabiner onto one of the ropes that Lieutenant Parry had attached to the stakes in the ground.

'See you down there,' he said, walking backwards over the cliff, holding the rope in front of him with his left hand and behind him with his right as Lieutenant Parry had shown the cadets.

The cadets peeked over the edge of the cliff to watch. The principal was heading for a wide ledge about ten metres below the top of the cliff. The waves crashed into the cliff wall thirty metres below that, sending a fine mist of sea spray onto the ledge. There was a carved staircase just to the side of the ledge with a handrail that extended all the way from the top of the cliff down to the water. A little further past the staircase the cliffs hollowed into a narrow bay with a small, sandy beach.

When Principal Metsen reached the ledge he landed in a low squat. He threaded the rope through a metal stake hammered into the ledge and called, 'On belay!'

'Now it's your turn,' said Lieutenant Parry, smiling at the cadets. 'Who wants to go first?'

'I go,' said Svetlana.

'There are two ways to go down the rock,' Lieutenant Parry explained as he supervised Svetlana securing the rope through her carabiner. 'You can either walk or you can make a triangle with your legs and bounce off the rock like this,' he continued, demonstrating on the flat ground. 'You won't be going that fast, but remember to bend your knees when you come back towards the rock.

We don't want any broken legs today. When you get to the ledge, squat right down like Principal Metsen did. That'll give the rope some slack and make it easier to unhook yourself. You ready?'

Svetlana took a deep breath and nodded.

'OK. Hold the rope in front of you with your left hand, behind you with your right, and walk towards the edge.'

'Backwards?' asked Svetlana.

'Yep.'

Svetlana backed her way to the edge of the rock.

'Now what I do?' she asked.

'Put your heels over the edge and lean back,' said Lieutenant Parry.

'Like this?' said Svetlana, leaning back until her legs were horizontal and her body was at a forty-five degree angle to the cliff face.

'That's it,' said Lieutenant Parry. 'Now either walk down the rock or make a triangle with your legs and bounce.'

Svetlana took off down the rock and reached the bottom in no time.

'Who's next? Jess?'

Jess clipped her carabiner onto the rope and walked backwards to the edge of the rock. When she got to the very edge, she leant back, drawing the rope firmly behind her to the left. Jess let her body tilt until her legs were horizontal with the ground but her torso was still upright.

'Lean back a little,' said Lieutenant Parry.

Gradually Jess played out the rope and angled her torso.

'OK,' said Lieutenant Parry. 'Down you go.'

Jess took a few tentative steps.

'Loosen up on the brake,' called Lieutenant Parry.

Still holding the rope tightly, Jess moved it slightly to her right. She then pushed herself off the rock and slid down a bit. It was easier than she had thought. She held the rope further to the right, pushed off with her legs and slid the rest of the way to the bottom.

Principal Metsen helped her unhook herself from the rope with a broad smile, although Jess noticed his eyes weren't smiling. 'Well done,' he said, pointing her to the stairs. Jess was already halfway up by the time Matt had leaned back over the edge, and he didn't seem to have moved when she got to the top.

Ben sidled over to Matt and made a very soft *bwaark-bwark-bwark-bwark-bwaaark* sound. Matt narrowed his eyes and pushed off.

'That's it,' said Lieutenant Parry. 'Keep those legs bent. Loosen up on the brake. You've got it. Who's next?'

Gradually each of the cadets had a turn.

'This time,' said Lieutenant Parry, setting up another rope, 'we're going to do it in pairs, racing to the bottom. And please, although it's a race, make sure you concentrate on your landing. I don't want any broken ankles or coccyges. In the case of a tie, the first person to unclip from the rope will be declared the winner, as judged by Principal Metsen. Pair up!'

Matt was absolutely stoked when Svetlana came up to him and asked him to be her partner. Emily just laughed.

'It's not because she fancies you, she just wants to win.'

'You keep telling yourself that,' said Matt, clipping himself on to the rope.

Lieutenant Parry blew his whistle and Svetlana was down the cliff and unclipping her carabiner before Matt had even made it over the edge.

Emily laughed herself silly, until she noticed Krivlyakaev laughing just as hard. She glared at him for a few seconds, then a cheeky grin came over her face.

'What's up?' asked Ben.

'Just wait till Art class,' said Emily mysteriously. 'We're up!'

Emily and Ben were toe for toe going down the cliff, but Emily managed to unhook herself fast enough to be declared the winner.

Lauren beat Jess down, no contest.

When all the cadets had regrouped at the top of the cliff, Lieutenant Parry said, 'Normally when we do this exercise we keep going with the knockout rounds until the fastest abseiler is left, but the stairs are about to get very wet, so we've just got time for some Australian rappelling. Who's up for it?'

'What's Australian rappelling?' asked Svetlana.

'Same thing as abseiling but you do it facing forward. Volunteers? Ivan?'

Krivlyakaev smirked, then hooked his harness onto one of the ropes and ran full pelt over the edge of the cliff. By the time the rest of the class had made it to the cliff edge to check on his progress he was unhooked and climbing up the stairs.

'Come on, Jess. Your turn.'

Lieutenant Parry helped Jess adjust the rope on her harness for the forward run down the cliff.

'Now, remember, it might look like you're falling–' said Lieutenant Parry.

'Oh, blimey!' said Matt.

'–but if you stop running, you'll stop moving down-wards. OK?'

'OK,' said Jess.

Jess walked over to the edge of the cliff and positioned her feet against the top corner. With her legs braced, she lowered her body forward until she was horizontal and looking straight down at the ledge.

'Everything all right, Jess?' asked Lieutenant Parry.

Jess looked at where Principal Metsen was standing on the ledge below her, and the water below that. It was a lot scarier going forwards, and she wasn't so sure she wanted to do it any more.

'It's not too late to chicken out,' said Lieutenant Parry.

A couple of the cadets started making clucking noises. That did it. Jess took a deep breath and lifted up one foot. Nothing happened.

'You're going to have to pull yourself down with your feet,' instructed Lieutenant Parry. 'Try and get some momentum by running.'

Jess took a few tentative steps. The rope only let her down as far as she pulled. She picked up the pace and ran down the cliff as fast as she could, landing on the ledge on her hands and knees.

'Quite a rush, eh?' said Principal Metsen, helping Jess to her feet and unbuckling her from the rope.

Jess got the feeling Metsen was sizing her up.

'Yeah. It's cool. Scary at first, but cool,' she answered.

Principal Metsen held his end of the rope taut.

'Better move,' he said.

Jess looked up and got a load of sand and gravel in the eyes as Svetlana ran down the cliff.

A few feet before the bottom Svetlana stopped running. Without using her feet to pull herself down the rock, she just hung in midair.

'Use your feet,' said Principal Metsen.

'I cannot reach the rock,' she called. 'Help me.'

126

Principal Metsen gave Svetlana some more slack on the rope and with a few jerks she made it to the ground, landing on all fours.

'Next time, don't stop till you get to the bottom,' said the principal.

'Hmph,' said Svetlana.

Jess was amazed by Svetlana's rudeness, but when she glanced at Principal Metsen he seemed genuinely amused, the corners of his eyes crinkling up that time.

As Jess was climbing the stairs up the cliff, she heard a helicopter. It was very close by. When she got to the top she turned and saw that it was hovering over the ocean, blowing huge concentric ripples over the surface. Then six black-clad figures leapt out of the helicopter, plummeting to the water below.

'Who's that?' Matt asked.

'Sophister years,' said Lieutenant Parry. 'It's a component of their mission-readiness certificate. At random times throughout the year we grab a bunch of them and do something crazy like drop them out of a helicopter in the middle of the ocean. No parachutes. No life jackets. Something for you to look forward to in a couple of years' time.'

'Great,' said Jess, wondering just how fearless she would need to become over the next three years.

9

ASSAULT

Towards the end of the second week, Jess was starting to feel a bit more on top of things. She was still ridiculously tired, but her body had gone into autopilot and she found she could complete morning Fitness Training without properly waking up, only switching on her brain after breakfast. The study load was incredibly demanding, but apart from Chinese, where she had absolutely no idea what was going on, she liked the secret-agent flavour the classes had to them.

Mathematics, which had a tendency to be dull at her old school, was always more than just about the numbers. The cadets were quickly taught the equations needed to work out complex problems in Physics, including how a cross wind would affect sniper fire and the blast radius of different bombs made of varying weights and types of explosive materials.

Miss Ball even managed to work a spy theme into the Music curriculum: the first two pieces she gave the transition-year orchestra to learn were the theme tunes from the James Bond and Austin Powers movies.

At first Matt was upset at being assigned the piccolo as an instrument, but when he discovered that he had a key solo in 'Soul Bossa Nova' he, literally, changed his tune. 'Size doesn't matter, it's what you do with it that counts.'

'Just keep telling yourself that,' said Emily wickedly, tooting loudly on her bassoon behind him.

Jess was quite happy to be seated next to Aidan in the violin section, and Ben looked like he'd explode with glee, banging loudly on his timpani while Krivlyakaev was limited to the occasional ding on the triangle in the percussion section.

Just about the only class where the cadets did things that weren't secret-agency was Art. As Jess took out her sketch of a terminator with half its skin hanging off she glanced across at Emily's homework.

'Is that …?'

'A hyena,' said Emily. 'I think it captures Krivan's personality perfectly.'

'Krivan? You lovebirds have nicknames for each other now?' teased Jess.

'I refuse to call him by his first name, and his surname's just too much bother. I think it's a good mix,' whispered Emily as Miss Kwan walked around the class, glancing at their sketches and making notes in her marking book.

'Right, class,' she said when she'd marked everyone's homework. 'Step two, which we will be doing today, is to make a clay sculpture of your mask on top of one of the positive moulds. Once the clay is dry, you'll make a negative mould of it by pouring a slurry coat of gypsum cement over it, then building that up with burlap strips. Then next week, after you've cleaned the negative mould, we'll pour some gelatin liquid into it, press the second positive facial mould on top and weigh it down. Once that's set, you'll have your prosthetic.'

'This is going to take forever,' said Emily, kneading a chunk of clay until it became pliable.

Not long into the clay sculpting, Jess was beginning to regret her terminator choice for Aidan's mask. The flap of skin was causing great problems. When it was too thin it broke off, and if it was thick enough to maintain its shape it just didn't look right.

'How are we going?' said Miss Kwan.

'Not so well,' said Jess, watching Emily etch fur lines into her perfectly sculpted hyena face.

'You have set yourself a challenge,' said Miss Kwan. 'What you can do to maintain the form is use some sculpting wire, like in reinforced concrete. It's giving Aidan's tentacles exactly the right amount of lift.'

'Oops!' said Emily, accidentally carving across the hyena's snout as she shook with laughter.

Ignoring her, Jess clipped off some lengths of wire and used them to hold the clay in place. She still wasn't happy with the result.

By the time Miss Kwan had finished inspecting everyone's sculptures and making suggestions, the bell rang.

'Alright, class,' said Miss Kwan, 'that's all we have time for this week. Please put your sculptures on the drying racks if they are finished, or in the humidicupboard if they still need more work. The Art Room will be open all week during homework hours if you would like to finish them off.'

Most of the class put their sculptures in the humidicupboard. Despite the sculpting wire, the flap of cheek skin fell off Jess's terminator mask when she set it down.

'Cheer up, Jess,' said Miss Kwan, helping her to reattach the flap of skin. 'I hear you're doing well in your other subjects. My office is always open between seven and eight in the evening for informal tutoring.'

Jess winced, only then making the connection that her two worst subjects, Chinese and Art, were both taught by Miss Kwan.

⬚·⬚·⬚·
·⬚·⬚·⬚

Jess continued to struggle in both classes, but she never seemed to have time to make it to any of the informal tutorials. However, she finally got a chance to prove herself in front of Miss Kwan midway through the term. On the morning of the day in question Jess and Emily got to the gym and were surprised to find the door locked and no one else around.

'Don't tell me Signora Enigmistica overslept and forgot to unlock the gym?' said Matt, coming up behind them.

'Not just Signora Enigmistica,' said Ben.

'Oh no,' groaned Emily. 'You mean this is the one day we actually get to sleep in and nobody told us?'

'Is that … chit-chat?' said Matt, moving out of Emily's reach as he spoke.

'I don't think that's it,' said Jess, ignoring Matt and Emily's subsequent hiss. 'We would have heard if there was a sleep-in, surely. It's not the kind of event you're likely to miss.'

'This red sign back here is pretty hard to miss too,' said a sophister cadet, tapping on a sheet of paper taped to the wall behind them which said, 'Pop quiz, rear lawn, 6:30 sharp!'

Jess, Emily and the boys followed the sophister to the rear lawn. The rest of the cadets were already gathered there, along with most of the staff. Unlike the cadets, the staff were relaxed, sipping on coffees and chatting to each other, apart from Signora Enigmistica and Miss

Kwan, who stood alone with a stopwatch and whistle at opposite ends of the lawn. The freshmen and sophisters looked serious as they jogged on the spot or did stretching exercises.

'Maybe we should follow their lead,' said Jess.

They had just started warming up when a whistle blew sharply.

'Good morning, cadets,' said Signora Enigmistica. 'We'll be doing something a little different this morning. Those of you who have been at the abbey a while will no doubt be familiar with our physical-education pop quiz.'

The transition years all raised their eyebrows at each other.

'For those of you who haven't done one of these before, let me explain,' continued Signora Enigmistica. 'We do a random fitness assessment every so often to measure your physical progress. We time your performance through an assault course. You must clear all the obstacles as instructed. If you fall off an obstacle, you must repeat it until you overcome it successfully. You will start in pairs in reverse alphabetical order, in timed intervals of two minutes. Ward and Tierney, you're up!'

A girl in green and a boy in red walked up to a banner that said *Start*. Traffic cones lined either side of a two-metre-wide course, disappearing into the trees. Signora Enigmistica blew her whistle and the pair began running.

'Sykes and Sykes!'

Ben and Matt stepped up to the start line and took off towards the trees when Signora Enigmistica blew her whistle.

'Sweeney and Sullivan!'

Two boys in red uniforms took their place at the start line.

'It's a shame they don't film it,' Emily said to Jess. 'I'd like to see how the boys are doing.'

'I'd like to know what the course is like,' said Jess, shaking out her neck, shoulders and arms to warm up her body as she jogged on the spot.

A number of other pairs were called to compete, then Signora Enigmistica said, 'McCarthy and Lyons!'

Aidan and Lauren walked to the start line.

'They're up to the L's. You'll be next,' said Emily, which did nothing to calm Jess's nerves.

'Lynch and Leclair,' called Signora Enigmistica.

Jess took her place at the start line next to a boy in a green uniform who was the size of a tank. She wondered how long she'd be able to keep up with him, if at all.

Signora Enigmistica blew her whistle and Jess was off, sprinting towards the trees. Just inside the thicket she came to the first obstacle: parallel tyres. Jess hopped nimbly between the tyres, placing her right foot then her left on the ground in the centre of each one. Her rhythm was smooth and she managed to keep up with the freshman as they reached the end together.

The next obstacle was a low net, strung barely a foot above the ground. Cylinders covered in wet purple paint hung down from the net at random intervals. The cadets in front had streaks of purple paint in their hair and on their uniforms as they crawled out the opposite end of the net.

Lynch dived down under the net and Jess followed, getting a faceful of sand. It was only then she noticed the fans either side of the net, which were blowing sand in all directions. Sand blew in her eyes, so she shut them tight and crawled forward on her belly, letting the noise of the fans guide her to the end of the net. Only when the sound of the fans was firmly behind her did Jess open her eyes.

Lynch was already up and running to the next obstacle, an artificial pond. Ropes hung vertically from a bar of wood over the middle of the water. To reach the rope, the cadets had to take a running jump. Ahead of her, Lynch leapt for the rope but it slipped out of his hands and he came splashing down in the middle of the lake. He stood up, waded back to the start and jumped again, grabbing the rope firmly and clearing the lake on his second attempt.

Knowing wet clothing would slow her down, Jess did not make the same mistake. She timed her jump perfectly and grabbed the rope at exactly the right spot, swinging to safety and landing on the platform on the opposite side of the water.

The platform faced a climbing wall. Lynch was already a metre or so up, but his wet clothing was heavy and making the wall slippery. His going was slow and Jess gained on him easily. Inches from the top, Lynch lost his grip and came sliding down the wall towards Jess. Although his foot brushed her upper arm, she held on tightly and managed not to fall.

When she got to the top, a series of pillars stretched out in front of her, like three-metre-high stepping stones. To Jess's surprise, Matt was climbing up one of the pillars, obviously having fallen off previously. Jess mapped out the path of stepping stones in her head, took a deep breath and began, leaping past Matt's pillar easily.

It wasn't until she was halfway across that she realised why he had fallen. Herr Klug was flying a remote-control plane around the pillars, deliberately dive-bombing the competitors. Jess swatted at the plane as it came near her, knocking her off balance. She wobbled wildly, tightening all her core muscles to regain her balance, as the plane circled for another pass. She waited until the plane had passed her by before leaping onto the next pillar. She quickly jumped the remaining pillars and leapt to the ground, landing in a somersault to absorb the impact of the three-metre jump. She sprinted through the trees, gaining on a sophister who had started several minutes ahead of her, and they burst out of the thicket onto the rear lawn in a dead heat.

'Jess – you did amazingly,' said Miss Kwan with surprise as she clocked Jess's time at the finish line.

As Jess looked for a sunny patch on the grass to stretch out her muscles and cool down, a purple boy loped towards her, his grin revealing purple paint on his teeth.

'Matt?' said Jess uncertainly as she propped herself up on her elbows.

'Nope,' said Ben, grinning even wider. 'He hasn't finished yet.'

'You beat Matt? That's fantastic!' said Jess, very proud of her friend.

'Not as fantastic as you,' said Ben. 'Look.'

He pointed towards the abbey. It was only then that Jess saw the scoreboard up against the wall of the abbey with the names and times of the top ten competitors. Her name was first, a full half minute ahead of the next competitor, and Ben was coming a solid fifth.

'Looks like all that work in the gym is paying off. Maybe you should thank Krivan–' said Jess, letting out a shriek as a cold dribble of water ran over her head and down her back. She glanced up to see Emily towering over her, wringing out her T-shirt over Jess's head.

'How's it feel to be the sporty twin?' asked Emily, squeezing a second lot of water from her T-shirt over Ben.

'Oh, Matt and I aren't competitive,' began Ben. Then he saw the sceptical looks on the girls' faces. 'OK,' he admitted, smiling more broadly than ever, 'it feels awesome.'

The names lower down the scoreboard were in constant motion, as more and more cadets finished the course. But Jess was still a good ten seconds ahead of second place.

'Keep moving,' said Miss Kwan, shooing exhausted cadets away from the finish line.

'This must be a big deal. Look who's here,' said Ben.

Lieutenant Parry and Principal Metsen were making their way across the lawn. Lieutenant Parry was looking less than happy until Principal Metsen drew his attention to the scoreboard. The lieutenant nodded towards Jess and Principal Metsen headed in her direction.

Jess turned to her friends and said, 'Say something to me, anything.'

'Here he comes,' said Emily.

'Miss Leclair,' said Principal Metsen.

'Hello, sir,' said Jess, turning to face the principal.

'That's a fine time you did this morning. Definitely a transition-year record. You should be very proud.'

'Thank you, sir,' said Jess.

Just then a muddy, purple blur barrelled into them, knocking the four of them over.

'Get off, you idiot,' Ben yelled.

Once Jess had got out of the scrum, she saw their attacker was Matt, sporting a graze on his arm and a cut above his right eye, as well as litres of purple paint and mud.

'Principal Metsen!' said Matt in alarm, as the principal brushed at some paint on his suit jacket.

'And you would be …?'

'Matt Sykes,' mumbled Matt.

'It's been a long time since someone's caught me unawares like that, particularly on school grounds, so fair play to you.'

Matt looked even more embarrassed.

'But for the long term, I suggest you take a leaf out of your friend's book here,' continued Principal Metsen, nodding at Jess. 'I've got my eye on you, Miss Leclair.'

He then went off to join Lieutenant Parry, who was talking to Miss Kwan, sending a shiver down Jess's spine that had nothing to do with the cold water from Emily's T-shirt dripping down her back.

'What happened to you?' asked Emily, turning to Matt.

'Let's just say that if Svetlana went for me even half as much as that evil remote-control plane did, I'd be a very happy man,' said Matt, collapsing on the ground. 'What was Metsen doing here anyway?'

'Congratulating my roommate for setting a transition-year record on the assault course,' said Emily proudly.

Miss Kwan blew her whistle as the last cadet crossed the finish line.

'OK, cadets. Hit the showers. Try not to drip too much purple paint inside the abbey.'

The cadets started heading back to the main building.

'Hang on,' said Emily. 'Don't you get anything for winning?'

'What do you want, Jess?' asked Lieutenant Parry, coming up behind them. 'A medal?'

'I didn't say anything,' said Jess, feeling incredibly embarrassed.

'You've actually set the bar pretty high,' said Lieutenant Parry, 'beating all the higher years. You do realise you have to improve on your time each time you do this?'

'Are you saying I shouldn't have done so well?' asked Jess.

'No, I'm saying you did a good job today, and I expect you to work just as hard so you can do even better next time. Remember, the principal's got his eye on you. See you after breakfast.'

10

BREAK-UP

The rest of autumn term went by in a flurry of classes, homework and workouts. In Fitness Training Jess noted that her sprint times were improving and she was able to do more repetitions with heavier weights. Plus she was able to keep up with the rest of the class in aerobics. On the rare occasion that she had time to glance in a mirror she had even noticed that her face was showing signs of the athletic look that the teachers and older cadets had.

Their final class of the term was Espionage 101. It was held in the multi-purpose room. Some chairs were set up in the first third of the room, with a room divider hiding whatever was in the remaining part of the room.

Lieutenant Parry was sitting on the teacher's desk in front of the room divider.

'Breaking and entering. Who can tell me some common tools of the trade?'

'Crowbar,' said Krivan.

'Glass cutter,' said Svetlana.

'Blow torch,' said Matt.

'Plastic explosive,' said Emily.

'OK,' said Lieutenant Parry. 'Not bad, *if* you want to make lots of noise and attract attention. May I remind you that you are training to be *secret* agents and secret agents do things quietly. Would any of those methods be undetectable if it were a heavily guarded premises?'

The class sat silently.

'Didn't think so,' said Lieutenant Parry. 'The best way to enter a heavily guarded building is during business hours, through the front door.'

'Won't the guards see you?' asked Ben.

'Absolutely,' said Lieutenant Parry. 'It doesn't matter if they *see* you, as long as they don't see you as a *threat*. How could you do this?'

'Flirt with guard,' said Svetlana.

Lieutenant Parry held up his hand as the class burst into laughter.

'Svetlana has a very valid point. Talking your way past the guards, be it by flirting or any other means, is one of the easiest ways. But try to keep your interactions short so they don't have much to remember you by. We'll be doing an interactive homework exercise on that. What else?'

'Fake ID,' said Aidan.

'Very good,' said Lieutenant Parry. 'In fact, a whole division of P.E.P. Squad specialises in creating fake IDs for all types of missions. And I believe you've already been doing some work on facial prosthetics. They're also useful if you need to impersonate someone who has access to a restricted area you need to penetrate. What about smuggling materials in? Specifically through a mag and bag?'

'What is mag and bag?' asked Svetlana.

'The type of thing they have at airports where you walk through a magnetic arch and have your bag X-rayed,' said Lieutenant Parry, sliding back the room divider at the front of the class to show such a structure. 'How would you smuggle something through this, Jess?'

'Um ...' said Jess, thinking quickly. 'Have a note from a doctor saying you've got a plate in your head if you want to smuggle in something metallic?'

'Which would be fine if the metallic thing you were smuggling was actually in your head. Most security details also run you over with a hand-held device and do pat-down searches,' said the lieutenant.

'Get your equipment from P.E.P. Squad research labs so it won't show up in an X-ray?' suggested Ben.

'We do that as often as possible,' laughed Lieutenant Parry. 'In fact, we invented ceramic knives. But there are some things that just can't be made out of undetectable materials.'

'Disguise it as something made of the same material,' said Lauren. 'Like placing something metallic in the frame of a wheelchair.'

'Very good,' said Lieutenant Parry. 'The wheelchair is also a good idea, as it's too bulky for most X-ray machines.'

'How about throwing it over the top or round the side, so it doesn't actually pass through the detector?' suggested Krivan.

'Excellent idea, although notoriously difficult to do undetected in practice,' said Lieutenant Parry, 'unless of course you have an accomplice who is very good at distracting the guards while you attempt the manoeuvre.'

'No problem,' said Svetlana, smiling smugly.

'Which leads us to the second part of our lesson. Lock picking,' said Lieutenant Parry, pressing a button so a room divider near the back of the room retracted to reveal twenty-four doors with multiple locks on them, incongruously arranged in a semicircle around a motorcycle.

'This is quite old school,' continued the lieutenant, 'but not every facility you need to penetrate will rely on electronic doors with card readers. Whether it's breaking into a room or a filing cabinet or a suspect's house, the basic principles of opening a keyed lock are the same.'

'What's the motorcycle for?' asked Krivan.

'A special treat for those who finish early. Sometimes when you're on a mission, it may be necessary to "appropriate" a vehicle to escape,' said Lieutenant Parry. 'Once you've penetrated a building and acquired the information you need, it's sometimes necessary to make a quick and unconventional getaway. A motorcycle is a great option, as it's fast and highly manoeuvrable.

'But back to lock picking. I like to think of it as an art form. You can generally pick any conventional lock with two long, thin pieces of metal. Take this hair grip for example.'

Jess watched intently as Lieutenant Parry prised open the hair grip and demonstrated how to pick each of the five locks.

'And voilà! It's open,' said Lieutenant Parry, opening the door. 'The locks on your doors are graded. The ones at the bottom are the easiest to pick. As you go higher, they get a little more complicated. Your task is to open all five locks, and when you've finished you can have a go at the motorcycle ignition.'

Jess thought she was making good progress with the locks and had just opened the third one when the roar of the motorcycle engine took her completely by surprise. Krivan revved the motor before turning it off.

'Piece of cake,' he said.

'Show off,' muttered Ben a little too loudly as he struggled with the fifth lock.

The final Saturday of term was reserved for parent–teacher interviews. Each cadet was assigned a time slot with their parents and mentor. Jess's interview was one of the last to be scheduled, at 2 p.m.

She was waiting in the abbey foyer when her parents' car rolled up the drive. After three months away from home she felt an urge to bolt out to them, but managed to remain calm and seated until they came into the abbey.

'Jessica!' squealed Mrs Leclair, running over to her and enveloping her in a tight hug. 'I've missed you so much.'

Jess was so glad to breathe in the homely smell of her mother that she didn't even mind that other cadets were watching.

'I've missed you too, Mum,' she squeaked. Mrs Leclair was squeezing her too tightly for her to talk properly.

'How are you, Jessica?' asked her dad, leaning around her mum and kissing her on the cheek.

Mrs Leclair let go and held Jess at arm's length.

'My goodness – what have you been doing?' exclaimed Mrs Leclair.

'What do you mean?' said Jess, slightly alarmed.

'You're all, I don't know, kind of sinewy. And look at those cheekbones. You're all grown up!'

'Dr and Mrs Leclair, I presume?' said Lieutenant Parry, shaking hands with them. 'Pleased to meet you. Come this way.'

Lieutenant Parry escorted them to his office. It was one of Jess's favourite rooms in the abbey. She, Emily and the twins had spent many hours there on Sunday afternoons discussing training, the other cadets and the staff, and musing about their futures. Despite its neat and professional appearance, the office had a very welcoming feel, a reflection of the man who occupied it.

Jess walked in and took her normal chair, furthest from the fire. Her parents sat to her right and Lieutenant Parry to her left. As Lieutenant Parry opened his mouth to speak there was a knock at the door.

'Come in,' said Lieutenant Parry.

Principal Metsen poked his head around the door.

'I'm not too late, am I?' he said.

'No, we're just getting started,' said Lieutenant Parry, with a tight-lipped smile.

'Dr Leclair, Mrs Leclair, lovely to see you again,' said Principal Metsen, shaking hands with Jess's parents.

All of a sudden, Lieutenant Parry's office didn't feel like a safe haven any more. Jess's parents shot each other a look and the lieutenant must have spotted the anxious expression on Jess's face.

'Principal Metsen, you don't usually–'

'Please, you can call me Vladimir,' interrupted Principal Metsen, smiling at Jess's parents, although there was something about his smile that struck Jess as smug, which made her feel decidedly uneasy.

'*Vladimir*, you don't usually sit in on our parent–

teacher interviews,' continued Lieutenant Parry, his voice sounding strained.

'But I wanted to tell Jess's parents personally how well she is doing,' said Principal Metsen. 'She achieved the best ever score on our placement test and has been out-performing her classmates across the board. You should be very proud.'

'Jessica, you never even hinted at this,' said Mrs Leclair proudly.

'A student of her calibre wouldn't,' continued Principal Metsen. 'But I will be keeping a close eye on her progress for the rest of the year. Now, I won't gatecrash any further. Have a safe trip home and rest up well on your holiday, Jess. Next term's going to be even tougher.'

And with that Principal Metsen left. Lieutenant Parry stared after him thoughtfully for a moment, then turned back to Jess's parents, refusing to meet Jess's eye. 'Well, Vladimir kind of stole my thunder,' he said, passing them a small booklet. 'Here is Jess's term 1 report. As you can see, she got straight As …'

As he continued talking Jess leant over to see the report. Chinese, Russian and Espionage 101 weren't listed. '… apart from a B+ for Art. Her theory is sound, but she needs to work a bit harder on her practical skills. Otherwise, spectacular results. All her teachers, myself included, say she's a delight to have in the classroom.

She's made a lot of friends and contributes well to group activities.'

'Well done, Jess,' said Mrs Leclair, patting her on the knee, while her father nodded at her.

'I am Jess's mentor here at the school,' said Lieutenant Parry. 'We have weekly informal get-togethers with three other students: her roommate Emily and Ben and Matt Sykes, also transition-year students. I like to think it's like a little family away from home. So I dare say I know Jess better than any of the other staff. She shows a mature approach to her studies and gets on very well with her peers. Is there anything you'd like to ask me?'

'Yes,' said Mrs Leclair. 'We haven't had a lot of opportunity to get to know Jess's friends or their parents. I understand that for the first term it's important for the children to get used to boarding school without too many reminders of home, but I was wondering if there's any opportunity for us to get more involved in the school community?'

Lieutenant Parry didn't even blink.

'We like to offer the same opportunities to all parents, but unfortunately, due to our geographic position, it's a substantial drive from Dublin, which puts couples such as yourselves at a disadvantage. We also have quite a few international students, so you can imagine the effort it would take for their parents to come here.'

'But surely—'

Lieutenant Parry pressed on.

'We do have a school-wide event for parents just before the Easter holidays, which we call Presentation Day. Student work is on display, all the food is prepared by the Home Economics class and we have performances by the Drama, Dance and Music classes of the various years. There is a prize-giving ceremony for the top students of each year, and the day culminates with the performance of the school musical. You are, of course, invited to attend and should get a chance to meet the other students and their parents then.'

Jess could tell that her mother wanted to say more but Lieutenant Parry continued.

'You do make a valid point, though. I'll tell you what. I'll put your suggestion to the school board in the form of proposing a parent mixer on the parent–teacher interview day for autumn term next year. It's too late for this year, unfortunately, but how does that sound?'

Mrs Leclair perked up. 'Sounds good,' she said.

'Is there anything further you'd like to discuss regarding Jess's progress?'

'I think this report speaks for itself,' said Dr Leclair.

'Well then, I wish you all a wonderful Christmas and look forward to seeing you refreshed for next term, Jess.'

'Thank you, Lieu– *Mr* Parry,' said Jess.

'He seems like a good chap to have as a mentor,' said Dr Leclair after they'd left the office.

'Yep, very encouraging,' said Jess.

She threw her suitcase in the boot. It was a lot fuller than when she'd arrived. As well as her formal uniform, it was packed with books for homework. Several of the teachers had set assignments over the holidays, including an essay on Art History, a lengthy French translation and a Mathematics worksheet. Miss Kwan had also set her some Chinese revision, with strict instructions to keep it out of sight of her parents.

It began raining heavily as they drove out of the grounds.

'It's forecast to be like this for most of the afternoon. It'll be a slow drive back, I'm afraid,' said Dr Leclair.

Great, thought Jess, steeling herself for hours of endless questions from her mother about her friends, classes and the food.

'Now don't get me wrong, I'm very proud of how well you're doing, and that Mr Parry seems to be a decent fellow,' said Mrs Leclair, right on cue, 'but I was rather hoping to meet some of your friends and their parents. Especially Emily and the twins.'

'Their interviews were scheduled earlier in the day, as they had to catch the one-thirty flight to Dublin,' said Jess.

'I wish we were on the one-thirty flight to Dublin,'

muttered Dr Leclair, who was not a fan of driving in the rain.

'They live abroad,' explained Jess.

'Yes, Emily's the South African girl. And where are the boys from again?' asked Mrs Leclair.

'Australia,' said Jess.

'Aren't you a little young to be hanging out with boys?' said Dr Leclair.

'Dad, I'm almost sixteen.'

'They're her classmates, Pierre,' said Mrs Leclair. 'Plus, they work them very hard at Theruse so they'd hardly have time for … Besides, Jess is way too young to worry about what you're worried about.'

'It's not her I'm worried about. Don't forget I was a teenage boy once,' said Dr Leclair.

'Times have changed,' said Mrs Leclair.

'Any homework for the holidays or are they letting you have a break?' asked Dr Leclair, changing the subject.

'As if,' snorted Jess. 'They gave me so much stuff to do I'll hardly have time to open Christmas presents.'

'That's lucky, because we haven't bought you any,' laughed Dr Leclair. 'Do you have much to do with the Krivlyakaev boy?'

'*Who*?' said Jess, wondering how on earth her father knew about Krivan.

'The client who recommended the school to me. His

name was Krivlyakaev. Alexi Krivlyakaev, I think. Eastern European bloke. Nice chap, but terrible teeth.'

Jess sat quietly while she processed the information. In her experience the words 'Krivlyakaev' and 'nice' didn't belong in the same sentence. At least now she knew who the mystery P.E.P. Squad recruiter was.

'Do you know him, Jess?' asked Mrs Leclair.

'Yeah,' said Jess. 'He and my friend Ben don't get on so well.'

'Well, everybody can't be friends with everybody,' said Mrs Leclair. 'What's that up ahead?'

A car had pulled over on the verge with its hazard lights flashing. Two youngish women were standing outside the car, flagging them down.

Dr Leclair pulled over.

The women ran up to the car and knocked on the driver's window. Dr Leclair wound down the window and both women started speaking at once in Russian.

'I'm sorry, I don't understand you,' said Dr Leclair. 'Do you speak English? *Parlez-vous Français?*'

'They're speaking Russian, Dad,' said Jess from the back seat. 'They have a flat tyre.'

Jess's parents looked at her in surprise.

'There are a couple of Russian kids I hang out with sometimes at school. I've picked up a few words,' said Jess quickly, trying to cover her mistake.

'*Flat tyre* was one of the phrases you happened to pick up from your friends in passing?' Dr Leclair said incredulously. 'I suppose I'd better help them. Pass me my mac.'

Red-faced, Jess passed him one of the raincoats folded next to her on the back seat, and her dad got out to help the women change their tyre. Several minutes later he returned to the car, dripping wet and covered in mud.

'I don't suppose you'd know how to tell them to get to a tyre shop ASAP to replace the flat?'

'I can try.' Jess grabbed her raincoat and went over to the women. When she got back into the car, her parents were gaping at her.

'What?' said Jess, peeling the drenched raincoat off.

'How much time do you spend with those Russian friends of yours?' asked Dr Leclair.

'I've picked up a few words,' said Jess again, thinking quickly. 'Shop, broken, new, tyre, pointing at my watch. It got the message across.'

'Impressive,' said Mrs Leclair.

Jess settled back into her seat as her father drove off, feeling her stomach churn. She wasn't even halfway home and already she'd nearly blown her cover, letting it slip that she could speak some Russian. It was a scary wake-up call to how careful she'd have to be – not just for the rest of the holidays but for the rest of her life.

11

AUDITION

Jess managed not to slip up for the rest of the holidays. Her body was still conditioned to waking at 6:15 a.m., so she managed to knock off an hour or two of homework every day before breakfast. She helped her mum around the house, went Christmas shopping with Saoirse in Grafton Street and totally forgot about her optimum-performance diet. Although she enjoyed being home, she missed the twenty-four/seven contact with her school friends, and by the end of the holidays she couldn't wait to get back to school for spring semester.

'Now you're sure you've got everything?' Mrs Leclair asked as they unloaded Jess's bags from the car boot in the Theruse Abbey car park.

'It's a bit late now if I've forgotten anything,' said Jess.

'Well, if you do need anything, then remember we're only a phone call away.'

'I know, Mum,' said Jess, feeling slightly guilty. Ever since her slip-up on the road home, it had gnawed at her slightly that she couldn't tell her parents the truth about what she was doing. But that was part and parcel of being a spy.

'OK, darling. I won't make a scene this time. See you on Presentation Day,' said Mrs Leclair, giving her a quick kiss and then driving away without looking back.

'They have to grow up some time,' said a wistful voice next to her.

'Em! How was South Africa?' asked Jess, giving her roommate a big hug.

'Absolutely stinking hot. You know it's summer there when it's winter here, and by summer I mean real summer, not the hour or two of sunshine you get here,' said Emily. 'How was Dublin?'

'Pretty boring, actually,' said Jess. 'The food was good though. Not a single fish-oil salad in sight.'

'We'll pay for that in training tomorrow, you realise?' said Emily.

'Yeah, that's tomorrow,' said Jess. 'Let's go and see if the boys are here yet.'

Jess and Emily dumped their bags in their room and knocked on Ben and Matt's door.

'Uh, just a second,' said Matt.

Emily grinned wickedly as she pulled out a hair grip and undid the lock. Then she and Jess burst through the door.

Matt and Ben were hurriedly tipping the contents of Ben's rucksack into his desk drawer.

'You brought sweets?' exclaimed Jess, grabbing a fizzy cola bottle from the collection and chewing on it. 'Isn't that against the rules?'

'Sometimes I just need a sugar boost,' admitted Matt.

'So do we,' smiled Emily, popping a rhubarb and custard into her mouth and immediately screwing up her face. 'What the …?'

'I actually like the tang with the creaminess,' said Jess, swallowing down her cola bottle and sucking on a rhubarb and custard. 'How about one of these to take the taste away?' she said, passing Emily a sour apple.

'You call these sweets?' said Emily, pulling a face and spitting it out again.

'We split this fifty–fifty,' said Jess, eyeing Ben and Matt.

'Yeah, like *that's* going to happen,' said Matt.

'Leave me out of it,' said Emily.

'OK, let me rephrase that. We split this fifty–fifty or we *tell*,' said Jess.

'Fine,' said Matt.

'That's not fair,' said Ben. 'Emily doesn't want any.'

'Those are my terms,' said Jess, opening a packet of Rolos.

'Ooh, chocolate!' said Emily, grabbing one. 'Fifty-fifty,' she continued, the chocolatey caramel sticking to her teeth.

'Take it,' said Ben, passing the girls his rucksack.

Jess and Emily scraped half of the sweets from the

drawer back into the rucksack, taking more than their fair share of the Rolos.

'Hey, I came across some interesting news over the holidays,' said Jess as she zipped up the rucksack.

'This sounds juicy,' said Emily, sitting on the end of Matt's bed with some milk teeth wedged between her upper lip and gum.

'Dad let it slip that a patient of his – my dad's a dentist – called Krivlyakaev first told him about Theruse Abbey.'

'Your dad's a dentist called Krivlyakaev?' said Matt.

'No, my dad's a dentist who has a patient called Krivlyakaev.'

'*The* Krivlyakaev?' asked Ben.

'Well, his dad at any rate,' said Jess. 'He said he had a son starting at the school.'

'So your dad does Krivan's dad's teeth. That makes you almost related,' said Emily.

'It's not just that,' said Jess. 'The first time Lieutenant Parry told me about P.E.P. Squad he said they'd arranged for a new patient to tell Dad about Theruse Abbey.'

'So Krivan's dad is a P.E.P. Squad recruiter,' said Ben.

'Which makes Krivan a second-generation spy,' said Emily. 'It's all starting to make sense,' she continued, frowning seriously, which looked anything but serious with the candy teeth poking out of her mouth. 'If his dad's a spy, then Krivan's parents know the truth about this place. They probably have big expectations of him.'

'Which would explain why he doesn't like being outsmarted or outrun by people like us,' said Matt.

'I still don't like him,' said Ben.

'I only said it *explains* his behaviour. It doesn't excuse it,' said Emily.

'But if all his dad does is recruit cadets, then he can't be that great a spy,' said Ben.

'I wouldn't say that around Krivan,' said Emily. 'He's just waiting for an excuse to clock you.'

'Anyway, Lieutenant Parry's a great spy and he recruits cadets,' said Jess.

'Oh, here we go,' said Emily. 'The Lieutenant Parry fan club again.'

'Hey, I'm not his fan club – I just said he's a good spy.'

'Who's a good spy?' said Lieutenant Parry, poking his head around the door.

Jess felt her face flush. 'Uh … Daniel Craig.'

'Controlling involuntary physiological responses is a study unit in Espionage 201. You'll learn all about it next year.' His eyes fell on the still-open drawer. 'What's this? Is that contraband I spy?'

'Uh, well …' Ben trailed off.

'Mmm. Sour apples, my favourite,' said Lieutenant Parry, grabbing a handful and popping them in his mouth. 'I'll make you a deal. You give me a supply of those and I'll pretend I didn't see any of this. So how was Christmas?'

'Good.'

'Warm.'

'Relaxing.'

'Great. By the way, Jess, Miss Ball would like to see you in the auditorium.'

'Me?' said Jess. 'Now?'

'Now.'

'OK. I guess I'll see you later,' said Jess.

She dumped the rucksack full of sweets in her dorm on the way to the auditorium, wondering why Miss Ball wanted to see her there rather than in her office. When she got to the auditorium, the stage was full of freshman- and sophister-year cadets doing a rehearsal of *The Wizard of Oz*. A small group of transition years was sitting on the ground in front of the stage limbering up, including Lauren and Aidan.

Miss Ball looked up as Jess walked in.

'Take five everybody,' she said, walking off-stage towards Jess. 'I don't know how this got overlooked, but I believe you're a very competent gymnast.'

Jess nodded.

'I also hear you do a bit of free running,' said Miss Ball. 'How long have you been doing it?'

'About three years,' said Jess, wondering how Miss Ball knew about it and why she cared.

'You must be pretty good at it. How did you get into it?'

'It allows for a bit more spontaneity than skateboard-ing.'

'Hmm,' said Miss Ball. 'What sort of tricks can you do?'

'Tricks?' said Jess. 'Um, I can run up a wall and do a somersault, dive off a two-storey building and land safely.'

Miss Ball nodded.

'Ever dangled off anything?'

'What do you mean?' asked Jess.

'Sliding down poles or doing Tarzan swings off–'

'Jungle vines? No,' said Jess.

'Would you like to give it a try?'

'I guess.'

'I'm not guaranteeing anything,' said Miss Ball. 'But if you can keep up with the dance routine then I think your gymnastic talents would really add to the production. As I've already explained to the others, for this production of *The Wizard of Oz* we'll be using the traditional score, but the performance will be more like *The Wiz* meets Cirque du Soleil. There will be lots of dancing and lots of aerials. By the end we want the audience to feel like they've been to Oz and back.

'We'll start dance and acrobatic rehearsals once we've finished blocking this scene, so use the time to warm up.'

Jess sat down with the other transition years and

started stretching out her muscles.

'Did you volunteer for this?' she asked Aidan.

'No,' he said, looking just as surprised as Jess felt. 'Miss Ball asked me to try out because I was on the gymnastics team at my last school. How was your holiday?'

'Too much food, not enough exercise.'

'I think we're going to pay for that this afternoon.'

While Jess was warming up she saw Signora Enigmistica in the wings, dressed in a black leotard and leggings, holding onto a ballet barre and swinging her leg from left to right, her toes pointing directly at the ceiling at the end of each arc.

'Signora Enigmistica, the stage is yours,' called Miss Ball a few minutes later.

'OK, monkeys,' said Signora Enigmistica, clapping her hands.

A dozen freshmen and sophisters assembled themselves into neat rows towards the front of the stage. Miss Ball gestured to the transition years to get up on stage and join them, so Jess and her friends took up places behind them.

'We'll start with some simple choreography. Just the first sixteen counts. Señor Carreras?' said Signora Enigmistica.

Señor Carreras, the Spanish teacher, played a short introduction on the piano, then Signora Enigmistica launched into the shortest and most complicated dance routine Jess had ever seen, including two spins, a leap and a forward roll, finishing with a split.

'Got it?' she asked when she'd finished.

The older cadets nodded.

Jess and Aidan looked at each other with blank expressions on their faces.

'This time do it with me. Señor Carreras?'

The music began again and Jess tried to keep up with the girl in front of her, failing dismally.

'One more time with me then you're on your own. Señor Carreras?'

Jess had the first eight counts down pat but spun the wrong way on count nine and ended up colliding with Aidan.

'Sorry,' she said.

'Give me some warning next time, OK?' he said, rubbing his shoulder and faking a wince.

'Now, let me see it,' said Signora Enigmistica. 'Señor Carreras?'

This time Jess managed to spin the right way and sort of complete the routine.

'Good work. Front line to the back. And music!'

Jess felt a little more nervous with people dancing behind her but managed to get through the routine with no mistakes. By the time it was her turn at the front, she was quite confident.

'Thank you,' said Signora Enigmistica. 'Now, let's test your acrobatics. Would the eight people on the right of the room please sit down. You'll get your turn in a minute. Now you eight. Who can show me a handstand?'

Jess and Lauren watched the eight cadets, including Aidan, as they did perfect handstands. Aidan turned his head and winked at Jess before pressing up onto his fingertips.

'Step down into a forward walkover,' said Signora Enigmistica.

The cadets did so in unison.

'Now a backward walkover.'

The cadets flipped over backwards.

'Can anyone do it without touching the ground?'

Four of them, including Aidan, did backwards aerial somersaults.

'Excellent.'

Jess was starting to feel intimidated.

'Now,' said Signora Enigmistica, moving towards the rear wall of the stage, 'who can run up the wall and do a sideways aerial somersault?'

The same four cadets tried, but only Aidan managed it without falling.

'Group two. I want to see the same thing from you.'

Jess was able to do the handstand and walkovers no

problem. She usually did aerial somersaults after a run-up on a sprung floor, but she managed OK – not the perfect gymnastic landing but Signora Enigmistica didn't seem to notice.

'Let's try the wall,' said Signora Enigmistica.

Jess volunteered to go first and did a perfect sideways somersault.

'Did you see the height she got?' she heard a freshman girl whisper to the boy sitting next to her.

Signora Enigmistica set tougher and tougher challenges: walking on hands along a three-metre metal bar, doing a springing cartwheel to land on another cadet's shoulders. Lots of acrobatic stuff Jess had never tried before but found she could do relatively easily.

By the end of the afternoon she had worked up quite a sweat and she was absolutely beaming, realising how much she'd missed doing gymnastics.

'OK, everyone,' said Signora Enigmistica. 'Come and sit down.'

'Congratulations everyone,' said Miss Ball. 'That was great work today. Based on what we have seen we'll be taking Caoimhe, Sarah, Emma, Lauren, Jack, Cian, Daniel and Aidan, and our lead monkey will be Jess.'

Jess jerked her head up in surprise.

'Now,' continued Miss Ball, 'there are only fifteen weeks until our performance. Rehearsals will be two to five each Sunday, with a few extras in the fortnight leading up to Presentation Night. Thank you again for your work today, and I'll see you next week at two if I don't see you in class first.'

Jess, Lauren and Aidan staggered together up the stairs to their dorms. Jess was relieved to see that Emily wasn't around, so she drew herself a nice hot bath and actually fell asleep in the tub. An hour later she woke up wrinkly and cold and had a quick shower to warm up before wrapping herself in a thick bathrobe.

As she opened the door from the bathroom to her dorm, Emily sprang at her, grabbing her by the forearm and bouncing up and down.

'Guess what? Guess what? Guess what?' said Emily, more excited than Jess had ever seen her.

Matt and Ben were sitting on Jess's bed, grinning.

'What?' asked Jess, pulling her robe more tightly around herself.

'We've found out something very interesting about Svetlana and Krivan,' said Emily.

'Listen to this!' said Ben, popping the earpiece from a ROACH into Jess's ear. Something high-pitched and discordant flooded her eardrum.

'What is that noise?' she said, yanking the earpiece out of her ear and twisting Ben's wrist around so she could see the armband display.

Emily shoved the earpiece in her own ear enthusiastically, then screwed up her face.

'I'm not sure but I think it's a balalaika,' she said.

'Svetlana and Krivan have been making not-so-beautiful music together,' said Ben.

The tiny image on the monitor showed Krivan and Svetlana sitting cross-legged facing each other, two long-necked string instruments with triangular bodies on their laps. As Jess watched, Krivan and Svetlana began opening and closing their mouths at the same time.

'What the …?'

'Oh, you should hear this!' said Emily, pulling the earpiece out of her own ear and poking it back in Jess's.

Krivan and Svetlana were singing, or trying to. Jess yanked the earpiece out of her ear. 'Glad you guys have been putting your time to good use.'

'Where were you anyway?' asked Emily.

'Trying out for the musical,' said Jess.

Emily and the twins looked at each other.

'Why?' asked Matt.

'Miss Ball insisted,' said Jess.

'And?' asked Ben.

'I'm lead monkey.'

'Lead monkey?' laughed Matt.

'The Wicked Witch of the West has monkey minions, and I'm the most important one. It's a pivotal role,' giggled Jess.

'What sort of stuff will you be doing?'

'Some acrobatics. With a tail and big ears.'

'Neat,' said Ben, popping the ROACH earpiece back into his ear before yanking it out again. 'It says a lot for the ROACH that it's able to withstand that sort of abusive treatment. I'm steering it home now before any permanent damage is done.'

'What a shame it's too late to put that in your assignment,' said Jess. 'Why do you still have a ROACH anyway?'

'Herr Klug was quite impressed with my assignment, so he let me keep one to perform some further tests,' said Ben proudly.

'You know, maybe it isn't transmitting properly and Svetlana really has a beautiful singing voice,' said Matt.

'She doesn't,' said Jess. 'You've heard her in Music.'

'She's like one of those sirens from Greek mythology, whose beauty and song lures sailors onto the rocks …' said Matt dreamily.

'That's it. Get out of my room,' said Jess. 'I've had a tough afternoon and I'm hungry, and I can hardly go to dinner looking like this.'

'OK. See you there,' said Ben, shepherding Matt out of the room.

'How did they get the ROACH to find Svetlana anyway?' Jess said as she towel-dried her hair.

'The way Matt follows Svetlana around, he could have easily slipped the ROACH into one of her pockets,' suggested Emily.

'Not that easily,' countered Jess. 'She never lets him get within touching distance.'

'Snuck it into her bag?' said Emily.

'Or maybe walked it under the door of her dorm,' said Jess, pulling her robe tightly around her as something scurried in under theirs.

Resisting the urge to step on it (mainly because she was barefoot), Jess picked up the ROACH with her thumb and forefinger and spoke directly to it.

'If I see this thing anywhere near my dorm again, not only will I squish it, I'll report you to Signora Enigmistica.'

There was an immediate knock at the door.

'Sorry. Don't know how that happened,' said Matt.

Jess dropped the ROACH into his outstretched hand and slammed the door.

'Can you believe that?' she said to Emily.

'I'd believe anything from Matt,' said Emily. 'The thing I want to know is how many more ROACHes have scurried in here without us knowing while we're getting dressed or having a shower?'

'I don't want to think about it,' said Jess shuddering, before rolling her towel up and shoving it against the bottom of the door frame.

12

HORSEPOWER

When the alarm went off at 6:15 the following morning, Jess felt like she'd never left. The morning training session was brutal, especially after the audition the previous afternoon, but nowhere near as tough as double Chinese. In the period before lunch, Miss Kwan was holding up pictures of people and asking the class to describe them. When it came to Jess's turn, instead of saying 'The girl is wearing a yellow skirt,' she accidentally said, 'The city is eating a boat.'

The whole class burst out laughing. Even Emily, who tried to be as supportive of Jess in Chinese as possible, had a fit of the giggles.

'This is too hard!' said Jess, exasperated, in English.

'No English in this class,' said Miss Kwan in Chinese. 'Please say it again.'

Jess racked her brain to come up with the translation.

'My tooth is pregnant,' she said in Chinese.

The class, including Miss Kwan, convulsed with laughter.

'What did I say?' an embarrassed Jess tried to say in Chinese, but it came out as 'Horse soup.'

The sound of the bell was barely audible above the raucous laughter, but Jess had been listening out for it and was already on her way to the refectory.

She was halfway through her meal by the time Emily and the twins sat down beside her.

'I'm so hungry I could eat a *horse*,' said Ben loudly.

Jess ignored him and kept on eating.

'Mmmm. *Soup*. I wonder what flavour it is?' said Matt, scooping a chunk of meat out of his broth and examining it closely.

Jess pretended she couldn't hear.

'Darn it!' said Emily. 'I forgot condiments. Does anybody else want *horse*radish sauce with their roast beef?'

'Hmph,' said Jess under her breath.

'What was that?' said Ben, leaning towards Jess with his hand cupped around his ear. 'I couldn't hear you properly. You're sounding a bit *hoarse*.'

'Enough!' said Jess loudly, finally looking up at her grinning friends.

'I've missed this,' said Matt.

'Yeah, good times,' said Jess, trying to keep a grumpy face, but failing.

'It could be worse,' said Emily. 'We had a whole heap of monkey jokes ready, but they'll keep until next time.

What've we got next?'

'Drama,' said Ben, consulting his timetable.

' 'I hope it's improv,' said Emily. 'I've got a lot more horse material up here,' she said, tapping her head.

To Jess's disgust, the Drama lesson *was* all about improv.

'Method acting,' began Signora Enigmistica, 'uses techniques to take on the true persona of your character to create a lifelike performance. In the post-graduation world, of course, lifelike will not be good enough. You must create a watertight performance when you are undercover if you want to fulfil your mission and stay alive.

'Most method actors draw on emotions and experiences from their past to identify with the role of their character. Since the average age in this classroom is sixteen – excluding myself from the calculation – that doesn't give you a lot of experience or emotion to draw on, so we need to circumvent the process.

'What I want you to do now is close your eyes and think about the first time you were scared, truly scared, by another person.'

Jess thought about a bully from primary school who had grabbed the front of her school jumper and shoved her up against a wall when she was six. Ever since then Jess had hated anything touching her throat.

'Now,' said Signora Enigmistica, 'I want you to imagine the scene you have just remembered from your *counterpart's* perspective. That man, or woman, or boy, or girl who scared you so much. Think about why they scared you. What motivated them? Did they enjoy scaring you? What would possess an individual to do such a thing?'

Jess thought hard. She'd always thought of the bully from primary school as nothing more than that. A bully. Trying to put herself in his shoes was completely distasteful.

'Think of everything you can remember about the person,' continued Signora Enigmistica. 'Their age, occupation, family status. How they may have perceived *you* at the time of the incident.'

Jess recalled what she knew about the boy. Suddenly something clicked. The boy who Jess feared had been the eldest in a single-parent family. He had probably been under additional pressure from his mother to help raise the younger children when what he really needed was parenting himself. Watching Jess playing happy families with her primary-school friends was probably more than he could bear. But she still hated him for what he had done.

'From the looks on your faces, I can see most of you have finished the exercise,' said Signora Enigmistica. 'You may open your eyes and come and take one of these character cards. They will have some basics like age, occupation, nationality, key events in your character's past, greatest desire and so on. You are to *become* that person for the remainder of the lesson.'

Jess couldn't believe it when the card she drew described a Polish heiress who was fixing horse races.

Emily had a field day. She hardly uttered a sentence that didn't contain the word horse. The whole class was in convulsions. Eventually an exasperated Signora Enigmistica made the situation even worse by saying, 'This is a serious exercise. That's enough horse play.'

Even the most diligent cadets fell out of character then, reverting to their fifteen- and sixteen-year-old selves.

The only thing that finally snapped Emily out of it was when Krivan galloped past them in the hall on the way to dinner, whinnying. After uttering some choice words to Krivan, Emily lowered her voice and grumbled, 'Honestly, some people just don't know when a joke's gone too far.'

Once they'd all tucked into their food, Lieutenant Parry pulled up a chair beside them. 'Mind if I eat with you guys?' he asked.

Jess and Ben shifted their chairs to make room for him.

'How was the first day back?' asked Lieutenant Parry.

Emily got a cheeky grin on her face and opened her mouth to say something, but quickly shut it again when Jess shot her a death stare.

'Great,' said Matt.

'Got much homework?' asked the lieutenant.

'Nothing we can't handle,' said Jess.

'Even better,' said Lieutenant Parry, handing out some printouts.

'What are these?' asked Ben.

'Pre-reading for this week's Fieldwork Fundamentals.'

'You mean,' said Emily, slamming down her paper, 'if we read this, we'll know what we're doing on Saturday?'

'Put it this way,' said Lieutenant Parry, 'if you don't read it, there's no way you're getting behind the wheel of a five hundred-horsepower race car.'

Jess held her breath, but the others were too excited about the prospect of gunning it around a racetrack to bother making any horsey comments.

By Saturday morning all the transition-year cadets were buzzing with excitement as they gathered in the foyer.

'I should be able to skip this one,' bragged Emily. 'I bet I can out-drive anyone here, including the instructors.'

'Why don't you go back to your dorm and skip it then, Miss Petrolhead, so we don't have to listen to you showing off?' said Ben.

'Do you think they'll give us regular cars or start us off in Formula 1 machines?' asked Matt, having visions of himself as James Bond, driving through the Alps in an Aston Martin.

'They've probably got their own P.E.P. Squad invisible spy cars,' said Jess.

A large bus with *Theruse Abbey* painted on the side drove up with Lieutenant Parry in the driver's seat. Herr Klug was seated at the front of the bus holding a microphone. During the twenty-minute drive to the speedway he kept firing questions at the cadets devised from the pre-reading material – from how internal combustion engines work to what gear the car should be in if you're travelling up a thirty-degree incline.

'Well, it's not invisible,' said Emily as they piled out of the bus and clustered around the American stock car sitting on the track. It had an internal cage around the driver and passenger seats and a reinforced roof.

'I doubt any of you will roll the car today,' said Lieutenant Parry, 'but, like everything we do, it's safety first. Emily, how about you take my friend Herr Klug here for a test drive?'

Herr Klug put on a crash helmet and gave Emily one to wear.

'Everyone else back behind this barricade,' said Lieutenant Parry, gesturing to the cadets to get off the track.

'Fast as you like,' Herr Klug said to Emily.

Emily gunned the engine and took off with tyres squealing. She sped around the racetrack, taking the curves smoothly. She flew across the finish line then did a handbrake turn which spun the car back to face the line, leaving four concentric circles of thick tyre marks and stopping with the front bumper exactly on the line.

'I've seen enough,' said Signora Enigmistica, stepping out of a black Ferrari which had drawn up next to the bus in the centre of the racetrack. 'Emily, come with me.'

'I get to drive *this*?' squealed Emily, making a beeline for the driver's side.

'Hardly,' said Signora Enigmistica, jerking her thumb at the passenger side.

Emily hopped in and Signora Enigmistica roared out of the stadium.

'OK, Jess. You're up,' said Lieutenant Parry.

Jess put her helmet on and slid into the driver's seat. Only then did she notice that the car had dual controls.

'Just in case we get into a serious spot of bother,' explained Herr Klug.

Jess turned the ignition.

'Now remember your theory lesson. Press in the clutch, put it into first gear, then let the clutch out slowly and ease down the accelerator – slowly!' said Herr Klug as the car bunny-hopped and stalled. 'Let's try that again.'

Jess turned the key in the ignition and the car leapt forward as the engine died a second time.

'Take the car out of gear first,' said Herr Klug.

'Right,' said Jess.

She did everything a little more smoothly this time and the car took off slowly.

'A little more pressure on the accelerator – I said a little,' said Herr Klug, as the engine roared in protest, 'now ease off the accelerator and clutch in, change to second, then let the clutch out sloooowly and press the accelerator gently.'

The car jerked forward but didn't stall.

'Better,' said Herr Klug. 'Now let's go a little faster and change up to third.'

Jess started to feel like she was getting the hang of it.

'Not bad,' said Herr Klug. 'We're almost back to the start line, so brake gently.'

Jess pressed on the brake and the car shuddered to a stop.

'Oops – forgot to remind you to put the clutch in when you're stopping. Keep that in mind next time.'

Jess got out of the car and passed the helmet to Matt.

Just then a helicopter soared over the speedway and Jess spotted two familiar-looking figures in the cockpit.

'Is that Emily?' shouted Jess over the noise as it roared past.

'She has car driving down pat, so we thought we'd give her a different sort of vehicle to try,' said Lieutenant Parry. 'Now off the racetrack.'

Jess scurried behind the barricade as Matt turned on the ignition.

'Was that Emily in the helicopter?' Ben asked as Jess joined the rest of the class.

'Yep. She's going to be unbearable this evening,' said Jess.

Surprisingly Emily was quite restrained.

'So how was it?' asked Jess, when Emily didn't volunteer any information.

'Signora Enigmistica made it look super easy, but in the split second I had the controls we nearly crashed,' said Emily.

'Really?' said Matt.

'Of course Signora Enigmistica would never have let that happen, but it was pretty scary,' said Emily.

'The winner of the South African Go-Karting Constructathon scared of driving a machine?' said Matt.

'Piloting,' snapped Emily. 'And this is totally different. For a start, when you build a vehicle you know exactly what its capabilities and weaknesses are. But that helicopter … did you know there are two rotors? The one in the tail stops the chopper from spinning out of control, but it also affects the main rotor, so flying straight is kind of like trying to balance on a basketball. Plus, if something goes wrong with a car, you stop. If something goes wrong with a helicopter, you plunge to your death.'

Jess looked at Emily sideways.

'You're messing with us,' she said. 'You loved it.'

'Yeah, I did,' said Emily, cracking a smile. 'I didn't want to make you all jealous. It's tricky but it's great. And I get to go up again next weekend.'

'Rather you than me,' said Matt. 'Heights aren't my thing.'

'Really? I never would have guessed from that abseiling exercise,' teased Emily.

⬛ ⬜ ⬛

Luckily heights didn't pose any problem for Jess. The following afternoon at the *Wizard of Oz* rehearsals, Jess and the other monkeys were sent to the gym, where Signora Enigmistica was waiting for them.

The whole floor was covered in crash mats and a complicated system of pulleys and wires was suspended from the ceiling.

'We're going to start today with some wire work,' said Signora Enigmistica. 'It should be familiar to most of you. We'll be using wires in the tornado scene at the start, the flying scenes for the Wicked Witch of the West and her monkeys and for the Tin Man when the witch casts a spell on him.'

Signora Enigmistica held up a wide, padded belt with a carabiner on it.

'These anchor belts will be sewn into your costumes. The carabiner attaches to the wire and the backstage staff will work the wires to, well, fling you around, I guess. Orla, you'll be the first one to use this in the tornado scene, so why don't you go first?'

While Signora Enigmistica helped Orla, who had the role of Dorothy, into the belt and clipped her onto the wire, Evan, the sophister who was playing the Tin Man, whispered to Jess, 'One of the Fieldwork Fundamentals you do in freshman year has you wearing a belt like that with a spring-loaded grappling hook attached to it. You have to shoot it to the top of the cliff, then press the *Retract* button and it pulls you up to the top.'

'Sounds cool,' said Jess as Orla flew over their heads, swirling as though she was in a hurricane.

'OK, Orla, could you do some freestyle swimming with your arms, like you're reaching for something to grab onto?' said Signora Enigmistica. 'Good. Now try to straighten from the waist – you're looking a little like a rag doll.'

Jess thought it all looked a bit difficult and was glad that no monkeys were involved in the tornado scene. As she watched the other actors have their turns, Jess got more and more nervous. Finally Signora Enigmistica called her up.

'Now, for the monkeys the belts are a bit different,' explained Signora Enigmistica as she helped Jess into a harness. 'These have two wires, one either side of your waist. This should allow you to turn somersaults in the air.'

'Yay,' said Jess nervously.

'I know you haven't done any wire work before, so let's start with some simple tugs.'

Signora Enigmistica nodded over to the side where Lieutenant Parry and Herr Klug were working the wires.

'Ready, Jess?' said Lieutenant Parry, then he pulled on the wire and Jess felt herself hoisted up into the air. She swung back and forth a few times, going higher and lower.

'How does that feel, Jess?' asked Signora Enigmistica.

'OK, I guess,' said Jess.

'Can you try turning a forward somersault?'

Jess was feeling a little light-headed but gave it a go. It was weird not having anything to push herself off.

'How about backwards?' Signora Enigmistica called.

Jess needed to grab onto the wires to still herself before changing direction. As she spun around, she noticed a new face in the room.

'Is this her first time on the wires?' Principal Metsen asked Signora Enigmistica.

'Yes, she's doing really well. They all are,' said Signora Enigmistica. 'Are you ready to come down now, Jess?'

'Yes, please,' said Jess, not particularly liking being the centre of attention when she was several metres up in the air.

Lieutenant Parry lowered her to the ground and helped to unhook her. Jess thought she saw him frown slightly as he glanced in the principal's direction, but as soon as she'd noticed it the expression was gone.

'Well done, Jess,' he said, then beckoned to the group of transition-year cadets. 'Aidan.'

Jess sat with Lauren while Lieutenant Parry hooked Aidan up and Signora Enigmistica talked him through the same basic moves. Aidan was a natural. Principal Metsen nodded at Signora Enigmistica and left.

After Lauren and the other novices had had a turn each, Signora Enigmistica called Orla and Evan back to practise some more complicated moves.

The rehearsal flew by.

'That was good work today, everyone,' said Signora

Enigmistica. 'I'll work with Miss Ball on the choreography for your flights, and we should have some really exciting moves for you next time.'

13

DUNEBOARDING

Spring was making a concerted effort to appear some weeks later as the cadets gathered in the foyer to be taken to the secret location of their next Fieldwork Fundamentals class.

Bang on nine o'clock, six jeeps rolled up. Lieutenant Parry poked his head out of the driver's window of the first one.

'Jess, Matt, Ben and Emily, with me.'

The four of them scrambled into the jeep, with Emily taking shotgun.

'Where are we going?' asked Matt.

'Wouldn't you like to know?' said Lieutenant Parry.

'That's why I asked,' muttered Matt under his breath.

They headed south, following the coast road.

'Any of you ride on a board before?' Lieutenant Parry asked after a while.

'Like hoverboarding?' asked Ben excitedly.

'Noooo,' said Lieutenant Parry. 'Like snowboarding or surfing?'

'We went snowboarding last season,' said Matt.

'I wasn't very good at it, though,' admitted Ben.

'How about you, Emily? Ever indulged in any non-motorised sports?'

'I've done some surfing,' said Emily.

'Jess? Any board experience?'

'I used to skateboard a bit before I got into free running,' said Jess.

'Great,' said Lieutenant Parry. 'We'll go a bit further on then.'

'Further on where?' asked Emily.

'Now that would be telling and by now you know that's not my style.'

Lieutenant Parry took a turn-off that put them on a dirt track towards the coast. The track was quite steep and came to an end at the top of a cliff. Lieutenant Parry parked the car and unbuckled his seat belt.

'OK. Everybody out,' he said, leaping out of the car and going to the boot. By the time the cadets had scrambled out of their seats he was sorting through some pairs of chunky lace-up boots.

'OK. Matt,' he said, throwing a pair on the ground, 'these are yours. Ben … Jess … Emily.'

'Snowboarding boots?' said Matt picking up his pair. 'What are we supposed to do with these?'

'Put 'em on your feet and clip 'em onto these,' said

Lieutenant Parry, pulling out some boards. They were about a metre and a half long and a shoe-length wide. They curved in towards the middle and up slightly at each end. There was what looked like a cross between a boot and a sandal spaced one third of the way in from each end. 'Watch the edges, they're sharp,' warned the lieutenant.

'But there's no snow,' objected Matt.

'No, but there's lots of sand,' said Lieutenant Parry, pointing over the ridge.

The other side of the ridge was a twenty-metre-high sand dune with a roughly ten-degree slope heading down to the beach below. The tide was coming in and the waves were large but breaking cleanly.

'Do the boards float too? That surf's cranking,' said Emily.

'Unfortunately not,' laughed Lieutenant Parry. 'But if you speak to Herr Klug about it he might get the guys at P.E.P. Labs to work on a surfboard/duneboard hybrid.'

'I think I know the answer to this, but once we get down how do we get back up?' asked Ben.

'You've got legs, right?' said Lieutenant Parry. 'Speaking of legs, can I get you to all line up next to each other, facing away from me?'

The cadets lined up. Lieutenant Parry walked up behind them and pushed Jess so hard in the back that she fell forward.

'Hey!' she yelled.

'What the …?' yelled Emily as she, too, was shoved forward.

'Oof,' panted Ben.

'Hey, man,' said Matt.

'Great, no goofies here,' said Lieutenant Parry.

'Care to speak English?' asked Jess.

'Goofy means right foot forward. You all stepped forward with your left foot to steady yourselves, which means you're regular foot, so you go down the mountain with your left foot forward on the board. Right,' Lieutenant Parry continued, pulling a screwdriver from his pocket, 'we need to set your bindings. Jess, step on here and slide your feet roughly shoulder width apart.'

Jess slid her boots into the bindings on the board. Lieutenant Parry moved the bindings in and out and twisted them a bit.

'Feel all right?' he asked.

'I guess,' said Jess.

'It'll probably feel a bit strange to start with. Unlike in skateboarding, both feet are fastened to the board,' said Lieutenant Parry, tightening Jess's bindings in place with the screwdriver. 'Emily, you're up.'

When Lieutenant Parry had adjusted all the cadets' bindings, he clipped his own duneboard on.

'Quick lesson. Stand with your knees slightly bent,

arms out to the sides, shoulders relaxed like this. To turn, *don't* throw your arms around – you'll just fall over. To go right, dig your toes into the sand. Kind of like sticking an oar in the water when you're rowing a boat. To turn left, dig your heels in.

'The board will start moving if the base is flat on the sand and reach maximum speed when it is facing straight downhill, so you might want to avoid that until you get your confidence up. Never let your right foot go forward, because you'll lose control and end up eating sand.

'To stop, just dig your heels or your toes in like you're turning, but dig in really hard. Ready? Let's do it!'

Lieutenant Parry pointed his board straight down the slope and took off, carving left and right effortlessly. Matt followed suit, gaining ground on him before the front of his board caught in an uneven patch of sand and he went head over heels three times before coming to a halt midway down the dune.

'What a *doos*,' laughed Emily, following cautiously at first, then gaining speed and confidence before swerving sharply in front of Matt, purposely spraying him with sand.

'Hmm,' said Jess nervously.

'I can teach you the way I learned snowboarding,' offered Ben, bouncing over to Jess on his board. 'But I have to warn you, I'm not very good.'

'You'll be better than me,' said Jess.

'I'll go down the slope backwards. Now you take my hands,' said Ben nervously, 'and when I say brake, dig your heels right in. Ready?'

'Ready,' said Jess.

She took hold of Ben's hands. They were quite sweaty.

'Stand flat on your feet,' said Ben.

Jess did as she was told, rocking the board slightly forward, and the pair of them started moving down the dune.

'How's that feel?' asked Ben.

'OK …' said Jess nervously.

'Wanna stop?' asked Ben.

'Yes, please,' said Jess.

'Then dig your heels in.'

Jess dug her heels into the sand hard. She stopped and was stationary for about half a second before falling backwards and landing on her bum.

'That's one way of stopping,' laughed Ben.

'Thanks for instilling me with confidence,' said Jess.

'Great. Now let's try it again …'

Slowly, and after several more tumbles (mostly as she tried to stop), Jess and Ben made it down the slope.

'Ready for another run?' Lieutenant Parry asked as soon as they got to the bottom.

'Sure!' said Matt. 'And a bit of advice for you all – if

you land on your face, keep your mouth closed. The sand may look clean and white but it tastes disgusting.'

The cadets unbuckled their boards and carried them back up to the top of the dune.

After a few more runs with Ben, Jess was getting the hang of it and actually helping *him* out.

'OK,' said Lieutenant Parry when they had all returned to the top of the dune again. 'Time trials.'

The cadets lined up along the ridge.

'On your marks,' said Lieutenant Parry, setting the timer on his watch, 'get set,' he held his arms up, 'go!' he said, dropping his arms.

Matt and Emily shot off down the hill, elbowing each other. Jess went wide to the right and Ben went out left. Emily's elbow shot out and Matt spun around before falling backwards down the slope. He skidded to a stop with his board pointing up the hill, then flicked his feet into the air, spun on his back and flipped himself upright in one fluid motion. He pointed his board down the slope and zoomed off again after Emily.

Meanwhile, Jess was carving a steady path down the hill without any tumbles, when she sensed a figure behind her. She didn't dare turn her head to check, fearing she'd fall. As the figure got closer, Jess could hear their board sliding over the sand. She bent her knees a bit deeper and leant forward, keeping her centre of gravity low so she could go faster. Just in front of her Matt had ploughed into Emily and they were both down. If she could hold Ben off, she'd win.

Jess carved left and she heard a shout. Sand sprayed over her back, followed by the sound of a body hitting the sand. The dune was a lot less steep now, and Jess had to point her board straight down to maintain her speed, slowing down under gravity as she met the wet sand of the beach.

She turned around to see Matt and Emily clambering to their feet and Ben cruising to a slow stop way over to the left side of the dune.

Lieutenant Parry was sitting on the dune, clapping, a few metres from where Jess had stopped.

'Were you trying to cut me off?' he said.

'Was that you? I thought it was Ben,' said Jess.

'Nice riding.'

Emily and Matt skidded to a stop between them.

'And wooden-spoon honours go to Matt and Emily. This was supposed to be a straight time trial, not snow-board cross,' Lieutenant Parry said.

'What can I say? I like to wrestle,' said Matt.

'Good work, everyone. You're looking pooped.'

'I'm knackered,' said Ben, dropping his board and falling on the sand.

'Well, the good news is that's all the riding for today,'

said Lieutenant Parry. 'The bad news is you've got one last hike up the hill. See you at the top.'

Lieutenant Parry balanced his board on one shoulder and started jogging up the dune.

'Show off,' said Emily.

The boys slung their boards over their shoulders and headed after Lieutenant Parry. Jess noticed Emily was limping.

'Are you OK, Em?'

'It's probably nothing. I slammed down on my knee pretty hard in that second crash with Matt. I'll be fine if I take it slow.'

Jess walked up the hill slowly with Emily, noticing her wince every now and again.

'I think you should go to the infirmary when we get back. Let me help you,' she said, taking Emily's board from her and letting her friend lean on her.

Back at the abbey, Signora Enigmistica was on nursing duty.

'This looks quite nasty,' she said, gently prodding Emily's knee and trying to bend it back and forth. 'You may have a bruised patella or torn ligament. We'll have to take you to the local hospital to be sure.'

'You mean there isn't a magic cream that can make it better overnight?' said Emily.

Signora Enigmistica shook her head.

'But look on the bright side: it's Sunday tomorrow so you won't miss any classes.'

Jess waved goodbye to Emily as Signora Enigmistica drove her out of the school grounds. Just as the car disappeared down the drive, another jeep pulled up. Krivan, Svetlana, Lauren and Aidan got out.

'Hey, Jess. What's up?' asked Aidan.

'Emily has to go to hospital for an X-ray,' said Jess.

'What happened?'

'She and Matt were going a bit hard on their last run.'

'Sounds nasty.' Aidan paused for a moment and then said, 'This'll probably sound a bit weird, but what are you doing now?'

'You mean other than enjoying the peace and quiet of my roommate-free dorm?' said Jess.

'Yeah, sorry, of course.'

'Why? Did you have something else in mind?'

'I'm really struggling with Arabic and, since you're not in the beginner's class, I was hoping that maybe if I helped you with Chinese you could help me with–'

'What's wrong with my Chinese?' Jess attempted to say in Chinese.

Aidan looked really confused.

'Why would a hamburger be wearing a dress?' he asked.

'Huh?' said Jess.

'That's what you just said, in Chinese,' said Aidan.

'Oh man, I'm hopeless,' said Jess, wishing the ground would just swallow her up. 'Yes, yes, of course I'll help you with your Arabic, although I think my Chinese is beyond hope.'

'Look at it this way, it can't possibly get any worse,' said Aidan.

'And to think I was going to share my secret stash of sweets with you,' said Jess in mock horror.

'You think you're the only one with a secret stash of sweets?' laughed Aidan.

'Well, no, because I have to share with Emily, and we only have one because we stole it from Matt and Ben, so that's at least three other people—'

'Jess, relax. I'll bring the sweets,' said Aidan, looking up at the sky. 'It's a nice day. Want to meet outside somewhere?'

'Wouldn't the library be more conducive to study?' asked Jess.

'You're not supposed to talk or eat in the library, remember?'

'Oh, right,' said Jess.

'There's never anyone out on the front lawn. No one to eavesdrop,' said Aidan.

'What are you implying about my Chinese?' said Jess.

'Actually, its more about my Arabic. It's a lot worse than your Chinese,' said Aidan.

'I doubt that,' said Jess. 'The front lawn would be great.'

'See you there after lunch.'

Jess went off to shower. Sand had managed to work its way into crevices she didn't even know she had.

'Hey, Jess, got any plans for after lunch?' Matt asked as they sat in the refectory.

'As a matter of fact, I do. Why?'

Ben and Matt looked conspiratorially at each other.

'We were kind of hoping you might have a go at our latest computer game,' said Ben.

'Your latest game? Is this what you get up to while I'm at rehearsals?'

'It's been in the back of my mind for a while, so it was fairly easy to slap together a beta version in a few days,' said Ben. 'The graphics are all low-res.'

'Hey – why do you want *me* to test out a game for you? Em's the gamer.'

Matt and Ben passed that look again. It reminded Jess of the way her parents acted when they were going to tell her something they knew she wouldn't like.

'This isn't a game for gamers,' said Matt. 'It's to try to lure non-gamers into the market.'

'*Attract* non-gamers, not *lure* them,' said Ben, noting the look of mistrust on Jess's face.

'You don't think I'm good enough to play your regular games?' said Jess.

'I told you this wouldn't go well,' Matt murmured to Ben.

'No, we're just trying to appeal to a broader audience,' said Ben. 'A lot of games are pure fantasy. We thought we'd try to ground this one in reality. Get the users to go on adventures that they could feasibly encounter in the real world. Like finding the secret passageway between a queen's bedroom and–'

'Let me stop you right there,' said Jess. 'You just said "real world" and "queen's bedroom" in the same sentence.'

'Technically it wasn't the same sentence,' said Ben. 'And this particular part of the game was written for people interested in European history.'

'Look,' said Jess, standing up, 'I really am flattered that you boys want to use me as your guinea pig but sorry – I've got a date.'

14

MAZE

'It wasn't a date!' Jess said for about the fourteenth time that morning.

'Sure it wasn't,' said Emily, favouring her right leg as she hobbled to Espionage 101. 'He took you to a romantic setting ...'

'The front lawn,' clarified Jess.

'Brought you chocolates ...'

'Oh, for goodness' sake, it was just a packet of Jaffa Cakes,' protested Jess.

'I bet he even walked you home afterwards ...'

'Of course he did. Everyone has to walk past our dorm room. And would you keep your voice down?' said Jess.

'And why is it that the first I hear about this date is over breakfast from Matt and Ben?' continued Emily, unperturbed.

'Because it wasn't a date,' hissed Jess and quickened her pace to show that the discussion was over.

'Why are we having today's lesson in the kitchens anyway?' asked Emily as they joined the cluster of transition-year cadets around the kitchen-access door from the refectory.

'Remember that movie with the great chase scene through the hotel kitchen?' Matt asked Ben.

'That's right. The guys were throwing knives, hot oil, boiling water, chilli paste – there are a lot of lethal weapons in the humble kitchen,' said Ben. 'One guy even pressed another guy's face onto a hotplate.'

'Charming,' said Jess.

'If you don't have the stomach for wounding bad guys, maybe you should consider another career,' grunted Krivan.

'Maybe you should keep your opinions to yourself,' said Ben.

'Or what? You'll come at me with a limp cabbage?' snorted Krivan.

Svetlana, who was standing next to Krivan, burst out laughing.

'Glad to see you're all in such good spirits for today's class,' said Lieutenant Parry, opening the kitchen door. 'Find a spot on one of the benches and put your aprons on.'

'Aprons?' said Matt.

'Sure,' said Lieutenant Parry. 'Cooking can get messy.'

'Cooking?' said Emily.

'What else were you expecting to do in a kitchen?' asked the lieutenant.

Once the cadets had all donned their aprons, Lieutenant Parry began.

'For the remainder of the term, our Monday-morning double periods will be what most other schools would call "Home Economics".'

'Seriously?' groaned Matt.

'There are several reasons for including Home Economics in the syllabus. As you know, at Theruse Abbey we tailor-make your meals so you can achieve your optimum physical performance. In these classes we will teach you about foods, their vitamin and calorific content and how to plan your own optimum-performance menu. Secondly, as all your meals are prepared and the course load is so heavy, there isn't a lot of opportunity for you to cook and cooking and learning about food safety is an essential life skill. We will teach you that skill. Thirdly, when we need to infiltrate a premises or event, one of P.E.P. Squad's preferred techniques is for our agents to pose as catering staff, so in addition to cooking and nutrition, you will learn how to be first-class waiters, bartenders and baristas. And before you ask – no, we will not be using real alcohol. Any other questions?'

'Are we marked on this?' asked Aidan's roommate.

'Absolutely,' said Lieutenant Parry. 'Flavour, technique and neatness of your workstation, so wipe up spills straight away. Now, let's start with our first recipe. Since breakfast is the most important meal of the day, we'll begin with an upmarket version of Eggs Benedict with salmon and rocket. At the end of each bench is a fridge. All the contents are clearly labelled for those of you who really have no clue. You will have to weigh and measure them yourselves. All the equipment you need is on the storage shelves under your bench. The recipe is on the whiteboard. Sing out if you need help.'

Jess got going. Her father typically spent Saturday and Sunday mornings whipping up the most fantastic brunches, and Eggs Benedict was a family favourite. The most complicated part of the recipe was making the hollandaise sauce, but her father had taught her a neat trick. Instead of putting the bowl with the sauce ingredients directly into the saucepan of gently boiling water, Jess rested it in a vegetable steamer over the pot instead.

'Nice work, Leclair,' said Lieutenant Parry on one of his rounds of the kitchen.

Emily, who was at the bench next to Jess, looked up. She was red-faced and sweaty and not in a good mood.

'Aargh! How do you do it without it going all lumpy?' yelled Emily, dumping her third batch of sauce in the bin.

'You have to whisk it the whole time and make sure the water's at a gentle simmer, not bubbling away quite so violently,' said Lieutenant Parry, adjusting the heat on Emily's cooker.

'OK, class,' he said. 'This is where it gets a bit like *Masterchef*. You have ten minutes to plate up before our taste testers arrive.'

'What?' said Matt, dropping a poached egg on the toast, which made it split its yolk and dribble all over the plate.

Jess carefully poured her sauce over the egg, smoked salmon, rocket and toast on her plate and took a step back. It looked appetising, but nothing like Ben's on the next bench over, which could have been the cover photo on a cookbook.

'Chefs, tools down,' said Lieutenant Parry when the ten minutes were up. 'Let's welcome our guest critics.'

With all the showmanship of the TV programme, the kitchen door opened and Signora Enigmistica walked into the kitchen, followed by Principal Metsen. They made their way around the class slowly, talking to the cadets, inspecting the cleanliness of their benches and finally tasting the food.

Signora Enigmistica sampled Emily's meal, while Principal Metsen cut into Jess's.

'The eggs are poached perfectly,' he commented, 'and as for the taste …'

He put a forkful of egg, salmon, rocket, toast and sauce into his mouth.

'I give you a solid nine for that, Miss Leclair,' he said, dabbing the corners of his mouth with a napkin and smiling at Jess before moving on to Ben's plate.

'Two Sykes,' said Principal Metsen, after he'd tasted both boys' dishes. 'One with great presentation, the other with fabulous flavour. Less vinegar next time,' he added in a stage whisper to Ben.

'OK, cadets,' said Lieutenant Parry when the food critics had finished making their rounds. 'The final stage in the cooking process is the clean up. The kitchen staff have one hundred and seventeen lunches to prepare, starting in fifteen minutes, and your workstations need to be spotless before they arrive.'

'What on earth would possess anyone to go on *Masterchef*?' said Emily, as she hobbled to their next class. 'That was the most stressful lesson I've ever had. I can't believe we have to do it all again next week.'

'Beats having to jump off a cliff,' said Matt. 'Just.'

'I'll tell you what, I'd rather cook a three-course meal for Metsen any day than do this test,' said Jess, as they got to their Chinese class where Miss Kwan was waiting at the front of the room with a pile of test papers in her arms.

'I'd imagine after all your *tutoring* yesterday, you'd be feeling quite confident,' said Emily, smiling evilly as she sat at her desk. Jess rolled her eyes and sat down as Miss Kwan started to hand out the papers.

⁘⁛⁘

The final weeks of spring term were the busiest Jess had had at the abbey. Regular classes and Fitness Training were full-on as usual, plus there were extra rehearsals and costume fittings for Presentation Day in the evenings, as well as first-year band practice during lunchtimes. Their final class for the term was a special Espionage 101 with Herr Klug in the multi-purpose room.

'Today you will be trialling a new device from P.E.P. Labs,' said Herr Klug, holding up a mobile phone. 'This looks like an ordinary smart phone, but we have a very special app installed called IseeU which allows you to locate living things through solid objects.'

'Sounds cool,' said Ben.

'As you've learnt in Biology, animals give off heat. The IseeU app uses this to show the location of animals, including humans, with a red dot on the map. Today we will be testing not only your ability to use this device effectively, but also your reaction times, by sending you into a maze,' said Herr Klug, drawing the cadets' attention to the high black partitions, with wires on the top leading up to the roof, which filled the majority of the room. 'However, this is no ordinary maze. The walls move. To make it even more interesting, we will also be playing laser tag. One group of four will be unarmed, wearing target vests and carrying a smartphone. The larger group will have guns, but no vests or phones.

'Emily, Ben, Matt and Jess, you can be the first target group. The rest of you, go around the back of the room to the south entrance of the maze. Grab a laser gun and go inside.'

'*Kif*!' said Emily.

'Eh?' said Herr Klug.

'Don't mind her,' said Ben. 'She's full of weird South Africanisms.'

'Right,' said Herr Klug. 'Your objective is to make it all the way through to the south entrance of the maze without getting shot. To your advantage, each laser gun takes ten seconds to recharge after being fired. So if your opponent misses you, you have time to make your escape. If and when you do make it through the maze, press on the big red button just outside the south entrance and the maze will be deactivated. In you go,' he finished, giving Ben a small tap on the shoulder.

Jess, Emily and the boys entered the maze. It was exactly like being inside a cave. The lighting was very dim. Matt immediately headed off to the left.

'Wait,' said Ben, his head bent over his detector. 'I'm just plotting the route … OK. We go left.'

Matt rolled his eyes and continued down the passageway, the others following.

Jess looked at her own detector. She zoomed right out so she could see the whole maze. She saw four dots moving down the passageway from the north entrance and a swarm of dots fanning out from the south entrance.

'Now turn right,' said Ben.

There was a low rumble. Just as Matt turned right, a wall slid down behind him, sealing him off from the others.

'Matt!' called Emily, banging on the wall.

Jess looked down at her detector. The map of the maze was changing. Now there were three dots on one side of the wall and Matt's single dot on the other side.

'What happened?' called Matt from the other side.

'Hang on,' called Ben. 'I'm just recalculating the route. Oh. You're now in the complete opposite direction to where we need to go. You're on your own, buddy.'

'And once again, Matt fails to get the girls.' Emily giggled.

'Hot spots coming our way,' said Ben. 'Let's go. Left up ahead.'

Jess and Emily followed Ben's instructions, keeping close together so they wouldn't get separated.

'Left again … Right up ahead, now left … Tsk!' said Ben as there was another low rumble and the maze reconfigured itself, leaving them standing in a T-junction. 'Every time we get close to the exit … I reckon Herr Klug has one of these too and he's doing it on purpose–'

'Run!' cried Emily.

While Ben was muttering and concentrating on figuring out a new route, Svetlana and Lauren had appeared from behind. Jess ran right. Emily ran left. Ben stood stock still, trying to calculate the best escape route and ended up getting shot.

Alone, Jess glanced at her detector. She was heading towards a dead end and two dots, presumably Svetlana and Lauren, were only one corner behind, following her. Jess ducked around the final corner before the dead end and waited. She could hear two sets of footsteps growing louder as they got closer. Then they were drowned out by the rumbling of the maze reconfiguring itself and suddenly there was a solid wall between Jess and her pursuers.

But there was no wall between her and the person directly in front of her.

'Jess!' said Matt. He was sweaty and panting.

'Oh, thank goodness!' said Jess. 'Svetlana and Lauren got Ben. I lost Emily.'

'Yeah, well Krivan would have got me if the maze hadn't just reconfigured,' said Matt. 'What's the best way out of here?'

Jess recalculated the route. They were only metres from the south exit, but if Herr Klug was manipulating the maze the way Ben thought he was, they'd never get there.

'Where did you say Krivan was?' asked Jess, noticing a dot on the other side of the wall from Matt heading directly north. It was only metres from a break in the wall that led to the corridor they were in.

'Through that wall–'

'Run!' cried Jess, as Krivan poked his head through the gap.

Jess and Matt ran directly south.

'Hot spots to the right, go left!' said Jess. 'Now right … right again …'

There was another low rumble as the maze reconfigured itself. A bright light appeared in front of them.

'The exit!' said Matt, heading straight for it.

'Wait!' said Jess, noticing a hotspot on her detector just to the left of the entrance.

But it was too late. Just as Matt reached the exit, Krivan stepped forward and shot him.

'Now you,' he said, pointing the laser gun at Jess.

She heard the whir of it recharging and looked on her detector for an escape route. A hotspot was rapidly moving down the corridor Krivan had come from, then it collided with him and knocked him to the ground.

'Go, Jess! *Oof*,' cried Emily, as Krivan grabbed her ankle, making her trip.

Jess started towards Emily, who yelled, 'Forget about me – hit the button!'

Jess turned around and ran towards the exit, hearing the familiar rumble that immediately preceded a reconfiguration. She rolled under the descending wall that threatened to seal off the south entrance and pressed the red button.

Immediately all the walls shot upwards, suspended from the ceiling by wires. A class of very dazed cadets was scattered about the room, waiting for their eyes to adjust to the sudden brightness. Emily and Krivan were still wrestling for the gun.

'Good work, Jess,' said Herr Klug. 'As for you two,' he continued, glaring at Emily and Krivan, 'the exercise is over. Although feel free to continue for your own amusement.'

Krivan got up immediately and glared at Emily, who had a cheeky grin on her face.

'At least I got to land a few punches,' she whispered to Jess.

Emily, Ben, Matt and Jess swapped their vests and phones for guns with the next group of four. It was a lot less nerve-wracking being the pursuer in the maze.

When the class was over Herr Klug said, 'Ben, could you come here, please?'

'Sure,' said Ben.

Matt, Jess and Emily went to leave, but Herr Klug called them back.

'This is very important news. Your friends should share it with you.'

The others looked at each other with their eyebrows raised and stayed to listen.

'I showed your ROACH report to the scientists at P.E.P. Squad research laboratories,' said Herr Klug, 'and may I say they were very impressed with your analysis, particularly your suggestion, fully accompanied by schematics, on how to record the output and pipe it to foreign devices, such as USB flash drives, mobile phones and laptops.'

'Fantastic,' said Ben.

'In fact, they were so impressed that they want you to trial the new version with your suggestions incorporated, the ROACH 2001,' said Herr Klug, pointing to a large box sitting by the door.

'It's a bit bigger than the last one,' said Ben.

'*Doch*, in fact it's smaller. The reason the box is so heavy is because they have also sent you the complete instruction manual with everything you need to know should you want to make your own improvements to the ROACH.'

Ben opened the box and lifted out the twelve-hundred-page instruction manual. Matt, Emily and Jess had to stifle a laugh at the look on his face.

'In there you will find circuit diagrams as well as how to use the advanced features of the ROACH. I thought it might make a nice little research project for you over the holidays.'

'Thank you, Herr Klug. That's very … generous of you,' said Ben as Herr Klug bustled off.

'Just as well you've been doing all those extra workouts,' said Emily.

'You can keep in shape over the holidays by bench pressing the manual,' laughed Matt.

'You know, for one of the world's most innovative research labs, you'd think they might do an online manual rather than pulp a whole forest to describe how something the size of my thumb works,' said Ben. 'Besides, by the time next term starts this whole thing'll be obsolete because I will have made so many improvements to the ROACH–'

'Enough with the ROACH!' said Emily, glancing at her watch. 'We've got final band rehearsal for Presentation Day in five minutes. Let's go.'

15

MUSICAL

There was a huge buzz in the refectory on Saturday morning. The cadets' families had been invited to lunch before the Presentation Day concert, and the transition years especially were excited to have their families coming to the abbey for a look around.

All the cadets, dressed in their formal Theruse Abbey uniforms, pitched in to get the school ready. Jess and her friends helped drag tables and chairs onto the front lawn for the welcome luncheon.

By eleven o'clock the first cars had started rolling up the driveway. Jess spotted her parents' car at once. She passed the plate of sandwiches she'd been carrying to Emily and ran over.

'Jess, I've missed you so much,' said Mrs Leclair, giving her a giant hug.

'Aiysha, remember you promised not to make a scene,' said Dr Leclair quietly.

'I only promised you and that doesn't count,' said Mrs Leclair over her shoulder as she held Jess at arm's length to look at her. 'How are you, darling? You're still feeling very sinewy.'

'That'd be all the exercise,' said Jess.

'You're actually looking quite lovely,' said Dr Leclair, giving her a quick kiss on the forehead.

'Are you going to introduce us to your friends?' asked Mrs Leclair.

'Sure,' said Jess, taking her parents over to where Emily and the twins had been re-enacting Jess and her parents' reunion behind their backs.

'This is Ben, this is Matt and this is my roommate Emily.'

'Are any of you monkeys in the musical as well?' Mrs Leclair asked.

'No, that's Jess's special thing,' said Matt.

'Actually the best roles are usually reserved for the sophister students, so Jess did really well to get lead monkey,' said Emily with a straight face.

'Look, Matt, Mum and Dad are here,' said Ben.

The boys headed off towards the car park.

'Jess said you hurt your knee, Emily. Are you all recovered now?' Mrs Leclair asked.

'Pretty much,' said Emily. 'But it'll still be a while before I play basketball again.'

'I thought you said she hurt it playing tennis,' said Mrs Leclair, turning to Jess.

'I *did* hurt it playing tennis,' said Emily quickly, 'but basketball's my favourite sport. I'm surprised Jess didn't tell you that. I've told my parents all about that weird free-running thing she does. Speak of the devil ...'

Emily ran off towards the car park. Jess wasn't sure whether she really had seen her parents or just wanted to get away from saying something else contradictory. They really should have worked better on their cover stories. It was a rookie mistake.

'Are we allowed to eat any of this food?' asked Dr Leclair, eyeing the tables.

'Pierre,' said Mrs Leclair, giving Dr Leclair a playful slap on the wrist.

'It was a long drive,' complained Dr Leclair.

'Feel free to start,' said Signora Enigmistica, coming up behind them. 'Marianna Enigmistica,' she continued, extending her hand to Jess's parents. 'I take Jess for Phys Ed and Drama. She's doing remarkably well. You should be very proud.'

'Oh, we are,' said Dr Leclair. 'Look, there's Alexi Krivlyakaev.'

Dr Leclair headed over towards Mr Krivlyakaev and Krivan. Mr Krivlyakaev looked more like a teacher than one of the other parents, as he had the same athletic build and chiselled facial features as the staff.

'Good to see you again, Alexi,' said Dr Leclair, shaking

Mr Krivlyakaev's hand.

'Dr Leclair,' he said. 'I trust you are happy with my recommendation?'

'Oh, yes. It's a wonderful school,' said Mrs Leclair. 'Aiysha Leclair.'

'And you must be Jessica,' said Mr Krivlyakaev.

'Hi,' said Jess, wondering why, of all the parents she had to meet, Krivan's father was the first. Her one consolation was that Krivan looked less than happy about it too.

'Is your wife here?' Mrs Leclair asked Mr Krivlyakaev.

'Er, no. Sadly she passed away just under a year ago.'

'Oh, I'm so sorry,' said Mrs Leclair.

'If you'll excuse us,' said Mr Krivlyakaev.

'I hope I didn't upset the poor man,' said Mrs Leclair as the Krivlyakaevs walked away.

'Dr and Mrs Leclair, lovely to see you again,' a suave voice said behind them.

Jess and her parents turned around to find Principal Metsen standing there.

'Principal Metsen,' said Dr Leclair, shaking the principal's hand.

'As I said the last time we met, please call me Vladimir,' he said, neither greeting nor even looking at Jess. 'I won't take up too much of your time, as I know how keen you must be to meet Jess's friends and their parents, but I just wanted to take this opportunity to congratulate you again on your daughter's results. She's continued to top most of her classes, and I'm expecting great things of her in the coming years.'

He finally flicked his eyes at Jess, momentarily making her feel like a wounded zebra being circled by a hungry lion.

'Nothing like a bit of pressure to make you work harder,' whispered Dr Leclair as the principal disappeared into the crowd.

They spent the rest of the morning mingling with cadets and parents from Jess's year. At one point everyone started moving in towards the auditorium. The freshmen had set up the artwork and science projects for display in the foyer.

'Jess, what a lovely painting of you,' said Mrs Leclair.

Jess was taken by surprise. Someone had indeed painted a portrait of her, but she certainly didn't remember posing for it. She was sitting by one of the cliffs, staring at the sea.

'Who's Aidan Lyons?' asked Dr Leclair, reading the card at the bottom of the painting.

At that moment Aidan walked up with his parents.

'Er, this is Aidan,' said Jess, introducing him to her parents.

'You've got an amazing talent there,' said Mrs Leclair. 'That's a great likeness of Jess.'

'You should have it,' said Aidan. 'Although I'm not sure if you'll be able to take it home today.'

'Thank you. What a lovely gesture,' said Mrs Leclair. 'But only if you're sure.'

'Now where's this alien mask I've heard so much about?' asked Mr Lyons, looking at the other displays.

'Attention everybody,' yelled Herr Klug in a loud voice. 'If you vould please take your seats in ze auditorium, ze performance vill begin in fifteen minutes. Vould all students please take your places backstage.'

'What is he doing?' Jess hissed to Aidan.

'Putting on a German accent to impress the parents,' whispered Evan, who was standing behind them and had seen Herr Klug do this other years as well.

Jess said goodbye to her parents and went backstage.

'Transition years,' called Ms Pimsleur, who was backstage manager, 'please gather your instruments and go on-stage. Remember, absolute silence.'

Jess picked up her violin and sat in her seat on-stage. Aidan, who was lead violin, sat next to her, accidentally kicking the music stand as he sat down.

'When did you do that painting?' whispered Jess.

'I wasn't spying on you or anything,' he murmured, paying great attention to righting the music stand and avoiding Jess's stare. 'I like to sit out on the cliff on weekends when the weather's fine, to get away from my roommate practising his trumpet. Sometimes I take my paints, and you just happened to pop into my head that day. Miss Kwan saw it and insisted on putting it on display today.'

'It's a great painting,' said Jess. 'Missing a few tentacles but otherwise very lifelike.'

Miss Ball stood in front of the orchestra, giving Aidan and Jess a stern look.

A firm set of footsteps tapped across the stage on the audience side of the curtain.

'Good afternoon, parents and friends of Theruse Abbey,' boomed Principal Metsen's voice. 'It is my great pleasure to welcome you to the formal part of the afternoon's proceedings. Both staff and students have had a tremendous year at the college so far, attaining top academic results, as you will see shortly. They are also a very artistically skilled group of students, something which we take great pride in here at Theruse. So without further ado, let the afternoon's entertainment begin.'

The footsteps tapped away.

Miss Ball held her baton high, nodded towards the wings and the curtain went up.

Jess focused on the music, keeping her bow in time with Aidan's.

When they'd finished the three pieces the curtain went down. Jess juggled her violin, music stand and chair and followed the rest of the orchestra off stage. She put her violin away and started to head for the changing area to get into her monkey costume, but Ms Pimsleur stopped her.

'You'll have to stay in uniform a little longer,' said Ms Pimsleur. 'Ben, Matt and Ivan, come over here with Jess. The rest of you can go and join your parents in the audience when the freshman dance number is over. Make sure you come back as soon as intermission begins to help with costuming and props.'

Emily waved goodbye as she followed the rest of the class to front of house.

'I wonder what this is all about,' said Jess.

'I think I can guess,' said Krivan.

'Of course you can,' muttered Ben under his breath, as Ms Pimsleur put a finger to her lips and stared fiercely in their direction.

The freshmen came backstage after their dance routine, and Ms Pimsleur pulled four of them aside. They looked confused at first then ran off excitedly to change into their school uniforms.

'They seem pretty happy about something,' said Matt.

'There's four of them and four of us – maybe this is a good thing,' said Ben.

Krivan just grunted.

Orla, Evan and two other sophisters Jess didn't recognise

from rehearsals also joined the group.

'It's going to be a quick costume change for you two, so I hope you have everything organised,' said Ms Pimsleur to Evan and Orla.

'Our pit crews are ready,' said Evan.

'Alright. Most of you know the drill. File up on stage left, wait until your name is called, then walk across stage to Principal Metsen. Transition years first.'

Jess, Krivan, Ben and Matt walked around to the left of stage. Lieutenant Parry was standing behind the curtain, where he couldn't be seen from the audience.

'What's–?' began Jess, but Lieutenant Parry put a finger to his lips and shook his head.

Principal Metsen was addressing the audience. A table was laid out with twelve books on it.

'I trust you've enjoyed the performances so far,' Principal Metsen was saying, 'and we have *The Wizard of Oz* to come, which will be the first musical directed by our new Head of Arts, Miss Lucinda Ball. I know she's done a terrific job.

'But now to the academic part of the day. It's no secret that we work our students hard, and they consistently achieve the highest results in the national rankings. So I can confidently say that the best students at Theruse Abbey are the best in the country. We like to reward our students for their academic achievement and for the effort they put in. Although final exams aren't until next term, the prizes awarded today are for the students with the highest and most consistent performance throughout the academic year.

'For our transition-year class, the award for Most Improved goes to Matthew Sykes.'

'Go, Matt!' said Ben, clapping Matt so hard on the back that he pushed him halfway across the stage. Matt shook hands with Principal Metsen, who handed him a book from the table.

'Third place for overall performance throughout the year goes to Benjamin Sykes,' said Metsen.

Jess gave Ben a tiny shove for good measure as he went on stage.

'Second place goes to Ivan Krivlyakaev.'

Jess also gave Krivan a shove so he wouldn't feel left out.

'Which means …' whispered Lieutenant Parry.

'And our highest achieving student, based on an aggregate across all disciplines for transition year, is Jessica Leclair.'

'Told you I know a good candidate when I see one,' said Lieutenant Parry, giving Jess a shove onto the stage.

Jess half jogged the rest of the way across.

Principal Metsen shook her hand.

'Congratulations, Jess,' he said. 'From what I hear you're as good or better than some of our freshmen.'

'Oh, I don't think so,' said Jess, looking at the book Principal Metsen handed her. It was a signed first edition of *Harry Potter and the Philosopher's Stone*.

Jess exited stage right and made her way out of the auditorium. Krivan and the twins were already tucking into the refreshment table, earning a dirty look from Señor Carreras, who was pouring champagne for the parents.

'Well done, Jess. You're smarter than all of us,' said Ben.

'They obviously didn't take Chinese into account,' said Jess.

'Yeah, that would have brought your average down big time. What book did you get?'

'Harry Potter. Signed first edition. You?'

'*A Brief History of Time*, signed first edition too,' said Ben.

'They're two extremes of reading,' said Jess.

'So different, yet so similar,' replied Ben.

The freshman and sophister prizewinners arrived, then the doors opened and people poured out of the auditorium.

'Oh, Jess, I'm so proud of you,' said Mrs Leclair.

'How long have you been keeping this a secret?' asked Dr Leclair.

'I only found out literally a second before you did. We

had no idea what was going on when they walked us up on stage.'

'Lead monkey, your presence is required in the dressing rooms,' said Emily, grabbing Jess by the hand and pulling her a little more roughly than necessary through the crowd to backstage.

'Hey,' cried Jess, snatching her hand back. 'What's your problem?'

'I can't believe my three best friends win these huge prizes without telling me,' grumbled Emily.

'We didn't know, Em,' said Jess as she stripped off her school uniform. 'It was as much a surprise to us as it was to you.'

'Oh, sorry. Well what really sucks is that it was Krivan up there with you three. It should've been me,' said Emily, helping Jess into the monkey suit.

'It probably would have been if you hadn't wrecked your knee duneboarding,' said Jess, sitting in front of a mirror surrounded by light bulbs. 'The physical component was really tough this term. Plus, Krivan probably gets a lot of home tutoring,' she added as Emily continued to frown.

'Hmmm,' said Emily, dotting dark-brown foundation cream around the edge of Jess's face. 'Anyway, I suppose since Krivan came second, if I'd beaten him then Ben would have missed out. He's such a nerd – I couldn't do that to the poor guy.'

'So wrecking your knee was really a magnanimous move,' said Jess as Emily attached the prosthetic monkey face to her head.

Emily stood back.

'They did such a good job on that mask,' she said. 'If you weren't still talking to me I'd think a real monkey was sitting in that chair. Have a banana.'

'Don't mind if I do,' said Jess, her voice quite muffled through the mask, suddenly realising she was ravenous while peeling the banana. She opened her mouth to take a bite, but the fruit crashed into the mask instead. 'Hey, I can't eat in this thing.'

'I know,' said Emily, smiling wickedly and wiping banana mush off Jess's prosthetic mouth.

'The performance is about to start. Places please, everybody,' said Ms Pimsleur.

'Too late to take it off,' said Emily grabbing the banana from Jess and taking a bite out of it herself. 'Break a leg. On second thoughts, don't. It really hurts.'

Jess watched most of the performance from the wings, safely out of sight of the audience. The staging was truly spectacular, and when it was her turn on-stage she had a hard time believing she wasn't flying through the air with a horde of genuine winged monkeys, doing the Wicked Witch of the West's evil bidding. But she was glad to take the prosthetic mask off after the final curtain call. It had made her face sweaty and itchy.

The dressing room was completely mad. There were clothes and costumes and excited cadets all over the place. Jess quickly got dressed in her casual clothes, then went to fetch her bag and meet her parents in the foyer, which was just as chaotic, full of cadets, teachers and parents.

'Darling, you were amazing,' said Mrs Leclair, rushing over to give her a big hug. 'At least, I think you were amazing. It was kind of hard to tell which monkey you were with all those amazing masks and costumes.'

'Thanks,' said Jess.

'Let's get out of here,' said Dr Leclair. 'I have to catch a flight to Kiev for a conference.'

'What's the conference?' asked Jess quickly.

'I've joined Dentistes Sans Frontières,' said Dr Leclair as they walked to the car. 'Kind of like doctors without borders but bringing dentistry to less privileged countries.'

'Sounds worthwhile,' said Jess.

'It's important to do something valuable with your life,' Mrs Leclair said. 'Have you given any thought to what you'd like to do when you finish school? With results like yours the sky's the limit.'

Jess wasn't surprised that her mum was able to keep up a monologue most of the way back to Dublin about the wealth of career possibilities that potentially awaited her.

She only interrupted when she noticed her father getting irritated.

'Actually, after today I'm thinking of applying to Cirque du Soleil,' said Jess, catching her father's eye in the rear-view mirror and winking.

'*What?*' said Mrs Leclair.

'On one of their touring shows. Sure, it's probably not as vital as healthy teeth, but I'd be able to bring joy to people who watch the show. Plus, I'd be able to do a college degree by correspondence.'

Her words had the desired effect and her mother sat in stunned silence for the rest of the journey home.

16

SKYDIVING

Jess wasn't one to make the same mistake twice. During the holidays she eased up a little on her fitness routine but didn't overindulge on the food. She wanted to be in top shape when she got back to school. With work experience and exams still to come, she had a feeling that summer term wasn't going to be easy.

Surprisingly both her parents had work commitments when it was time for her to go back to school, so she caught the train to Tralee. Lieutenant Parry picked her up at the station. Emily was also in the minibus, having arrived at Cork Airport a couple of hours earlier.

'What sort of contraband have you two brought this time?' asked Lieutenant Parry.

'Huh?' said Emily innocently.

'I know there are sweets in your bag. I can smell 'em,' said Lieutenant Parry.

'How could you possibly? I haven't even opened a packet yet!' said Emily.

'And you have just failed your first RTI class,' laughed

Lieutenant Parry.

'What?' said Emily.

'Resistance to Interrogation. In sophister year we teach techniques to resist interrogation if you are captured by the enemy. You fell at the first hurdle.'

'So you couldn't really smell the sweets?' asked Emily.

'No,' said Lieutenant Parry, still laughing. 'But now that I know they're there, I want my share.'

'That's hardly fair,' said Emily.

'Don't forget I witnessed what happened to the boys' stash at the start of last term. It's entirely fair,' said Lieutenant Parry.

'I've been travelling for almost twenty hours. I'm sleep deprived,' protested Emily.

'Sleep deprivation is a common interrogation technique that you'll have to learn to overcome,' said Lieutenant Parry.

'*Hayibo!*' muttered Emily.

Lieutenant Parry glanced at Jess in the rear-view mirror but she just shrugged.

'So what sort of cool stuff will we be learning in Fieldwork Fundamentals this term?' asked Jess.

'What would you like to learn?' replied Lieutenant Parry. He turned to Emily. 'See how I resisted Jess's attempt at interrogation by just deflecting the question?'

Emily muttered something even less comprehensible

and sulked for the rest of the drive.

Lieutenant Parry dropped the girls at the foyer of the abbey.

'I'm going to leave the unpacking until later,' said Emily, dumping her bag at the end of her bed. 'Let's go see if the boys are here yet so we can restock our supplies.'

Jess was about to knock on Ben and Matt's door when Emily grabbed her wrist. She took a hairgrip out of Jess's hair and undid the lock. Then she held three fingers up, then two, then one …

'Gotcha!' yelled Emily and Jess as they burst through the door.

Matt was lying on his bed with his hands behind his head.

'What took you so long?' he asked lazily.

'Where are the sweets?' demanded Emily.

'Where's Ben?' asked Jess.

'Where do you think? Off to find Herr Klug to show him all the improvements he made to the ROACH over the holidays. He was pretty obsessed with it.'

'What was I obsessed with?' asked Ben coming into the room.

'The ROACH,' said Matt, rolling his eyes.

Ben's eyes literally sparkled.

'I just spoke to Herr Klug and he said my suggestions all look pretty good, so he's going to show the guys at

P.E.P. Labs first thing.'

'I don't suppose one of your suggestions was to make it a more attractive-looking bug?' said Jess. 'What's wrong with your common garden-variety ladybird?'

'Two things. One is that the necessary electronics won't fit inside something as small as a ladybird. Yet. And two, cockroaches are found all over the world, while ladybirds are only found in a few regions and only in summer. So the ROACH is far more inconspicuous.'

'But far more likely to get squashed by someone who hates cockroaches,' argued Jess.

'I proposed a much tougher exterior for the new model and found a way to make the components liquefy on squishing so it looks like cockroach guts,' said Ben proudly. 'Thanks to you. I never would have thought of that if you hadn't flattened it in class.'

'I like to think of myself as a muse,' laughed Jess.

'Get any more Krivan goss over the holidays?' asked Matt.

'Actually,' said Jess, 'did any of you notice that only his dad was at Presentation Day? My mum asked him where his wife was, and he said she'd died about a year ago.'

'Do you think Krivan's mum was in P.E.P. Squad too?' asked Emily.

'You're friends with him, why don't you just ask him?' said Ben.

'Hey,' said Emily. 'I'm not friends with him. I'm just trying to work out what makes him tick. *Know your enemy,*' she said, tapping the side of her nose.

'Whatever,' muttered Ben.

'If his mum was in P.E.P. Squad, and she got killed on a mission, that could explain some of Krivan's attitude. Now if only we knew someone who could hack into P.E.P. Squad's computers and look it up for us ...' said Emily, shifting her stare to Ben.

'No can do,' he said, looking extremely glum. 'Lieutenant Parry said that if I ever made just one keystroke suggesting I might be trying to hack the system, Matt and I would be out of here with a Memory Wipe chaser.'

'You never told *me* that,' said Matt.

'Never saw the need,' said Ben.

'I'd say on a need-to-know basis, that's something I needed to know,' said Matt, sounding annoyed. 'What other secrets have you been keeping from me?'

'Hey – I think everyone should just focus on the problem at hand,' said Jess.

Everyone looked at her inquiringly.

'Where are the sweets?' she said, diving for Matt's desk drawer, which was so full of goodies it was almost jammed shut.

'I can't believe you put them in the same place,' groaned Ben.

'I thought it was the last place they'd look!' said Matt.

'Know your enemy,' laughed Emily wickedly, taking handfuls from the drawer.

The combined stash of sweets and lack of *The Wizard of Oz* rehearsals on Sunday afternoons gave Jess a lot more energy and time to get on top of her studies. She and Aidan met up every Saturday for their Arabic/Chinese language tutorials, and Jess was now regularly making it through Chinese classes without the whole class laughing at her mispronunciation.

With a little over a month until exams, the transition years gathered in the abbey foyer on Saturday morning for their final Fieldwork Fundamentals class.

'Do you think we're going somewhere today?' asked Ben.

'Don't get your hopes up,' said Emily. 'We're probably doing suicide runs all the way to the gate and back.'

The sophister cadets were also with them, with knowing looks on their faces.

'Whatever they've got planned for us today, the sophisters are in on it,' said Emily. 'Look at them!'

Jess tried to catch Orla and Evan's eyes but they studiously refused to look at her.

'They're ignoring me on purpose,' said Jess. 'Whatever it is, I can tell it's going to be bad.'

Just then a bus pulled up – not the normal Theruse Abbey minibus but a regular coach.

'We're all going to the same place by the looks of it,' said Ben.

They piled onto the bus. Jess and Emily purposely sat in front of two sophister girls who were known to be gossip queens, but no amount of eavesdropping helped them figure out what the coming class was about.

'Oh, no,' said Emily as the bus turned a corner.

'What?' said Jess.

'I've just worked it out. Matt's gonna hate this,' said Emily.

'Why?' asked Jess, listening in to the sophisters' conversation about whether cotton or synthetic underwear was better when travelling with limited laundering facilities.

'We're heading for the airfield where Signora Enigmistica takes me flying, so I'm guessing we're doing …'

'Skydiving!' said Niamh, the sophister-year girl sitting behind Emily, checking her watch. 'Who said eighteen minutes? Oh, that's right. I did. Pay up.'

All the sophisters started digging in their pockets and passing money around.

'What's going on?' asked Jess.

'We had a tote on how long it'd take one of you to figure out what we're doing. I've made a killing!' said Niamh.

'Skydiving? As in jumping out of a plane?' said Matt, turning pale.

'We've also got a tote running on how many of you will chicken out,' said Niamh, winking.

'But why are you guys here?' asked Jess.

'Even at this school they're not going to let you just jump out of a plane with nothing but a parachute. You're doing tandem jumps. With us!'

The bus pulled up outside a hangar.

Lieutenant Parry got out of the driver's seat and spoke to the cadets.

'I can see by the looks on some of your faces that the cat's out of the bag. You are indeed doing tandem skydiving today. It sounds scarier than it actually is, and with the amount you transition years have done this year, it'll be a piece of cake.

'We've paired each transition cadet with a specific sophister cadet based on size and weight. The sophisters will be your tandem master. Every year some pairs ask if they can change. Every year we say no. So please listen carefully for your partner's name, then go and get your gear from the hangar.

'Jess Leclair and Orla Ryan.'

Jess and Orla stood up and walked off the bus.

'I'm so glad I got you,' said Orla to Jess's surprise. 'You've had so much experience on those theatre wires that this should be a cinch.'

'There's a slight difference between being on belay a couple of metres above a stage and just leaping into thin air hundreds of metres up,' said Jess. 'Not that I don't trust you. You've probably done this hundreds of times.'

'Not quite that many,' admitted Orla. 'We practised with dummies last week, just to get used to the weight, but this will be the first time I've taken a live human on a tandem jump. Oops! I wasn't supposed to tell you that until after the jump,' said Orla, clapping her hand over her mouth.

'Just as long as whoever Matt's got can keep it a secret,' said Jess, wondering how her acrophobic friend was coping with the idea of jumping out of a plane.

Jess looked around the changing room and noticed that Matt, who was looking decidedly green, was paired with Evan.

'Evan's solid,' said Orla.

Once everyone had their gear on, Lieutenant Parry made them do a few drills, lying belly down on the ground with arms and legs spreadeagled.

'Most importantly, transition years, keep your feet up when you're landing,' said Lieutenant Parry. 'Now, there's a lot of you so we'll have two plane loads. If anyone's feeling particularly nervous, now's the time to tell me.'

Matt and Lauren put up their hands.

'Anyone else?' said Lieutenant Parry.

If anyone else was feeling nervous they were either too embarrassed to admit it or too petrified to move.

'You two, first plane with everyone to my left,' said Lieutenant Parry, sticking his arm out in front of him to divide the room in two. Jess and Orla were also in the first plane load, along with Ben and Emily and their partners.

'There are two lights in the back of the plane: a red light and a green light. It's pretty simple. When the red light is on, it's not safe to jump. When the green light goes on, the pair I choose jumps. Any questions?'

The transition-year cadets were silent.

'Any questions from the sophisters?'

No one said a word.

'Alrighty then. Don't just stand there, get moving.'

The first group of cadets walked over to the plane that was waiting outside the hangar with its propellers spinning. Ms Pimsleur was in the cockpit.

'Do all the teachers know how to fly a plane?' Emily asked her partner, Niamh.

'*We* all know how to fly a plane,' said Niamh. 'Apparently it's a useful skill for field agents to have.'

'Can't wait!' said Emily.

They sat down on the row of seats that went along the walls of the cargo hold.

'Better belt up,' said Orla. 'The take-off is more dangerous than the skydiving.'

Jess fastened her seat belt, feeling relaxed by Orla's confidence.

Once everyone was on board and the cargo door was closed, the plane taxied slowly to the runway. The frequency of the propellers increased and the plane rolled down the runway, gaining speed and then taking off.

'It feels different going sideways, doesn't it?' said Jess.

Opposite her, Matt was turning a horrid shade of green.

'Will you be OK?' Jess shouted over the noise of the plane's engines.

'He'll do great,' said Evan, smiling reassuringly at Jess.

After a few minutes the plane levelled off.

'We're at our cruising altitude. Get ready,' said Ms Pimsleur through the PA system.

Still seated, the sophisters strapped themselves to their transition-year partners' harnesses. Jess felt Orla check and tighten all her straps.

Lieutenant Parry stood up and released the door. The wind was quite strong and took Jess by surprise.

'Sorry – I should have warned you about that,' yelled Orla.

'First pair, Matt and Evan, get ready to go,' said Lieutenant Parry.

Matt and Evan stood up and shuffled over to the door. Lieutenant Parry double-checked Matt's harness before giving them the go ahead.

The light went green.

Evan put his arms around Matt's chest and stepped out of the plane. The pair disappeared.

'Next, Lauren and Monica.'

Lauren and Monica shuffled over, had their straps checked and waited for the green light.

'Go!' said Lieutenant Parry.

They stepped out of the plane and disappeared.

'Ben and Howard.'

As Ben stood up, his face turned green and he made a spewing face.

'Hold it in,' said Howard.

Ben took a deep breath and steeled himself.

'You're supposed to be the twin who can handle heights,' yelled Jess, just loud enough for Ben to hear.

'You OK, Ben?' asked Lieutenant Parry as he double-checked Ben's harness.

Ben nodded.

'If you do need to spew, point your head up.'

'OK,' muttered Ben weakly.

The light went green and Howard shuffled forward

until they were out of the plane.

'Jess and Orla,' said Lieutenant Parry.

Jess and Orla shuffled to the door.

Jess glanced down and felt her breakfast make a bid for staying up in the plane while Lieutenant Parry checked her straps.

The light went green.

'Let's go,' said Orla, making Jess step out of the aircraft into nothingness. They spun in the air as they dropped away from the plane. The absence of the noisy engines was a relief. Then the sound of whistling wind built up and Jess felt the flesh on her cheeks billow in the breeze caused by their descent, as her arms and legs were blown back behind her.

Suddenly there was a sharp tug as the parachute deployed, jerking them into an upright position.

'Are you OK?' asked Orla.

Jess had almost forgotten she was there.

'Yeah. This is great!' exclaimed Jess, looking at the distant ground below them.

'You can see the abbey over there,' said Orla, pointing right.

For a moment the scene reminded Jess of her Google Maps search for Theruse Abbey all those months ago. At the time she had no idea how much her life would change in less than a year.

'We've got about a minute to go,' said Orla. 'When we get close to landing, pull your legs right up like you're going to sit on the ground.'

Jess looked back down. When they were free falling they'd been so high that they didn't seem to be getting any closer to the earth, but now the ground was approaching quite quickly.

'Legs up – legs up – legs up!' shouted Orla.

Jess pulled her legs up just in time, feeling Orla's knees pummel one thigh then the other as she landed.

'You can stand up now,' said Orla, staggering slightly under Jess's weight. 'How was that?'

'Great!' said Jess, looking up at the other parachutes still on their descent with a slight pang of jealousy as Orla unclipped her.

'Now for the not-so-fun bit,' said Orla, 'packing up the parachute.'

Jess was helping Orla repackage the 'chute when suddenly there was a scream. Jess recognised the voice and a shiver ran down her spine.

'Em!' yelled Jess, running towards a black and yellow parachute that still had some of its form as it came to rest on the ground.

Emily was lying facedown on the ground, her knee twisted at an awkward angle. Niamh was lying on top of her, trying to unbuckle the harness.

Jess rolled them over and Emily shrieked in pain.

'Em,' said Jess.

'This hurts,' cried Emily. 'This really, really hurts.'

Jess had never seen Emily cry before. It was unsettling to say the least to see her normally self-assured roommate sobbing.

'Go get a teacher,' Jess yelled at Orla while she held her friend's hand.

Signora Enigmistica was there in seconds. She took one look at Emily and whipped out her phone.

'We need an ambulance,' she said, dialling.

She gave the address of the airfield to the operator.

Emily started to panic.

'It's OK, Emily,' soothed Signora Enigmistica. 'You'll get medical help faster this way than if I flew you to hospital by helicopter myself.'

She turned to Jess.

'I'm sorry, Jess, but only one person gets to ride in the ambulance with her, and according to protocol it should be a teacher.'

'Can I stay with her until then?' asked Jess.

'Of course,' said Signora Enigmistica.

Lieutenant Parry arrived with a cold pack, which he asked Jess to hold in place on Emily's rapidly swelling knee, then the teachers cleared the field of cadets and parachutes. A short while later Jess heard an ambulance siren approaching. By then Emily had gone into shock.

The paramedics raced towards them and tried to examine Emily.

'I can't get any sense out of her,' one said to the other. 'Get the morphine. Can someone else tell me exactly what happened?'

A tearful Niamh tried to explain, but she was so upset that the second paramedic ended up treating her for shock while the first one injected Emily with morphine.

Within a few minutes Emily was in the ambulance, giggling.

'See you at school.' Jess waved as the doors closed on Emily.

Jess was too worried about Emily to concentrate on any homework that afternoon. She, the twins and most of the transition years and sophisters had gathered in the foyer of the abbey, waiting for the teachers to return from the hospital, with or without Emily.

Shortly after three o'clock, Signora Enigmistica's black Ferrari pulled into the car park.

The students ran out to mob Signora Enigmistica and Lieutenant Parry as they stepped out.

'Her knee's dislocated,' said Lieutenant Parry. 'She'll need surgery but she should make a full recovery.'

Niamh was most concerned.

'I feel so bad,' she said.

'It wasn't your fault,' said Jess. 'That knee's been a bit weak since she hurt it duneboarding.'

'At least she'll enjoy the sleep-ins while she gets to skip Fitness Training,' said Matt.

'Sleep-ins?' said Lieutenant Parry. 'No way. Emily will need to do lots of physiotherapy to get her knee back in action, as well as making up for the classes she'll miss while lazing around in hospital. Speaking of which, don't any of you have homework to do?'

'He's right,' murmured Evan as the cadets made their way back to their dorms. 'I broke my arm last year and I still had to get up at 6:15 for physio. Then my first proper day back they did a pop quiz and I got in trouble for not beating my previous time. It totally sucked.'

Jess went into her dorm and flopped onto her bed. The room seemed strangely empty. Although she and Emily got on like a house on fire, Jess normally cherished the moments of solitude she got on the rare occasions she had the room to herself. Now the absence of Emily made it feel suffocating and Jess had to get out.

She wrenched the door open and walked straight into Aidan.

'I was just coming to see if you were up for tutoring this afternoon,' he said, holding up a packet of Gummi Bears.

'Sure,' said Jess.

Aidan raised an eyebrow at her.

'*Dang ran*,' she repeated in Chinese.

'Your pronunciation's getting much better,' Aidan said as they headed for the back stairs. 'I would have known what that was even without the English translation first.'

When they opened the door, a crowd had gathered.

'What's going on?' said Jess, running down the steps.

Three figures were squaring off in the middle of the crowd.

'Just saying,' growled Krivan.

'Maybe you'd like to keep your opinions to yourself,' said Matt.

'Maybe you'd like to join your friend in hospital,' bellowed Krivan, hurling himself towards Matt.

But before he could reach Matt, Ben side-tackled Krivan, throwing him to the ground.

Krivan rolled on top of Ben and drew his fist back, but Matt barrelled into him and pinned him in a half nelson.

'Break it up,' said Lieutenant Parry, appearing out of nowhere and hauling the boys to their feet. 'I don't know what started this, but all three of you can explain it to Principal Metsen. Now.'

Lieutenant Parry herded the boys back into the abbey.

'What'd we miss?' asked Aidan.

'We could waste time speculating on it now or wait for the full report at dinner,' said Jess. 'There's a spare seat at our table.'

'There might be three spare seats depending on what sort of mood Metsen's in,' said Aidan.

As it turned out, the boys made it to dinner.

Ben and Matt looked from Jess to Aidan and back again.

'This is just too weird,' said Matt. 'You've got to at least talk with a South African accent.'

'*Eish brah*,' said Aidan.

'Sounds good enough to me,' said Ben.

'So? What was all that with Krivan?' asked Jess.

'The limp cabbage dissed the ROACH,' said Ben.

'What language is he speaking?' Aidan asked.

'Herr Klug gave Ben the ROACH to work on as a special project,' explained Jess. 'Ben made all these fabulous improvements. But what's that got to do with Krivan?'

'His dad apparently heard about it and gave him grief for being upstaged,' said Ben. 'Since he can't beat me on an intellectual level, he sank to insults and then violence.'

'And let's face it, mate, he's been waiting for an excuse to crack you one all year,' said Matt.

'The way I remember it, he went for you first,' said Ben. 'Why was that?'

Matt smiled.

'I guess he's jealous of me and Svetlana.'

Jess and Ben stopped eating and looked at Matt.

'So you're …?'

'Getting closer,' said Matt, grinning.

'Don't you think you should be focusing on something other than girls this close to exams?' said Aidan.

'That's rich coming from you,' said Ben.

'Ben!' said Jess.

'That's OK, I can take a hint,' said Aidan, shoving in his final forkful of food and taking his tray back to the servery.

'Did Krivan smack you one in the head?' said Jess angrily. 'Aidan and I are just friends.'

'Sure,' said Ben, grabbing his tray and stalking off.

Jess looked at Matt.

'What can I say?' said Matt. 'Benny's a sore loser too.'

It was a very subdued group in Lieutenant Parry's office that Sunday afternoon. At first Jess was glad to see Ben, as he hadn't shown up for breakfast or lunch, but when his grouchiness became apparent she began to wish he'd skipped mentor group as well.

Their mood didn't escape the lieutenant. 'You're a

cheerful bunch this afternoon,' he said. 'Tell you what, how about I get a pass for you guys to go visit Emily later?'

Jess perked up immediately but Ben maintained his surliness.

'Alright. What's going on?' said Lieutenant Parry, leaning back in his chair and eyeballing each of them.

Jess, worried that he might withdraw the offer to visit Emily if nobody spoke up soon, said, 'Ben's imagining things that aren't there and getting his knickers in a knot over nothing.'

'Care to comment, Ben?' asked the lieutenant.

'No,' said Ben, not meeting anyone's eye.

'OK, guys,' said Lieutenant Parry, almost sighing. 'We're getting to the pointy end of the year. People are getting injured, stress levels are sky rocketing, otherwise level-headed kids are lashing out … It happens every year. The thing I need you guys to do is remember to work as a team. You've been a great support to each other all year. Don't stuff it up now, especially with work experience just around the corner. Can you do that for me, Jess?'

'Sure.'

'Matt?'

'I've got no problem,' said Matt.

'Ben?'

Ben scowled at Lieutenant Parry, then looked over at Jess.

'Fine,' he said.

'Great,' said Lieutenant Parry. 'Anything you guys want to discuss?'

The cadets shook their heads.

'You'd better get back to studying then, while I sort out the paperwork for our visit to Emily. We've just finished drafting the Espionage 101 final paper and it's a doozie.'

17

BRIEFING

With no Fieldwork Fundamentals class, the following Saturday Jess and the twins were enjoying a leisurely breakfast when they were joined by a familiar face.

'Emily!' said Jess, leaping up so quickly that she bumped the table and made everyone's breakfast slop off their plates.

'Easy,' said Emily, her crutches almost slipping out from under her due to Jess's bear hug. 'My knee's not that strong yet.'

'Why didn't you tell us you were coming?'

'I wanted to make a grand entrance, which I'm regretting now,' said Emily, wincing slightly as she sat down.

'So how was it in the real world?' asked Matt.

'Not so relaxing,' said Emily. 'Lieutenant Parry came to visit every day with a mountain of homework. I still had to do all the assignments and I'll have to do the labs I missed when you guys are doing Fitness Training classes.'

'Speak of the devil,' said Ben as Lieutenant Parry strode over to their table.

'Don't you four have somewhere to be?' he asked.

'Don't think so,' said Matt.

'Seriously?' said Lieutenant Parry. 'I can't believe a single one of you hasn't remembered.'

Jess, Emily and the twins frowned at each other, but then Ben's expression cleared. 'Work-experience week!' he said.

'Great to see you all so well prepared for your first mission,' said Lieutenant Parry. 'Meet me out front in ten. If you're late, you'll miss out and fail the year.'

Jess and the twins sprang out of their chairs.

'That goes for you, too, Harris.'

'Seriously? With this knee?'

'The doctors discharged you, didn't they? That tells me you're good to go. Now get going.'

Emily swung after the others on her crutches as they went upstairs to pack their rucksacks.

'What do you think our mission's going to be?' asked Matt.

'I hope it doesn't have anything to do with pushing us out of a helicopter into the sea,' said Ben.

'That's only for sophisters,' said Jess, slowing down for Emily. 'If hoppity here's tagging along it can't be anything too strenuous.'

'See you out front,' said Emily as she and Jess went into their room.

A few minutes later they were walking through the foyer to the meeting point when Ben stopped short.

'You've got to be kidding me,' he said.

Krivan was waiting right where Lieutenant Parry had told them to gather, a hold-all at his feet. His expression soured when he saw the four of them approaching.

Lieutenant Parry drove up in a plain white minivan.

'What are you waiting for? Hop in.'

'All of us?' said Ben, as Krivan slid the back door open and climbed inside.

'You must be desperate to fail, Sykes. Yes, all of you,' said Lieutenant Parry.

Ben sat in the seat furthest away from Krivan as the others piled in. Lieutenant Parry hit the accelerator the second they were all belted in.

'What's our mission?' asked Emily, rubbing her palms together eagerly.

The lieutenant pressed a button in the middle of the steering wheel and some screens in the back of the headrests flickered into life, displaying the face of a man in his late fifties. He had white hair, piercing blue eyes and a slightly dishevelled appearance.

'We're doing reconnaissance in the Bavarian Alps, looking for this guy,' said Lieutenant Parry.

'Who is he?' asked Krivan.

'Cameron Hess. He's an ecotechnologist. He has

251

designed several closed, self-sustaining ecological systems,' said Lieutenant Parry, as the picture on screen changed to an aerial photograph of what looked like the top half of a giant glass soccer ball. 'His most recent experiment, Biosphere 3, was the prototype for a Martian spaceport scheduled for construction in 2030.'

'*Was* the prototype? What happened to it?' asked Jess.

'Just one month short of its two-year anniversary the Science Foundation pulled the plug on funding. Biosphere 3 staff had started asking serious questions when all the plants started dying mysteriously. Many of the animals weren't looking too great either and one of the human workers had to be hospitalised. It's believed that Hess had been using the biosphere as a laboratory to develop a virus that would be so deadly its release into the atmosphere would cause a mass extinction event.'

'You mean ...?'

'If that thing got out, we'd all be deader than the dinosaurs,' said Lieutenant Parry. 'No plants, no animals, no humans.'

'What a psycho!' said Emily.

Lieutenant Parry made a non-committal noise.

'What happened to Hess?' asked Matt.

'He disappeared. The intelligence community thinks he's continuing work on the virus in a secret laboratory.'

Something about the tone of his voice prompted Jess

to say, 'But you don't think so.'

He met her eyes briefly in the rear-view mirror. 'I know Hess – or at least I did several years ago. This all seems completely out of character for the man I knew. But people change. So, at the moment I'm reserving judgement and following orders.'

'Wait a minute,' said Matt. 'This guy sounds like he's really dangerous. Why assign the mission to a group of work-experience students instead of real agents?'

'Don't worry,' said Lieutenant Parry, smiling. But Jess noticed the usual twinkle in his eye was absent. 'We're not going after Hess himself. We're just investigating one of the suspected laboratory sites. Recent intelligence suggests that Hess plans to release the virus imminently so we need to locate him asap. If our reconnaissance proves this site to be Hess's lab, we may have to confiscate the virus and take it back to P.E.P. Squad research labs for analysis.'

'That still sounds like pretty heavy-duty stuff for transition-year work experience,' commented Ben. 'Wouldn't it be safer if we just did the reconnaissance and then some real agents did all the … um … dangerous stuff?'

'I only said we *may* have to steal the virus. As I said, there are several other possible sites where it could be. Anyway, I'll be with you every step of the way. If my

253

assessment is that the situation is too dangerous, then I'll get you out of there and call in the big boys. Besides, four of you got awards for topping your year. The fifth one of you can pilot a helicopter. The powers that be seem to think that this is the perfect work-experience assignment for you,' said Lieutenant Parry, pulling a face like Emily eating her first rhubarb and custard.

'But you don't,' murmured Jess.

Lieutenant Parry glanced at her again.

'Hang on,' said Emily, breaking the silence. 'Did you say helicopter?'

'Those helicopter lessons weren't just for fun, you know,' smiled Lieutenant Parry.

'Cool!' said Emily, leaning back in her seat and brightening up considerably, while Matt turned a delicate shade of green.

Lieutenant Parry tapped on the steering wheel to bring up a picture of a Bavarian castle set against a snowy backdrop. 'This is our target, Altganz Castle, one of several suspected locations of Hess's secret laboratory and hideout.'

'It doesn't look very secret,' commented Jess, looking at the picture of the grandiose castle.

'The safest place to hide something is in plain sight,' said Lieutenant Parry. 'What else do you notice about this picture?'

'It's covered in snow,' said Krivan. 'Is it a file photo?'

'It was taken yesterday, in fact,' said Lieutenant Parry. 'In that part of the Alps there's always snow cover.'

'So what's the plan?' asked Matt.

'From the intel that I have, it looks like Altganz has extremely tight security – motion-sensitive cameras, laser-web window nets and armed guards posted at every entrance.'

'Breaking in sounds impossible,' said Jess.

'It is. So we get in the same way we've taught you to approach heavily guarded premises. Through the front door,' said Lieutenant Parry, grinning.

'Hang on. Are you saying we're just going to knock on the portcullis and the armed guards will simply let us walk in?' said Matt.

'If we stick to our cover, they can't refuse,' said Lieutenant Parry.

'What is our cover?' asked Krivan.

'All of us, bar pilot Emily, will be taking a little snowboarding holiday. You four will be normal, slightly spoiled teenagers. I'll be your guide, a career snowboarder,' said Lieutenant Parry.

'I think we can pull that off,' said Ben. 'But how do we convince them to let us in?'

'We'll say that one of you has been injured and we need somewhere to stay for the night.'

'I'm confused,' said Emily. 'I thought I was flying the chopper?'

'You are. I didn't mean you would be the injured person. In fact, it would be foolish to take someone actually injured into such a dangerous situation in case we need to make a quick getaway. We'll just make up someone's leg to look like they've sprained their ankle or twisted their knee or something. Whatever you feel most comfortable with, Ben, since Miss Kwan tells me that you're the most artistic one in the group. It'll just look like a heliboarding holiday gone wrong.'

'I hate to put a dampener on this whole leaping out of a helicopter thing, but just say one of us *does* get injured?' asked Matt.

'Pilot Emily will be on stand-by to fly anybody out while the rest of us proceed with the mission,' said Lieutenant Parry.

He drove the van off-road through a thicket of trees, stopping at the edge of a flat, grassy field. At first glance it looked completely empty apart from an orange windsock. The field was surrounded by a chain-link fence topped with barbed wire. 'Everybody out,' he said.

The cadets grabbed their packs and followed the lieutenant along the fence until they reached a padlocked gate with a sign saying 'Private Property. No Unauthorised Access'. Lieutenant Parry unlocked the padlock and held the gate open for the cadets before closing it after them and re-padlocking it.

'This way,' he said, striding over to a large shed completely hidden in the trees on the edge of one end of the field. The cadets had to jog to keep up with him, Emily bringing up the rear. A strange box hung on the outside of the shed, next to a huge roller door that took up almost the entire side facing the field. Lieutenant Parry put his face directly in front of the box. A faint laser shone out and fanned across his face. Then the roller door slid open.

'No way,' said Matt when he saw what was inside the shed. 'This is an airfield?'

'I thought that the big orange windsock might have given it away,' said Lieutenant Parry over his shoulder as he walked towards the eight-seater plane sitting in the middle of the hangar. He climbed the steps and looked at the cadets. 'What are you waiting for?'

The cadets hurried up the steps behind him and took their seats in the back as he closed the door.

'You're here with me, Emily,' said Lieutenant Parry, patting the co-pilot's seat. 'Your in-flight training starts right now.'

'*Cool!*' said Emily, changing seats and running her fingers lightly over the aircraft controls.

'Has everyone got their seat backs upright and tray

tables stowed?' joked Lieutenant Parry as he flicked some switches.

The aeroplane's propellers roared into life and they taxied out of the hangar.

'Where's the runway?' asked Ben, looking at the expanse of grass in front of them.

'We're light enough that we just need a grass landing strip,' explained Lieutenant Parry, gunning the engines and shooting the plane forward.

Jess thought the trees at the far end of the field were approaching more quickly than she'd like, but the plane lifted off with metres to spare. They took off to the north and Jess craned her neck to look down on Theruse Abbey. Cadets were dotted all over the lawns, making the most of the sunny Saturday morning despite the fact that the exams were only weeks away. Then the plane banked east, heading for the continent.

Lieutenant Parry levelled the plane out, explaining to Emily what he was doing. When he was happy that she knew enough, he said, 'Keep her on this bearing at this altitude.'

Emily grabbed the wheel in front of her and watched the dials diligently.

'It is now safe to access your in-flight entertainment units,' said Lieutenant Parry to the others, pressing a button to activate a screen in the middle of the instrument panel and the individual screens in the headrests in front of each cadet. A single word flashed up: *Equipment.*

'What gadgets do we get?' asked Ben, practically bouncing in his seat with enthusiasm.

'Glad you asked,' said Lieutenant Parry, displaying a photo of a pair of snow boots on the cadets' screens. 'Gear's in the back. We've got state-of-the-art P.E.P. Squad first-issue avalanche assault gear. The soles of your snowboard boots are hollow and filled with special P.E.P. Squad plastic explosive: Peptex. Nine times more powerful than Semtex. There's enough Peptex in a pair of boots to blast the entire castle off the top of the hill. Hence the term avalanche assault.'

'Um, I don't want to sound dumb or anything, but what happens if we slam our boots really hard, like when we're jumping out of a helicopter for instance? Won't our feet explode?' asked Matt.

'No,' said Lieutenant Parry. 'Peptex only goes off when a five-thousand-volt charge is applied to it. For that purpose, we have remote detonators, which I'm sure you're all familiar with.' He brought up a picture of the ROACH armband console on the screens.

Krivan clucked his tongue impatiently.

'This is the ROACH 2002. As I'm sure Ben could tell you, it has a remote destruct mechanism that causes it to short circuit, producing a five-thousand-volt charge. The components liquefy, making the ROACH undetectable and coincidentally igniting any Peptex it's in contact with.'

'You're drifting a bit too far south, Emily,' he continued, correcting the course slightly. 'Try and hold it here.'

'Sorry,' said Emily.

'Next,' said Lieutenant Parry, bringing up a picture of a pair of ski goggles with fluorescent orange lenses, 'ski goggles. The lens is made of an experimental material which allows you to see unobstructed through airborne water molecules including rain, sleet and snow. We'll be able to board with perfect visibility, even in a whiteout. There's also night mode, so you can see in the dark, and binocular mode, which gives you magnification by a factor of twenty.'

The ski goggles were replaced by a picture of a rucksack.

'These are your packs. The piping around the rucksack is a highly tensile copper-titanium alloy. A single strand can hold up to five hundred kilos. Perfect for an impromptu abseil or tying up prisoners.'

He then brought up a photo of some strange-looking thermal underwear. Unlike the kind you would buy in shops, this was a one piece that enclosed the feet and hands and also had a hood attached to the collar. It didn't look dissimilar to the suit Jess had worn in the VR booth for her entrance exam, with the exception that the hood on this one covered the entire face, except for the eyes.

'Bullet-proof undergarments,' he said. He reached into his pocket and pulled out a swatch of material which he passed to Jess.

'You've got to be joking,' she said, scrunching the soft, lightweight material in her hand before passing it around.

'I'm serious,' said Lieutenant Parry. 'Our agents wear this on all their missions. With a different TOG rating, of course.'

'What's a TOG?' asked Krivan.

'It's the system used to measure how warm a duvet or sleeping bag is,' explained Lieutenant Parry. 'There's no better protection than P.E.P. underwear, and it covers more of the body than a bulky bullet-proof vest. Plus, it's an electrical insulator so it'll protect you from tasers too, and the unique weave of the fibres acts as a gas mask.'

'Well, I don't know about you guys but I *always* look for that in a pair of undies,' said Ben, laughing.

'And now, on the off-chance that we have to seize and transport the virus,' Lieutenant Parry continued, bringing up the next picture, 'a Thermos. It's shock-proof and hermetically sealed. Any questions?'

'Do I get any gadgets?' asked Emily, her eyes not leaving the instrument panel.

'Other than the underwear and the chopper? We each get one of these,' said Lieutenant Parry, bringing up a picture of a mobile phone. 'This is exactly what it looks like – a regular top-of-the-line smart phone with touchscreen, sixteen-megapixel camera, GPS, Bluetooth and so on. You name it, it's got it. Plus a few P.E.P. Squad extras,' continued Lieutenant Parry, grinning. 'It operates over the P.E.P. Squad satellite network using a special protocol that makes communications impossible to intercept. I've uploaded the most up-to-date floor plans of the castle I could find, although there may be some additional secret passageways. There's also an infrared detector. When we're close by we'll be able to scan for security guards and lab staff by their heat signatures. The app is the same one used in the laser-tag maze exercise you did with Herr Klug.'

'So what's the plan?' asked Jess.

Lieutenant Parry brought up a topographical map of the area surrounding Altganz Castle. 'Tomorrow evening Emily will drop us here, two kilometres away from the castle on the opposite side of the peak, about an hour before sunset,' said the Lieutenant. 'We'll snowboard along this trail – which is quite wide and flat – and approach the castle from the south.

'Once we get to here,' he continued, highlighting a heavily-treed section of the trail, 'we can use the phones to scan the castle interior from the cover of the trees. If any of Hess's men spot us and come to question us, we can say we're just taking photos. So make sure you take a few happy snaps first.

'Whether they notice us or not, by the time we get here,' he said, pointing to where the trail neared the castle, 'it should be close to getting dark – and freezing. If they have any human decency at all, they'll let us in.'

'And given that they might be terrorists bent on destroying the planet, what happens if they don't?' asked Krivan.

'Then I suddenly find I can get a signal on my phone, call "mountain rescue" and we use our night-vision goggles to ski on to here where Emily comes to pick us up,' said Lieutenant Parry, pointing to a spot further down the trail.

'So we just give up if they don't let us in?' asked Jess.

'No. That's when we move to Plan B, which I will explain as and when we need it,' said Lieutenant Parry, 'but for the time being let's stick to Plan A.

'Now if they do let us in, they'll most likely restrict us to this area here,' he continued, highlighting a group of rooms on the ground floor at the front. 'If Altganz really is Hess's hideout, I'd assume that the laboratory would be underground, in the former dungeon.'

'How do we get to it?' asked Matt.

'That's where the nose and mouth covering of the hood comes in. As well as being bullet-proof, it doubles as a gas mask. Which will come in handy once I release the Sleeping Beauty potion.'

'Sleeping Beauty potion?' laughed Emily.

'P.E.P. Labs' airborne sleeping draught, potent enough to put a castle full of people to sleep.'

'Seriously?' said Ben.

'I just need to open my Thermos in front of an air-conditioning vent, and we'll be the only people in the castle left conscious for a good two hours. Plenty of time to break into the lab, steal a sample of the virus if it's there, destroy all the security tapes and escape.'

'What happens when the bad guys wake up and realise the virus is gone? Won't they be even keener to release what they've got into the world?' asked Jess.

'We have agents in Salzburg and Munich standing by. When I activate my Thermos to release the Sleeping Beauty potion, it automatically activates a beacon, so teams will come in to arrest everyone on the premises before they wake up.'

'Impressive back-up,' said Matt.

'Possibly highly necessary in this case,' muttered Lieutenant Parry. 'That's Plan A in a nutshell.' He continued with his usual bravado. 'Any questions?'

'Yeah,' said Ben. 'If we have back-up coming, why do we need to do anything more than knock out the bad guys and wait for the cavalry to arrive?'

'Because you'll not always have back-up on a mission,

and this is a good chance to practise all your new skills. Now, once we land we'll head for a nice little guesthouse I know, not too far from Altganz. Obviously, whenever we come into contact with any civilians we do not mention P.E.P. Squad, the mission or even Theruse Abbey.'

'So what can we talk about?' asked Matt.

'The usual teenage stuff: computer games, pop music, acne cures, whatever,' said Lieutenant Parry. 'If you reach into the pouch below your tray table, you'll find your phones in there. Emily, you can get yours when we land. They've got slightly different covers, so if we do get caught and searched, the phones won't look out of place. They're currently in flight mode, and I'd appreciate your leaving them that way until after we've landed, but feel free to personalise them in any way you choose. I shouldn't need to tell you that black mission protocols apply. Those phones are not to be used for communication with anyone outside the people in this plane. Got it?'

'Got it,' chorused the cadets.

18

SNOW

Jess had been dozing for a good half hour when Lieutenant Parry said, 'We are now commencing our descent into Germany. Please ensure you have your hand luggage securely stowed, your seat belt tightly fastened across your lap and hold on really tight because the runway's covered in snow and this might get a bit hairy.'

A light snow was falling as the plane bumped down on the small snow-covered landing strip without incident and taxied to a reasonably well-camouflaged hangar. Lieutenant Parry flicked a switch in the cockpit and the hangar door started rolling up. 'Nothing beats having a remote-control garage door in weather like this,' he commented.

An Audi Q7 was inside the hangar waiting for them. Lieutenant Parry taxied to a stop so that the fold-out steps in the aeroplane's door lined up perfectly with the rear of the car.

'Here we are,' he said. 'If you could each grab a bag of equipment on your way out, I'd be most grateful.'

The cadets formed a line with Krivan at the back grabbing equipment bags and passing one to each of them.

Lieutenant Parry opened the plane door. The outside temperature was freezing.

'Fresh powder should make our snowboard trip tomorrow a little easier,' said Lieutenant Parry, rubbing his hands together.

'As long as it doesn't freeze overnight,' said Ben.

'Always the pessimist,' said Lieutenant Parry. 'Maybe when you take a job in P.E.P. Labs after graduation you could work on a ski or snowboard that turns ice into powder snow. Make things easier for us field agents.'

Ben merely grunted as he shouldered a sack of equipment.

When the Audi's boot was fully loaded, the cadets piled into the car and the lieutenant drove out of the airfield and onto a small road that wound round the mountains. Before long Lieutenant Parry pulled off the minor road onto an even smaller one. A short while later they arrived at a classic Tirolean-style Wirtshaus. It had a wooden, sloping roof, whitewashed walls and wooden window boxes spilling over with geraniums.

'Now remember,' said Lieutenant Parry as he parked the car, 'no talk of anything even slightly related to you-know-what, even when you think you're in private in your hotel rooms, until I give the all clear.'

The cadets nodded and unloaded their bags from the car. They waited in the lobby, talking about the benefits of Clearasil over Nomorezits while Lieutenant Parry spoke to the proprietor in flawless German. He came back with four keys, giving one to Emily, one to Matt, one to Krivan and keeping one for himself.

'They've started serving dinner already, so come down to the dining room once you're settled.'

Jess and Emily put their bags down in their room without saying much, then went to meet the others at dinner. The boys and Lieutenant Parry were already seated in wooden chairs with love hearts carved into the back, reading the menus.

'What's Kasspatzen?' asked Ben.

'Egg noodles that are solid like gnocchi, but a lot smaller, with melted cheese and crispy onion on top,' said Lieutenant Parry.

'Rindsgulasch?' asked Krivan.

'Beef goulash. A slightly spicy, tomatoey sauce, but not as tomatoey as Italian food,' explained Lieutenant Parry.

'And Leberkäse?' asked Jess.

'Translates directly as liver cheese, but it's a kind of meatloaf.'

'I'm going with the schnitzel,' said Emily.

'Me too,' said Jess.

'I'll have the meatloaf,' said Matt.

'I'll give that gnocchi stuff a try,' said Ben.

'Rindsgulasch,' said Krivan.

Lieutenant Parry called the waiter over and ordered for them.

'So how good are you all at snowboarding?' he asked loudly, giving them a wink.

They spent the rest of the meal chatting about adventure sports, or in Emily's case misadventure sports, without a single mention of P.E.P. Squad. When they'd finished dessert, Lieutenant Parry herded them upstairs. He knocked on Jess and Emily's door a few moments later.

'Grab your stuff and we'll pay the boys a visit. You too, Ivan,' he said, knocking on the next door.

Jess and Emily picked up their bags and went to the twins' room. When Ben opened the door, Lieutenant Parry put a finger to his lips and walked into the centre of the room, gazing at his mobile phone.

'We're clear,' he said.

'This phone's also a bug detector?' said Ben.

'P.E.P. Labs have developed more apps than you can find on the iTunes Store,' said Lieutenant Parry. 'Let's get the equipment sorted.'

He gave the cadets a practical rundown of all the gadgets they'd seen pictures of on the plane and helped Jess and the boys set the bindings on their snowboards. Then he talked them through the mission one more time.

'OK,' he said finally. 'I think we're good to go. Any questions?'

Jess thought the plan was pretty straightforward, but Krivan had several questions that seemed to grow more trivial as the evening wore on. Finally, when he'd run out of things to ask, Lieutenant Parry enquired if the others needed any further clarification.

They yawned and shook their heads.

'Great,' said Lieutenant Parry. 'See you at breakfast. Seven sharp.'

Emily unlocked the door to the girls' room and flopped down on her bed.

'Krivan was acting weird tonight. I don't see how the snail population in this particular region of the Alps is going to affect the mission,' she said.

'I admit that was a bit excessive, even for someone with a snail allergy. But I kind of got the feeling that there was something else he wanted to tell us,' said Jess thoughtfully.

'I'm glad he stopped when he did then,' said Emily, rolling over to face the wall.

'I'm going to have a shower. Do you need the bathroom first?' asked Jess.

Emily waved a dismissive hand at her.

Jess hopped in the shower and let the hot water soak into her muscles. When she came back into the bedroom, Emily was fast asleep. Jess climbed into bed but, unlike

Emily, she was unable to sleep and lay awake, tossing and turning. Both Lieutenant Parry and Krivan seemed to be disturbed by something and that made Jess worried.

She pulled her mobile phone under the duvet, so the light wouldn't disturb Emily, and reviewed the mission plans.

Despite her relatively sleepless night, after a morning going over the plan in detail again, by lunchtime Jess was eager to get going. The other cadets could hardly sit still they were so pumped.

'Are you all looking forward to the snowboarding?' asked Lieutenant Parry over lunch, raising his eyebrows to indicate they could only speak in general terms.

'You bet,' said Emily.

'The latest weather report says that the area got a dump of powder snow last night and no further falls are expected until we're down the mountain, so it'll be gnarly riding,' the lieutenant continued.

'Sick!' said Matt.

Lieutenant Parry looked at the others.

'How about you three?' he asked them.

'Can't wait,' said Ben.

Jess flicked her eyes briefly at Krivan before nodding.

271

'That's what I like to hear,' said Lieutenant Parry, standing up. 'Emily, I'll meet you outside in ten. Ben and Matt – you know what you have to do. Jess and Ivan – you get some free time.'

Back in her room, Jess looked over the equipment. A snow-covered empty field with a reasonable incline lay next to the Wirtshaus. Now would be as good a time as any to practise her snowboarding. She slipped out of her jeans and put on her ski pants, jacket and snowboard boots. Then she grabbed her snowboard and went outside into the field. When she had walked all the way up the hill, she strapped her boots into the bindings of her snowboard and took off down the slope, coming to an abrupt stop as the front of her board hit a patch of snow and flipped her onto her face. She groaned and wondered if it shouldn't be her that was supposed to be injured, since her boarding skills seemed to have gone from bad to worse.

The sound of muffled laughter made her look up.

'I'm sorry,' said Krivan, 'but that was hilarious. Would you like a few pointers?'

Jess's first reaction was to tell him exactly where to shove his pointers but, realising she could really use the help, she swallowed her rebuke and said, 'Yes, please.'

Krivan walked with her to the top of the hill. Jess went to clip on her bindings, but Krivan placed a hand on her arm to stop her.

'Take a look at the snowboard first. If it's flat on the slope, there's no grip at all and you will just slide. So you need to lean the sides of your feet into the slope to carve. Keep your knees bent, hands out wide towards the edges of the snowboard to keep your centre of gravity low.'

Krivan clipped on his snowboard and Jess followed his lead.

'Now, I'm going to go slowly. Do exactly what I do.'

Jess followed Krivan as closely as she could. He was a good snowboarder and a patient teacher.

As they got to the bottom and unclipped their bindings he said, 'Much better. Could I talk to you for a second?'

'Sure,' said Jess, then feeling her jacket vibrating she said, 'hold on a minute.' She reached into her pocket and pulled out her mobile phone. It was Lieutenant Parry and the reception was so terrible she could barely hear him.

'Mind scooting over to the side?'

'What?' asked Jess. A relatively loud hum was making it difficult to hear.

'Look up!'

Jess gaped. Only a few metres up the hill a helicopter was hovering. 'How can a helicopter sneak up on you? They're usually pretty noisy.'

'Its an EC155. Shrouded tail rotor, blue-edge rotor blades. That bird's a stealth machine,' said Krivan.

'I suggest you move,' Lieutenant Parry continued on

the phone. 'Landings are always the most dangerous part of the flight and we don't have the most experienced pilot on board.'

Krivan and Jess grabbed their boards and ran to the side of the field. As the helicopter came in to land, its rotor stirred up the fallen snow so the whole thing was covered in a swirling, white cloud. Jess put on her ski goggles and could clearly see Lieutenant Parry and Emily sitting in the cockpit with headsets on.

Lieutenant Parry waved them over.

'What did you want to talk about?' Jess asked Krivan as they approached the helicopter.

'Never mind, it will have to wait,' he replied, as Parry opened his door and shouted, 'Hop in.'

Jess and Krivan ducked under the rotors and climbed in.

'Headsets,' said Lieutenant Parry, gesturing at the one he was wearing.

Jess and Krivan put on their headsets as Lieutenant Parry said, 'Take her up, Emily.'

Emily took the helicopter smoothly into the air and headed towards the first ridge of mountains. The view over the Alps was beautiful. Lieutenant Parry drew their attention to the invisible border between Austria and Germany.

'We've even got enough fuel to get to Venice if any of you fancy a quick pizza,' he said.

Emily smiled but didn't deviate from the programmed path.

'OK, coming up on the right is Altganz Castle,' said Lieutenant Parry.

It looked just as it had in the slides – the fairytale castle that may or may not be hiding a sinister secret.

'Later on you'll be setting us down behind that peak over there,' continued Lieutenant Parry, pointing to a rounded peak with a thick covering of snow. 'Now, head south-southeast so that we can scoot on back to the heliport without the dudes in the castle realising we've doubled back on ourselves.'

Emily flew the helicopter over a ridge which was down-wind from Altganz so that both the sight and sound of the helicopter would be unobservable from the castle. After a safe distance she took the chopper back to base.

'That was great flying, Emily,' said Lieutenant Parry as Emily set them down. 'Let's go see how the twins are doing.'

Ben had done a spectacular job on Matt's right ankle. The shape of the swelling and the colour of the bruise reminded Jess of the time she'd sprained her ankle when a competition gymnastics vault had been set at the wrong height. She hadn't been able to walk properly for two weeks afterwards.

'Awesome bruise,' said Lieutenant Parry to Ben. 'But

you might want to make it a little more purple, since it's supposedly fresh today,' he advised.

'That'll be the second layer,' said Ben, wiping a darker purple shade over the yellow bruise. 'I did the yellow in indelible ink, so if we get stuck in Altganz for some reason, Matt can wash off this outer layer and it will look like the bruise is healing naturally.'

'Full marks for forward thinking,' said Lieutenant Parry, glancing at his watch. 'It's time to eat. Come and join us when you're ready.'

Jess tried to hang back with Krivan to give him an opportunity to voice whatever it was he'd wanted to tell her earlier, but Emily chattered at them non-stop all the way to the dining room. When she finally stopped talking and looked at her menu, Jess looked expectantly at Krivan but he shook his head, indicating the other diners in the room.

Lieutenant Parry noticed the tension in the cadets' faces. 'I know you're nervous,' he said, 'but you need your energy at that altitude and temperature, so order big.'

He'd just finished ordering from the waitress when Matt and Ben appeared in the doorway. Ben was supporting Matt whose face was contorted in pain. Ben was taking most of Matt's weight as he hobbled over to the table. Then Jess realised that, although Ben had been fashioning the prosthetic on Matt's right ankle, he was limping on his left.

'Oh, no!' groaned Lieutenant Parry, who had also noticed. 'Don't tell me you've hurt yourself for real?'

Matt's face broke into a grin.

'Nope! Just wanted to make sure I could pull it off,' said Matt, doing a quick little jig to show off. 'If I can fool you guys into thinking I'm in real pain, I can definitely fool a bunch of mad scien–'

Before he could get any further, Lieutenant Parry cleared his throat loudly and shook his head almost imperceptibly. 'And just for the record,' he continued in an undertone, 'rather than geeky scientists, they're probably burly armed mercenaries who wouldn't hesitate to shoot a wounded teenager to put him out of his misery.'

Matt sheepishly eased himself into the seat next to Emily.

Lieutenant Parry made an effort to keep the conversation upbeat through dinner, recounting imaginary snowboarding experiences, including crashing out of the half-pipe in the qualifying round of the Winter Olympics.

'OK, suit up. It's time to hit the slopes,' said Lieutenant Parry when they'd all finished.

They went upstairs to change. Jess had to strip off almost completely to put her bullet-proof underwear under her ski outfit.

'Ready?' asked Emily.

'Ready,' said Jess, zipping up her jacket and shouldering her rucksack.

'Don't forget your snowboard,' said Emily as Jess stepped out the door.

Jess went to take the board from Emily, but Emily held on to it for a moment. 'You be careful out there, OK?' she said, giving Jess a hug.

'You fly me there safe and I'll take care of the rest,' promised Jess.

They went downstairs to meet the others in the foyer, then all trooped out to the helicopter together. Lieutenant Parry rode up front with Emily while Jess and the boys piled into the back with their snowboards across their laps.

When they all had their seat belts and headsets on, the helicopter rose into the air. The weather conditions were perfect, so Emily flew along the route they had taken on the way home from their earlier flight. The view was again spectacular and Jess was just as excited seeing it for the second time.

A few minutes later they arrived at the starting point of the snowboard run and Emily touched down gently.

'Go straight back to base and no detours to Venice,' said Lieutenant Parry to Emily as they piled out of the helicopter. 'We might need you to come back for us in a hurry.'

'Right on,' said Emily, waving at them as she took the chopper up.

'OK, team, this is the real thing,' said Lieutenant Parry as they all strapped on their snowboards. 'Off-piste riding on virgin snow. I'll go first. Try to follow my tracks as closely as possible. Ivan – you're the most experienced, so you take the rear. Let's do it.'

Lieutenant Parry sprang to his feet and carved out a path down the mountainside with Ben and Matt close behind him. With some difficulty, Jess got to her feet, then lost her balance straight away, crashing down, as always, on her bottom. Krivan scooted down beside her.

'I'll give you a hand up this time,' he said, pulling Jess to her feet, 'but if you're planning to fall lots, it's easier to roll onto your knees first and then get up facing into the mountain.'

Jess had barely made it a few metres down the slope when she toppled over again. Following Krivan's advice, she tried to roll onto her front but her board was stuck in the snow.

'Lift your legs up, then roll,' said Krivan, flopping down on the snow and demonstrating.

Jess followed his lead and got to her feet easily.

'Alright. Let's try this again …'

Jess took off slowly, Krivan following a short distance behind. Whenever she felt herself start to go off-balance, she steadied herself by throwing out an arm.

'Stop laughing at me!' she yelled at Krivan, who was

cackling loudly behind her.

When Jess was riding more smoothly, Krivan moved up beside her and began, 'That thing I wanted to talk to you about ...' but trailed off when they rounded a curve in the trail and saw Lieutenant Parry and the twins lying in the snow waiting for them.

Jess cruised to a perfect stop before overbalancing and landing hard on her bottom.

'What was the hold-up?' asked Lieutenant Parry.

'Jess has a somewhat unconventional riding style,' said Krivan.

'I knew it was a risk bringing a girl on this trip,' said Lieutenant Parry, smiling broadly. Just as he'd finished his sentence, a snowball hit him smack on the nose.

'Did you throw that, Leclair? If only you could snow-board as well as you throw ...'

'Just watch me,' said Jess, getting to her feet and taking off down the mountain shakily.

'Hang on, sister,' said the lieutenant, cruising ahead of Jess to guide the team down the safest path. After another ten minutes the trail led into a copse of trees and he came to a stop. Moving to the far edge of the copse he took out his phone and scanned the castle, while the others took pretend holiday snaps. They then gathered in the centre of the copse.

'There certainly seem to be plenty of people inside, but not too many for our gas to knock out.' He turned to the students. 'OK, this is it. The final run. Once we're clear of these trees, we'll be in sight of the castle, so we should assume that we are being watched. Ivan, Jess and Ben, take the lead. Matt, I'll ride close to you, just in case that ankle gives you too much bother,' he said with a wink. 'It's starting to get dark. Let's go!'

Krivan leapt to his feet and rode a few metres before crashing down. He rolled over, his face contorted with pain.

'What did you do?' asked Lieutenant Parry.

'I don't know, I was going fine, then I must have hit a patch of uneven snow or something. My board flipped and I think I twisted my knee,' said Krivan.

'Take your board off and see if you can put any weight on it,' said Lieutenant Parry.

Krivan unclipped his board and tried to stand, but fell down in pain before he was even halfway up.

'It's no use. My knee's totally screwed.'

'Can we carry him down?' asked Jess.

'You know it's against protocol to take an injured agent into an active operation,' said Lieutenant Parry.

'That didn't stop you bringing Emily,' countered Jess.

'Without completing work experience, she would have failed transition year,' said the lieutenant. 'Besides, she's well away from any potential confrontations with gun-toting assassins.'

'That's reassuring,' muttered Ben.

'So does Ivan fail now?' Jess persisted.

'No, I'll assess him up to the point of his injury.'

'But we can't just leave him here,' said Jess.

'Actually, we can,' said Lieutenant Parry. 'It'll only be for a short while. I'll text Emily to come and get him.'

'It's against mountain protocol to leave someone injured alone,' said Krivan flicking his eyes at Jess.

'I'll stay with him,' she volunteered.

Lieutenant Parry stared at Jess for a moment, before exhaling loudly. 'You'll fail your work experience,' he said.

'Isn't work experience all about rehearsing what we'd do in the field on a real mission? This is what I'd do,' replied Jess.

Ben looked at her incredulously.

'Jess, he'll be fine,' stated Lieutenant Parry, clearly annoyed. 'Are you coming or not?'

She shook her head.

'Well I hope you enjoy being back at that snooty Dublin girls' school next year. Right, boys. Let's go,' said Lieutenant Parry, jumping to his feet and sliding down the trail without a backward glance. Ben and Matt followed, shaking their heads.

Once they were out of earshot, Jess turned to Krivan and said, 'Now that I've totally screwed up my future career prospects, would you mind telling me what's really going on?'

19

PLAN B

'And it better be good,' said Jess, standing over Krivan with her hands on her hips.

'Something's not right here,' said Krivan, getting to his feet.

'What do you mean?' asked Jess.

'This whole work-experience mission. It's bogus. Parry knows it but for whatever reason he won't go against orders. You heard how doubtful he sounded during the briefing.'

'Sure, but if he really thought there was something wrong–'

'Plus, I've got some extra intel about the mission,' said Krivan, totally surprising Jess.

'What sort of intel?'

'Well, you know how Herr Klug gave Ben a ROACH 2001 to test? He gave me one too. But mine kind of went AWOL,' said Krivan, pulling his phone out of his pocket. 'I lost track of it in the abbey somewhere and, although I couldn't get it to come back, I could still pick up its transmissions. I uploaded them all onto a USB flash drive and just before we left I received this.'

Krivan plugged the flash drive into his phone and angled the screen so Jess could watch the recording. The ROACH was somewhere very dark, with a faint, eerie light. Even though she couldn't see much, what Jess heard chilled her more deeply than the sub-zero Alpine air.

'*Our guests are due to arrive at Altganz on Sunday. Then it will only be a matter of days until the project is complete*,' said a male voice Jess didn't recognise.

'*Excellent. This will be the true dawn of the bioweapon age*,' said a second voice.

The men laughed.

'*Once we go public, there will be copycat attempts.*'

'*With P.E.P. Squad's resources at our fingertips, they won't be hard to neutralise.*'

'That's it,' said Krivan as the recording stopped.

'You're saying that's a recording of two people talking to each other in Theruse Abbey?' exclaimed Jess, horrified.

'That's one possibility. Another is that it recorded a phone conversation on loud speaker,' said Krivan.

'So, at a minimum, at least one person from P.E.P. Squad knows that Altganz is the real location of Hess's lab!'

'And Lieutenant Parry and the twins are heading straight into a trap.'

'Why didn't you play them the recording?' asked Jess.
Krivan hesitated.

'I wanted to. Believe me. But I kept quiet because I can't be sure that Lieutenant Parry's not in on it.'

'What? That's ridiculous!' Jess exploded. 'Lieutenant Parry's one of the most decent adults I know! And what about Matt and Ben?'

'Stop yelling so loudly,' said Krivan calmly. 'You'll cause an avalanche. The lieutenant is a professional spy and, if he is one of the good guys, then I'm sure he'll be able to deal with whatever the Altganz people throw at them and keep your friends safe. Plus, I've got a Plan B of my own.'

'Let's hear it,' said Jess.

'Whoever is behind this knows we're coming, right?'

'Right.'

'So when Parry turns up with only two teenagers, instead of four, they'll most likely send someone back up the trail to look for us. Presumably on a snowmobile, as they're faster than skis, particularly uphill.'

'Well that's a comforting thought,' said Jess, not liking the idea of an armed terrorist, who was far more proficient at moving on snow than she was, pursuing her over the mountain.

'Actually, it is,' said Krivan, taking off his rucksack and drawing out the piping. 'We have the element of surprise. Help me string this up between these trees.'

Jess helped Krivan stretch the piping across the trail in the middle of the copse and secure it to trees either side.

'That should stop anyone who's coming for us, at least long enough for us to get a couple of punches in. Or, in your case, a couple of well-aimed snowballs.'

'What? And give away my position so they know where to shoot? I'm not liking Plan B much so far.'

'It's highly unlikely they would fire a weapon with all this snow,' reasoned Krivan. 'It could start an avalanche. My guess is they'll rely on using brute strength to subdue us. If we can catch them off-guard then we have a better chance of winning the fight.'

'I hope you're right,' said Jess, crouching down and beginning to make a stockpile of snowballs. 'What happens after we catch them off-guard?' she asked.

'Depends on how many there are,' said Krivan, helping Jess make the snowballs. 'We could probably take down three between us. But any more and we'll be stuck. On the plus side, if they bother to interrogate Parry and the Sykes boys about our whereabouts they'll find out I'm injured. And because we're only teenagers they'll probably underestimate the threat we pose. That should keep the numbers down.'

'Then what?'

'We immobilise them. We can tie them up with the rucksack piping, steal the uniform of the one closest to my height, then I'll return to the castle with you as my prisoner.'

'Enthusiastic as I am to enter the castle as your prisoner,' said Jess, 'won't they notice they're short a couple of guards and a prisoner?'

'Not if I tell them that the other two are off pursuing … me,' said Krivan. 'Or that things got ugly and the death score is 2:1.'

'What about the minor point that you don't look or sound like any of the guards?'

Krivan smiled.

'That's why I have this,' he said, reaching into his rucksack and pulling out an oval-shaped piece of latex. 'Prototype from P.E.P. Labs. Instapros. You smooth it over someone's face, let it cool for thirty seconds to set it, then remove, turn inside out and, voilà, it's the perfect prosthetic.'

'Where did you get that?' asked Jess.

'My parents are – well, now just my dad is actually a P.E.P. Squad operative,' said Krivan. 'Sometimes he brings cool stuff home from work. I thought it might come in handy to bring it along.'

'What about the voice thing?' asked Jess.

'You know I can impersonate anyone,' said Krivan, mimicking Jess's voice perfectly.

'So let me get this straight,' said Jess. 'We engage one

of these homicidal maniacs in polite conversation and then ask him to keep still while we make an impression of his face, then knock him unconscious?' The muted sound of a chopper interrupted their conversation. 'That'll be Emily. Should we call her off?'

But before Krivan could reply the helicopter flew over their heads. Jess and Krivan ran to the edge of the copse where they had a clear view of the castle from the safety of the trees. The helicopter landed on a helipad on the roof of the castle. They used their ski-goggle binoculars to watch what happened next. A man they didn't recognise, dressed in a red-and-black uniform, got out of the chopper, then turned and yanked Emily out. Her hands were bound behind her back and her face was so pale that her freckles stood out in stark contrast. The man led Emily inside.

'Horseradish root!' said Krivan. 'That means they'll be coming for us any second.'

'And to think I was worried about failing work experience,' said Jess, pointing to the base of the castle where a lone man on a snowmobile, also dressed in red and black, was heading up the mountain towards them. 'At least there's only one of them. Looks like you were right about them underestimating us.'

'Quick, into position,' said Krivan.

Jess ran back and hid beside her cache of snowballs

while Krivan ran across to the other side of the trail, jabbing furiously at his mobile phone.

The whine of the snowmobile's motor drew closer. Jess grabbed a snowball. Krivan put his phone away and held up a finger to signal *not yet*.

The snowmobile zoomed into the trees and the wire caught the rider under the chin. He was flung several metres backward through the air and landed head first in the snow with a sickening crunch, his body twisted in an awkward position. The snowmobile cruised to a stop a few metres up the mountain.

'Go!' cried Krivan.

He and Jess sprinted towards the snowmobile driver, who wasn't moving. When they were a few feet away, Krivan put out an arm to stop Jess.

'He might be faking it. Throw one of those at him,' he whispered, gesturing to the snowballs Jess had in each hand. 'See if he reacts.'

Jess aimed for the only patch of skin she could see between the man's collar and hairline and made the perfect hit. The man didn't flinch.

'Is he even breathing?' asked Jess.

Krivan walked slowly towards the fallen man, Jess two paces behind him, ready to jump in to help if the guy put up a fight. Krivan reached down and felt for a pulse at his neck, then shook his head.

'Oh God,' said Jess, horrified. 'We killed him.'

Krivan gingerly turned the body over. The man flopped onto his back lifelessly, his head tilted at a very odd angle to his body, an ugly red gash across his throat, his still-open eyes staring blankly into space. Krivan turned away quickly and retched.

Jess waited until he'd finished vomiting, then whispered, 'At least his eyes are the same colour as yours. Are you really up for this?'

'There's no going back now,' said Krivan, wiping his mouth with the back of his shaking hand. 'We need to hurry before they send out more men to look for this guy.'

He took out the Instapros and put it over the man's face but his hands were shaking so much that Jess took over. She piled snow on top of the latex.

'Thirty seconds,' Krivan reminded her.

'I know,' said Jess, going to the man's feet and undoing his boots. 'You'd better start stripping off too.'

When the thirty seconds were up, Jess peeled the mask off the man's face, then stripped the red and black uniform off his body, trying not to think about what she was doing.

Krivan put the clothes on quickly, still shaking.

'They're a good fit but you need to get control of yourself,' observed Jess.

'I'll be all right in a minute,' said Krivan, strapping on the man's gun holster. 'It's just the cold.'

He felt inside the pockets of his new uniform and found a mobile phone. 'Sweet. His phone's in Russian so let's hope the working language at the castle is Russian.'

'What about your voice?' said Jess. 'We don't know what he sounds like.'

Krivan looked back at the phone and then pressed a button. Holding it up to his ear he listened for a moment and smiled. 'Excellent. He's personalised the outgoing voicemail message,' said Krivan in a voice half an octave deeper with a heavy Russian lilt. 'Give me your rucksack.'

'Is that what he really sounded like?' asked Jess.

'Absolutely,' said Krivan. 'Now give me your rucksack.'

'What for?' asked Jess, passing it over.

'Seriously, Irish girl?' continued Krivan in his impression of the guard's voice. 'I'd hardly take you prisoner without confiscating all your spy gadgets.'

'Then give me yours,' said Jess. 'Or at least let me keep my phone and the ROACH.'

'Good thinking,' said Krivan, undoing his own ROACH wristband and stowing it in the rucksack. 'You keep your phone. I'll chuck mine in, but first I'll set up call-forwarding from my phone to the guard's phone,' he continued, keying numbers into his P.E.P. Squad mobile.

'While you're at it, can you shoot me a copy of that

ROACH transmission? We'll need it for evidence and the more copies we have of it on the more devices the better.' As Krivan was sending her the media file, Jess looked back at the semi-naked corpse lying in the snow. 'Should we bury him?'

'We don't have time for that but we should definitely hide him,' said Krivan, dropping his mobile in Jess's rucksack. 'I'll take the head.'

Before lifting the body, he picked up the prosthetic mask from the snow. He flipped it inside out and then, pulling a switchblade from his pocket, cut spaces for his eyes, nostrils, mouth and eyebrows. He pulled it over his face, pressing it down tightly at the edges and around the spaces so there was no indication that it wasn't his real face.

Jess found it freaky to say the least to be looking at two identical versions of the same face, one on a live human and one on the corpse they were carrying. They dumped the body in the trees, where they also stashed Krivan's clothes and rucksack.

'Now to make this look authentic,' said Krivan, tying Jess's arms behind her with some plastic cable tie he'd found in the guard's pockets.

Krivan drove the snowmobile down to the same castle gate from which it had emerged and revved the engine until a guard opened the gate from inside.

'Where's the other one?' the guard demanded in Russian.

'Dead on the mountainside,' answered Krivan in the same language, using the deep voice he had rehearsed.

The guard nodded and waved them through.

Krivan drove inside, parking the snowmobile next to another one in the courtyard, then pulled Jess off the back in the same manner as the helicopter pilot had dragged Emily out of the helicopter.

Another guard emerged from the castle and went to frisk Jess.

'I've already done that,' said Krivan, stepping between Jess and the guard and tossing Jess's rucksack at him. 'She was carrying this.'

'Put her downstairs with the others,' said the guard, turning and heading for a door on the other side of the yard.

'Looks like you got the voice thing right,' Jess murmured.

Krivan pushed her ahead of him, muttering, 'Let's just hope Parry didn't make any mistakes with that floor plan.'

They walked through a door to their left and found themselves in the kitchen from which, according to the plan, they should find access to the dungeon level. A staircase at the rear of the kitchen led down to a T-junction at the bottom. A long, dark corridor headed off to the right, while a locked steel door only accessible via a card reader blocked the way to the left.

'So far so good. Let's try this way first,' said Krivan, marching Jess down the dark corridor, which was lined with a number of barred cells. The air was chill and damp. Jess was glad she had got to keep her ski jacket and pants.

Another red-and-black uniformed guard stood at the very end of the corridor, right in front of a cell. Three teenagers were inside. Krivan made a show of herding Jess roughly towards it.

'Jess! Thank goodness you're OK. What's going on? Where's Krivan?' cried Emily, jumping up and running towards the bars.

'Silence!' bellowed the real guard in heavily accented English.

'I've been told to relieve you,' Krivan said in Russian.

The guard unlocked the cell and held open the door.

'Check for bugs,' Krivan whispered to Jess as he shoved her roughly into the cell.

After closing and locking the cell again, the guard passed a bunch of keys to Krivan before striding down the corridor towards the stairs.

The other three crowded around Jess in a giant group hug. 'I'm so glad you're all right,' said Emily.

'Hang on – Emily, what are you doing here? And where's Lieutenant Parry?' asked Jess, using her hard-earned acting skills to look concerned and pretending not to know what was going on in case anyone was watching or listening in – and also to fool her friends for the time being.

'They knew we were coming,' said Matt. 'They let us in all friendly-like and as soon as they closed the portcullis a heap of guards jumped us, took our equipment – and I mean all our gadgets, it was like they had an inventory or something – and tied us up. Then they dragged Benny and me down here. Emily arrived not long afterwards.'

'They were waiting for me back at base. As I was powering down the helicopter they stormed the cockpit, took me prisoner and one of them flew me back here,' explained Emily.

'And the lieutenant?' repeated Jess.

'Dunno,' said Ben anxiously. 'I didn't realise he wasn't with us until they locked us in here. Maybe he's locked up somewhere else. But what happened to you? And where's Krivan?'

'We were waiting for Emily to come pick us up but that guy came for us instead,' Jess said, pointing at Krivan in his guard's uniform. 'Krivan put up a great fight but the brute pushed him into a deep fissure in the mountainside.'

'Holy crap!' said Ben. 'Is he …?'

'There's no way he could have survived the fall,' said

Jess brokenly, as if fighting back tears. She wished Signora Enigmistica could see her now.

'Jesus,' said Matt. 'I can't pretend I liked the guy but I wouldn't have wished that on him.'

Outside the cell, Krivan snorted.

'Bloodthirsty killer,' Emily muttered.

'I can't believe they killed him,' Jess said, slumping to the floor, pulling her knees up and resting her head on them. Her hair falling down either side gave her enough cover to fish the phone out of her inside pocket and she used the app to do a quick bug scan. The only transmitters the program picked up was a series of three cameras, positioned along the corridor. Fairly sure there were no listening devices within earshot, she decided to bring the others up to speed. She slipped the phone back in a pocket and then let out a loud sob.

'Jess,' said Emily, concerned, 'it's going to be OK. We'll get out of here.' She sat down beside her friend and put an arm around her shoulders. Ben and Matt came over too and crouched down in front of her.

Jess looked up and eyeballed each of them.

'None of you is to react to a single word I say, do you understand?' she said quietly and urgently.

Other than tiny nods, Emily and the twins didn't move.

'Krivan's not dead,' Jess whispered.

'What do you–?' began Matt loudly but Jess gave him a death stare. 'Sorry,' he whispered.

'He's standing right outside the cell,' continued Jess.

The other three turned at once to look at the guard.

'I said not to react!' hissed Jess. 'Geez, if I was marking this work-experience assignment you'd all fail.'

'Jess, did you hit your head? That guy's not Krivan,' said Ben.

'Yes I am,' said Krivan quietly in his own voice, turning his body slightly so that the cameras couldn't see that he was talking to them. 'I take it we're clear?'

'Just three optics in the corridor. Double-check 'em?'

Krivan nodded, then took a slow stroll down the corridor.

'What the …?' said Matt.

'He's wearing a prototype P.E.P. Labs mask,' said Jess.

'His leg seems to have made a remarkable recovery,' observed Ben.

'And where'd you get the uniform?' asked Emily.

'We killed the real guard,' mumbled Jess.

The other three stared at Jess open-mouthed.

'I think I must've hit *my* head – did you say you *killed* someone?' exclaimed Emily.

'It was an accident,' said Jess, her voice cracking for real this time. She took a deep breath before continuing. 'But on the upside I've got a phone and a ROACH and, as long as we can keep them hidden from those cameras, we should be able to find out what's really going on here.'

'So when did you two come up with this private plan of yours?' asked Ben.

Jess had never seen him look so disgusted.

'Krivan sprang it on me when I stayed back to wait for Emily with him.'

'And you don't think *he* might have an ulterior motive?' whispered Ben as footsteps echoed along the corridor.

'Optical only, as far as I can tell,' said Krivan. 'Love the nickname, by the way. Which one of you geniuses came up with Krivan?'

'That was me,' said Emily sheepishly.

'Maybe this will explain things,' said Jess. 'Ben, shuffle over here.' Ben slid around so that he was close to her, with his back facing the camera. Using his body as a screen, she retrieved her phone again and played them the recording of Krivan's ROACH transmission from Theruse Abbey.

'Where'd that come from?' asked Ben.

'You're not the only one who gets special assignments from Herr Klug,' murmured Krivan.

'Krivan's ROACH picked this up inside Theruse Abbey,' said Jess. 'We were sent here for a reason and it's got nothing to do with work experience.'

'Then why are we here?' asked Ben.

'I don't know yet,' said Jess. 'But it might help if we could find that laboratory. Or Lieutenant Parry. Do you want to drive, Ben?' Jess offered, shielding her left arm from the cameras as she passed him the ROACH.

Ben took the ROACH without a word, skilfully guiding it out of the cell and along the corridor.

'Lieutenant Parry said he thought the lab would be underground. Try behind the steel door at the base of the steps,' suggested Emily.

Ben guided the ROACH around the door, looking for a gap between the brickwork and the steel frame.

Jess, who had a partial view of the ROACH display, was surprised. 'That thing goes vertical now?'

'Just one of my many improvements,' replied Ben. 'However, the ROACH is too large to get through any of the cracks. We're just going to have to sit it out until the door opens.'

'Told you it should have been a ladybird,' said Jess quietly so only Ben could hear.

The faintest of smiles played about Ben's lips.

20

CAVALRY

The steel door remained shut for what seemed like an eternity. The cadets were tired, hungry and bored. Finally the sound of footsteps clattering down the stairs echoed along the corridor.

On screen Ben watched as a man in the red-and-black guard uniform slid a card over the reader and the steel door opened. He guided the ROACH onto the back of the man's boot and they both disappeared behind the door. 'We're in,' he said.

Jess had to quell her urge to move around and look over Ben's shoulder for a better view of the ROACH display, because the corridor cameras were still active.

'Was Em right? Is it the lab?' she asked.

'I only have a dark view up a trouser leg at the moment,' said Ben. 'He's stopped at another door. I can hear a beep. Moving again. It's brighter now, wherever it is.'

The man took a few more steps, then came to a standstill. Ben guided the ROACH off his boot and made it climb a wall and scuttle over the ceiling before coming to rest, shielded by one of the overhead lights.

'Bingo. It's a lab,' said Ben. His excitement at finally doing something seemed to have dispelled his dark mood. 'There's a central room that's all glassed off. Inside it are big fridges – I can't quite see what's in them – microscopes, specimen bottles and some weird-looking equipment on the benches. Everyone in there is wearing a biohazard suit. And in the rest of the room … I don't believe it!'

'Don't believe what?' said Matt, as Ben just stared at the screen.

'It's Lieutenant Parry. He's looking a bit roughed up, but he's sitting at a computer, not tied up or anything.'

The cadets looked at each other.

'What sort of expression is on his face?' asked Emily quickly. 'Disgust? Disbelief? Fear?'

'Yeah, right. Like Lieutenant Parry's scared of anything,' said Matt.

'Well, he's frowning,' said Ben. 'But it's one of those concentration frowns. It looks like he's working. His eyes are darting round a bit.'

Jess tried to avoid the 'I told you so' look Krivan was sending her.

'Woah, *he's* looking a bit the worse for wear,' said Ben.

'Lieutenant Parry?' asked Jess.

'No. Cameron Hess!' said Ben. 'He's got skinny, and

wrinkly, and kind of bald. I barely recognised him. They're talking. I'll try to get the ROACH closer to them and pipe the output through the phone.'

Ben connected the ROACH display to the mobile and activated speakerphone, holding the phone in front of him so everyone else could see what was on the display and hear what was going on.

The cadets watched the ROACH's view of the lab on the phone's screen while Krivan kept an eye out for any movement down the corridor.

'*So this is definitely the molecular structure of the BS3 virus?*' a tinny version of Lieutenant Parry's voice asked.

'*Yes. It took us over a year to isolate it and recreate it synthetically, but it mimics the progression of the pathogen in Biosphere 3,*' replied Hess.

'Mimics?' said Krivan, who was straining to hear what was going on from outside the cell. 'Why would they need to mimic it?'

'*And the antidote?*' asked Lieutenant Parry.

'*I'm afraid that's why they've brought you in, old friend,*' said Hess. '*My employer is particularly anxious for an antidote.*'

'*I'll bet. When a virus like that occurs spontaneously once, who's to say it won't happen again? All biosphere experiments should have been put on hold until the origin of the virus in Biosphere 3 was identified and an antidote developed.*'

'So Hess didn't invent the virus,' commented Emily.

'*Unfortunately my employer's reason for developing the antidote is not to prevent the recurrence of such catastrophes,*' sighed Hess.

The lieutenant looked at him sharply. '*What do you mean?*'

Hess looked around nervously and waited for a guard walking past to move out of earshot.

'*You can tell by the treatment you and the teenagers have experienced that my employer is no humanitarian,*' he continued so quietly that Ben had to turn the volume to maximum so they could hear him. '*Wayne, we've known each other a long time. If it weren't for my family's safety, I wouldn't have anything to do with this.*'

'*Your family? Has somebody threatened them?*' asked Lieutenant Parry.

Hess nodded.

'*I've been stalling as long as I could, but now they've brought you in …*'

'*Why have I been brought in, exactly? I'm no scientist.*'

'*No, but you do have one of the most brilliant analytical minds on the planet. I've been working on this close to fourteen hours a day, seven days a week, since they closed down Biosphere 3 eighteen months ago. I'm getting burnt out. And to tell the truth, I'm not even sure I want to create an antidote under these conditions. However, with my research and your ability to figure things out, your boss seems to think you'll crack this in no time,'* Hess said.

'What do you mean? My boss has nothing to do with what's going on here,' said Lieutenant Parry.

'Au contraire,' said a third voice joining the conversation.

Ben swivelled the ROACH around to identify the speaker and almost dropped the phone. Standing behind Cameron Hess and Lieutenant Parry was none other than Vladimir Metsen.

'I have everything to do with what's going on here,' continued Metsen.

Lieutenant Parry gaped him.

'You're Hess's employer?' Lieutenant Parry said slowly.

'You catch on quick,' said Metsen.

'Why?' asked the lieutenant.

Metsen smiled. *'You're a smart chap, Parry. I know I've been on your radar for a while. So why don't you pull together everything you think you know about me and figure it out.'*

Slowly the expression on Lieutenant Parry's face changed to one Jess had never seen before. If a human was capable of shooting poison from their eyes then the lieutenant would have been soaking Metsen with it.

'Now it all makes sense, those sudden unexplained business trips and late-night phone calls to Germany and the Middle East. You're planning to use the virus as a weapon,' spat Lieutenant Parry.

'*And Wayne Parry does it again,*' said Metsen, clapping slowly.

'*But why? You're supposed to be one of the good guys,*' said the lieutenant. '*You set up P.E.P. Squad to prevent things like this being developed.*'

'*And I'm still one of the good guys.*'

Hess laughed incredulously.

'*This virus is to help P.E.P. Squad achieve our goal,*' Metsen continued. '*To help us win the fight.*'

'*We're already winning the fight. We've saved thousands of lives from terrorist plots,*' said Lieutenant Parry, shaking his head.

'*But we've lost some good agents too. Think about it, Wayne. This weapon is the ultimate deterrent – far more powerful than nuclear weapons or any other type of chemical or biological warfare. With the antidote at hand, we can unleash it safely–*'

'*Safely?*' yelled Hess.

'*… and turn it on and off as we see fit,*' Metsen carried on, ignoring him.

'*As who sees fit? The United Nations?*' asked Parry.

'*Well … me,*' said Metsen.

'*And who, exactly, are you planning to unleash it on?*' asked Lieutenant Parry.

'*Depends,*' said Metsen thoughtfully. '*The usual terrorist cells, of course. Plus corrupt governments in the Middle East and Asia. And maybe the North Americans if they get too big for their boots.'*

'No matter where you release it, you'd be harming innocent civilians as well,' said Hess.

'Collateral damage,' said Metsen. *'Although the majority of civilians in a democracy can hardly be called innocent.'*

'You're insane,' said Parry. *'This is not the P.E.P. Squad I signed up for. You can count me out.'*

'I'll be counting you in for a little longer,' said Metsen, smiling smugly. *'Perhaps it slipped your mind that I have four of your precious students in a cage on the other side of that door? I would hate for them to become collateral damage too.'*

'Collateral ... did you say four?' said the lieutenant sharply.

'Oh, did I forget to tell you? You must have guessed we would reunite the rest of your little team. Emily was easy to take with her injury, but I have to admit, after watching her progress through the year, I thought your star pupil would put up more of a fight. Quite disappointing. And as for the Krivlyakaev boy, well ... I just hope the bad news won't break his father – he is a very useful operative.'

'What did you do to Ivan?' said Lieutenant Parry coldly.

'Oh, I can't take the credit. It would seem he resisted my guard's kind offer of shelter, preferring to perish on the mountain.'

All the colour drained from Lieutenant Parry's face.

'*This is my fault. I knew something was wrong with this assignment from the moment you gave it to me. I should have followed my gut and stayed the hell away from here.*'

'*That's the trouble with you ex-army types. Always so quick to follow orders,*' sneered Metsen.

'*I swear if you hurt any more of those kids–*'

Metsen cut him off. '*Oh, they're safe enough. For now. But I can't guarantee they'll stay that way for long if you don't start producing results.*'

'That's it,' said Krivan. He dialled a number on his phone and shouted '*We have what we need. Go, go, go!*' into it in Russian.

There was an explosion, followed by machine-gun fire from the floors above.

'What's going on?' Jess yelled to Krivan.

'The cavalry's arrived,' said Krivan, moving to unlock the cell door, but dropping the keys in his excitement. 'I contacted Dad from the Wirtshaus last night. He got in contact with Parry's strike teams in Munich and Salzburg, and they've been on standby since we rigged up the trap for the snowmobile. They texted to say they were in position when I went to check out the cameras. Now we have Metsen's confession on tape, it's time to roll.'

Just as Krivan found the right key, loud footsteps clattered down the hallway towards them. Krivan quickly turned and drew his gun. Vladimir Metsen was hurtling towards them, a crazed expression on his face.

'Open the cell,' he barked at Krivan.

Puzzled, Krivan unlocked the cell using his left hand, his gun still clasped in his right.

Metsen entered the cell and grabbed Jess, dragging her outside.

'Kill the others,' he ordered Krivan in Russian.

Krivan raised his gun.

'Ivan! You can't!' Jess screamed.

'Ivan *Krivlyakaev*?' shrieked Metsen, shoving Jess so hard she ploughed head first into the wall. He then lunged at Krivan, who was distracted by the sight of a stunned Jess slumping to the floor, and with one hand grabbed the gun from him and with the other ripped the prosthetic off one side of his face.

'Well, well. Little Ivan Krivlyakaev. I don't know how you pulled that off, but you can take the secret to your grave.'

Metsen raised the gun and rapidly fired four shots, hitting Krivan, Emily, Ben and then Matt in the centre of the chest. As each was hit they were thrown backwards by the force of the bullet and fell to the ground, lifeless.

Jess's ears were ringing from the shots and she still felt woozy from her impact with the wall. She barely noticed Metsen's hands on her as he hauled her up and dragged her down the corridor. As they neared the staircase, Jess became aware of another noise, something high-pitched and whiney. It took her several seconds before she realised the noise was coming from her own throat.

'If I'd known you were going to be a screamer, I would have shot you and taken one of the others,' growled Metsen, forcing Jess up the stairs.

Jess didn't even try to resist. The shock of watching Krivan, Emily, Ben and Matt being shot in front of her in cold blood was more powerful than Memory Wipe in making her forget all her secret-agent training.

'Why don't you then?' Jess sobbed.

'Why don't I what?' said Metsen distractedly, steering Jess down a hallway.

'Shoot me!'

'Tempting as that is, you're more use to me alive than dead at this point,' grumbled Metsen, swiftly changing direction and ducking into an alcove, clamping a hand firmly over Jess's mouth so she could not cry out.

A pair of men, dressed in white camouflage suits and with guns drawn, raced past them. Once their footsteps had receded, Metsen clasped Jess close to him like a human shield and headed for another flight of stairs.

He's heading for the roof, Jess thought to herself, her training starting to kick through the fog of grief inside her head. *Once he gets there, he'll be free and I'll be dead.*

That thought jolted Jess into action. She put every-thing she'd learned in self-defence classes into practice: stamping hard on his foot and trying to use his own weight against him to slam him into the wall at the side of the stairwell, but she barely even managed to slow him down. Metsen may have been manic, but years of training meant he could easily counter all of Jess's moves.

Realising she couldn't overpower him physically, Jess switched tactics.

'It'll never work,' she said.

'Excuse me?' said Metsen, slowing his pace ever so slightly.

'Even if you make it out of here, no one from P.E.P. Squad is going to go along with this.'

'So you think you've figured it out, huh? Not everyone in P.E.P. Squad has such high ideals as yourself,' laughed Metsen, pushing Jess up another flight of stairs.

'Well the people I know–'

'The people you know are trained killers. Lying to their families about what they do. Do you really think I can't spin this so that the majority of my hand-picked minions won't think this is the greatest weapon of all time?'

'They'll agree that it's powerful, but that's its only greatness,' said Jess. 'You try to do what you've said you'll do with the virus and P.E.P. Squad will hunt you down.

You haven't built yourself an army of mercenaries: you've built yourself a moral compass who will take you out rather than have you play chicken with a deadly virus.'

'The blissful ignorance of youth,' mused Metsen almost dreamily, before fixing Jess with a hard stare. 'Believe me, after being operatives for long enough to see their colleagues, their friends, die on missions, there aren't many in P.E.P. Squad who would willingly risk their lives when a deterrent like BS3 is available.'

'The teachers would,' said Jess.

'I wouldn't base your knowledge of P.E.P. Squad personnel on Theruse Abbey staff. Remember the saying: those who can, do; those who can't, teach.'

'Some of us still have what it takes to survive in the field,' boomed a voice from below. 'It's over, Metsen. Let her go.'

Metsen whirled around, holding Jess in front of his body, one arm around her throat and his gun pressed against her head. Had he not been holding her so tightly, Jess would have fallen down the stairs in shock.

Standing on the landing below them was Lieutenant Parry. But unlike those of the man Jess had seen moments before on the phone display, Lieutenant Parry's clothes were ripped and his face was covered in blood, as were the knuckles on both hands.

Metsen laughed.

'Or what? You're unarmed and I have the world's deadliest weapon in my pocket,' said Metsen. He shifted his gun into his other hand, ramming the barrel into the base of Jess's jaw, and extracted a vial from his jacket. 'BS3 virus. No known antidote. Don't think I won't use it.'

Then Jess saw another expression she'd never before seen on Lieutenant Parry's face. Fear.

'That's got your attention, hasn't it?' laughed Metsen.

'You can't. You don't know what it could do if released into the atmosphere ...'

'I've got a pretty good idea,' said Metsen, pulling a balaclava out of his pocket and yanking it over his head. Jess recognised the material of the balaclava. It was the same as her P.E.P. Squad-issue thermal underwear.

Lieutenant Parry laughed.

'That won't keep you safe, Metsen. Don't forget, I've seen Hess's research. The virus structure is finer than the weave of the material. It'll get through and kill you too.'

Metsen cocked his head and looked at Lieutenant Parry.

'You're bluffing,' he said.

With a sudden movement, Metsen went to strike the vial against the wall. A shot rang out and Metsen fell backwards, letting go of the vial. Jess dropped to her knees and thrust out a hand, catching it millimetres before it could hit the floor and shatter.

She looked down the stairwell and couldn't believe her eyes. On the landing below Lieutenant Parry, a red-and-black uniformed guard with half his face peeling off was holding a weapon, pointed just to the right of Jess where Vladimir Metsen had been standing seconds before.

'That's for my mother,' said Krivan, starting to shake uncontrollably.

Jess and Lieutenant Parry bolted down the stairs to Krivan, taking care not to slip on the trail of blood seeping out of the hole in Metsen's forehead. The lieutenant took the gun and eased Krivan down to a sitting position.

'Ivan, thank goodness, I thought you were dead,' said Lieutenant Parry.

'So did I! I saw you get *shot*,' exclaimed Jess.

Krivan ripped his shirt open to reveal a silver disc in the middle of his black thermals, saying, 'Bullet-proof underwear, remember?'

Jess gasped with relief. 'Does that mean Emily and the boys are OK too?'

'I didn't wait to check,' said Krivan. 'I had to save you.'

Jess was torn. Her first instinct was to run back to the dungeon to check on her friends but she owed Krivan, who had single-handedly saved the mission, not to mention Jess's own life, and so she felt she should stay with him. Then a door burst open and the decision was made for her.

'*Ivan!*' cried Mr Krivlyakaev, barely recognisable in his camouflage gear, sinking to his knees and clasping his son tightly. Krivan buried his face in his father's shoulder and started to sob.

Lieutenant Parry whispered quietly to Mr Krivlyakaev, then grabbed Jess by the upper arm and walked her back towards the dungeon.

'Jess,' he whispered quietly, his lips touching her ear, 'I cannot begin to explain to you how important it is that you tell *no one* that Ivan shot Metsen. Is that clear?'

Jess nodded.

'There's no telling what Metsen's cohorts may do to him if they find out. Nice work snatching the vial, by the way. Now catch me up on what's been happening.'

As they made their way back to the dungeon, Jess quickly explained everything that had happened since Krivan had faked his injury, including the accidental death of the snowmobile rider, the ROACH reconnaissance and Krivan's request to his father for help.

'Wow,' said Lieutenant Parry as they strode along a corridor linking the roof staircase to the dungeon staircase. 'Krivan handled the situation like a pro, but why didn't he come to me?'

'He, er, wasn't entirely sure you weren't in on it,' said Jess.

'That poor kid,' said Lieutenant Parry. 'He worked

that all out single-handedly, got shot, saved our lives, the mission and clocked up two kills which will probably haunt him for the rest of his life. That's a heck of a day for a sixteen-year-old.' He turned to look at her. 'How are you doing?'

'I don't want to think about that right now. Let's go see if the others are all right.'

As they reached the lower corridor, Jess's legs started moving as if they had a mind of their own. She sprinted down the corridor, towards the moaning sounds of two boys and a girl, in pain but very much alive. Jess cried with relief as she tried to hug them all at once.

'How are they?' Lieutenant Parry asked Dr Hess, who was tending to them.

'They'll be sore at the impact points, both from the bullets and where they landed, but no serious damage has been done.'

'Good to hear it,' said Lieutenant Parry.

'Wayne, you're a sensible man,' said Hess. 'I know that your current employment is of a somewhat … secretive nature, but I why did you bring children into this mess?'

'I was under orders,' said Lieutenant Parry.

'Whose orders?'

'Orders from the most secret spy network in the world.'

Hess raised an eyebrow.

'Come to think of it, our research arm would really

benefit from a mind like yours,' continued Lieutenant Parry.

'That's good news, given that I'm assuming my "employment" contract here has been effectively terminated,' said Hess. 'But what about my research staff?'

'I have a special drink for your research staff,' said Lieutenant Parry. 'It's called Memory Wipe. No long-lasting effects, but they won't remember a thing from the time they began working on the project once we administer it. What do you say?'

'Bottoms up,' said Hess.

EPILOGUE

It was a very subdued group of cadets that sat down to a late supper at the Wirtshaus. Jess in particular noticed Krivan's absence, made all the keener as the others kept asking questions about their break-in to the castle and the showdown with Metsen on the staircase, which of course she had to lie about.

The questions didn't let up the following day either. But this time they were posed by professional P.E.P. Squad agents during a regulation debriefing. Jess, Emily, the twins, Lieutenant Parry, and presumably Krivan, were interviewed individually and then asked to confirm each other's accounts. At the end of the day they were brought together in a room, although Krivan was still absent. A man Jess didn't recognise, wearing a suit and tie, stood before them.

'I hardly need to tell you that what happened at Alt-ganz Castle is not a typical work-experience assignment. We have never before placed our cadets in such serious danger, and we have never before had to deal with such a crisis at top-management level.

'For the moment we think it best to keep the details of what happened here, including Vladimir Metsen's involvement, classified. You are not to breathe a word of what happened here to anyone, including each other, once you leave this room.'

The man handed out some stapled A4 pages to each of them.

'These are your official cover stories. You spent the last three days at Dublin Airport, working with customs. You have five minutes to read through them and ask me questions.'

Neither the lieutenant nor the other cadets had questions, so they were dismissed and sent home. Jess did have one burning question which she was afraid to ask. What had happened to Krivan?

She was still pondering this eighteen hours later, as she crossed the finish line of the assault course at Theruse Abbey and collapsed.

'That was disappointing, Leclair. You only managed to shave one second off your previous time,' said Lieutenant Parry.

Jess lifted her head off the ground and glared at him. He dropped his voice and continued, 'How are you holding up?'

'I'm OK, I think.'

'You know I'm here if you need someone to talk to.'

Jess smiled gratefully and nodded, and the lieutenant walked away.

'How was your work experience?' asked Aidan, coming over and offering Jess a hand up.

'Pretty dull, really,' said Jess. 'I can't wait to get to do something a little less routine next year.'

'Jess,' called Svetlana, coming over with a towel around her neck.

'Hi Svetlana,' said Jess.

'I haven't seen Ivan since he came back. Do you know if he's okay?'

Jess paused ever so briefly.

'He had to go back to Russia. Some family crisis. Quite handy our work experience was at the airport so he could get a flight straightaway.'

Svetlana's eyes narrowed. 'Funny, that's what Matt said. Word for word.'

'What was that about?' asked Aidan as Svetlana walked away.

'Beats me,' said Jess, glad that her red face from running disguised her sudden blush.

'So when did you get back?' asked Aidan.

'Late last night,' said Jess.

'Did you hear the news?'

'What news?' asked Jess.

'Metsen's dead. Apparently some terminal disease he'd been hiding for years. I wonder who the new principal's going to be?'

Jess glanced over at Lieutenant Parry and raised an eyebrow. 'I know a good candidate when I see one.'

Later that evening, when Jess finally sank down into her own bed, body and mind completely exhausted, one last thought snaked into her consciousness, making her eyelids fly open. Whose was the second voice on the ROACH tape and what were they planning now?